FLEE

# J.A. Konrath and Ann Voss Peterson

**THOMAS & MERCER**

The characters and events portrayed in this book are fictitious. Any similarity to real persons, living or dead, is coincidental and not intended by the author.

Published by Thomas & Mercer
P.O. Box 400818
Las Vegas, NV 89140

ISBN-13: 9781612185125
ISBN-10: 1612185126

*If the adrenaline doesn't kill you, she will*

# Not too long ago...

*"Whenever possible, avoid engaging the enemy,"* The Instructor said. *"If engaged, run. Fighting should be your last resort. Patriotism has its place, but it costs millions of dollars to train people like you. You're more valuable than the mission. If things go sour, flee."*

**This is fun** I typed. Then I hit enter and waited for the reply. It popped up on my computer screen a moment later.

*No pressure, but are we ever going to meet IRL?*

I took the last sip from my bottled water and tried to ignore the jitter under my rib cage. *In real life. He assumes I have one.*

I tossed the empty over my shoulder without looking. The sound it made confirmed I'd hit the garbage can.

**How do I know you're not some lunatic stalker? Or even worse, weigh eighty pounds more than your jpg?**

I'd been chatting with Victor9904 almost daily for the past two weeks. I liked him, and he was the first guy I had ever hooked up with online that I wanted to meet in person. That alone made me a little nervous. Dating, for me, was complicated. Except for stretches of time when I was abroad, I kept to a tight routine. Cruising bars looking for men wasn't part of that routine.

*Do you have a webcam?* he typed.

Another jitter, this time tougher to ignore. Chatting online was one thing. Letting him see me was riskier.

**Yes. But I haven't showered yet this morning.**

*<grin> Neither have I. You chicken?*

I smiled. **I don't scare easily.**

*OK. I'll set up a private webcam chat room and send you the URL. Give me a minute...*

**Sounds good.**

I didn't rush to the bathroom to check myself in the mirror, but I may have moved a little quicker than normal. My dark hair was shorter than I would have preferred, but it never got in my face and was easy to manage and conceal. I finger-combed it, deemed it fine, and wiped a toast crumb from the corner of my mouth. I was wearing what I'd slept in, an old tee and some baggy sweatpants. Since I'd already told him I hadn't showered, changing into nice clothes and putting on makeup would be disingenuous.

Besides, if a guy couldn't accept the way a woman looked when she woke up, he wasn't worth waking up next to.

Not that I was planning any sleepovers.

Sex, on the other hand...it had been too long.

I wandered back to my computer, sat down, and noted my pulse was a tiny bit faster than normal. My webcam was built into the monitor. I switched on the application, and a few seconds later, Victor IMed me the address. I typed in the URL, and then there he was, filling my computer screen, smiling boyishly.

He was actually cuter than his JPG. Blond hair. Strong chin, covered in stubble. Broad shoulders. Around my age, early thirties, and his blue eyes were several shades lighter than mine.

He said something, which I lip-read to be, *Good morning, Carmen. Nice to finally see you. Are you wearing a Cubs T-shirt?*

I unmuted the picture and adjusted the volume.

"Yes, I am." I smiled. "Is that going to be a problem?"

Victor stood up, revealing the White Sox logo on his jersey. Behind him I could make out a sofa, but the room details were blurry beyond that. With the sound level up, I heard his cat, a calico named Mozart, meow in the background.

"I'm a season ticket holder." His voice was deep, rich, pure Chicago South Side. He sat down, grinning. "But I'm willing to work through this if you are."

I shook my head, feigning disapproval. "I dunno. Season tickets? I'm not sure I could get over something like that."

"Are you asking me to give up the Sox when we haven't even had a first date yet?"

"If I did ask, what would you say?"

He rubbed his chin. "On one hand, I don't want you to think I'm a pushover. On the other hand, if this is what you look like before a shower, giving up the Sox doesn't seem like that big a sacrifice."

I granted him a smile for that one. "You should see me juggle."

We stared at each other for a few seconds.

"This is the first time I've ever used a webcam for something other than business." He leaned forward, like we were talking over a coffee table. "It's weird. Intimate, but distant at the same time."

"I agree." I took a breath and a plunge. "Dinner would be better, I think."

"Are you free tonight?"

I pretended to consider it. "Yes."

"I could pick you up. Have we reached a level of trust where you're willing to tell me where you live?"

"Let's meet someplace." Only one person in the world actually knew where I lived, and I wanted to keep it that way.

"You like German food, right?"

I nodded, remembering I'd mentioned that during our very first text chat.

"How about Mirabel's on Addison?" he said. "Six o'clock?"

"Looking forward to it."

"Me too. But now it's almost nine, and I'm on call. Gotta get ready for work."

"Off to save some lives?"

"I'm hoping for a slow day. Maybe I'll get lucky and no one in Chi-town will dial nine-one-one during my shift. But if I do have to heroically spring into action," he winked at me, "I'll be ready."

"See you later, Victor."

"See you, Carmen."

He switched off the camera. I initiated my tracking software, locating his IP address. It was the same one he always used. Previously, I'd hacked his ISP and gotten his billing information, and from there it had been easy to run a background check. Victor Cormack, as far as I could research using both public and private records, had been telling me the truth about his job, his education, his past. On the surface, he was a normal, average person.

But anyone checking out my identity would assume the same about me.

I erased my Internet footsteps, deleting cookies, clearing the cache, and reformatting the C drive. A pain in the ass to do every time I went online, but a necessary one. Then I wiped the keyboard clean with a spritz of Windex and began my morning workout.

Halfway into it, my encrypted cell phone rang. I finished my 239th push-up, slid the sweaty bangs off my eyebrows with my forearm, and padded over to the breakfast bar to answer it. Only one person—the same person who knew my address—had this number. A call meant work. And work couldn't be refused. The phone was even waterproof so I could take it into the shower.

I hit the connect button on the touch screen and waited, habit making me tune in to my surroundings. I could smell traces of the green pepper omelet and wheat toast I'd had for breakfast, along with a slightly sour odor coming from the sink telling me dishes needed to be done. The ambient sounds were unremarkable; the thermostat kicking on, the hum of the fridge, the ticking of a wall clock hanging over my computer, pigeons warbling outside.

"Is Velma there?" The familiar voice was digitally altered and sounded slightly robotic. I'd never heard his real voice, never met the man it belonged to.

I closed my eyes, shutting off part of me. The part that had just chatted with Victor. The part that was going to go shopping later for a new pair of running shoes. The part that read books and watched television and was normal as normal could be.

Then I slipped into the other part.

"Velma's on vacation in Milan, can I take a message?"

A pause, then, "It's over, Chandler."

"Jacob? What's over?"

Jacob wasn't his real name any more than mine was Chandler.

"We're over. Blown."

I processed this. "I thought no one knew—"

"Things have gotten ugly, fast. You need to go to ground. I'll contact you at ten thirty hours."

My skin prickled. *Go to ground.* This was bad.

"How long do I have?"

"Five minutes. Maybe less. And…I assume you know about Cory."

That was a name I hadn't heard in a while. The fact that I'd never discussed Cory with Jacob, or pretty much anyone else, didn't faze me. Jacob knew everything about everyone.

"I know that two weeks ago he killed four guards and escaped maximum security," I said, reflexively checking the front door. "I've been keeping an eye out for him, but he doesn't know where I live or my current name."

"I'm looking at a satellite image of your building. A black sedan just double-parked in front. Two people, a man and a woman. Infrared coming back…they're both armed. Get out, now. And don't answer your phone, it's about to ring."

My normal phone rang. I checked the caller ID. It was Kaufmann, calling three days before his scheduled time.

"Ten thirty," I said to Jacob, hanging up.

Kaufmann would have to wait.

Training took over, sparing me the indecisiveness inherently brought on by panic. The innumerable days of practicing insertion and extraction, fight and flight, and the prep work necessary to execute flawlessly constituted ninety percent of my job.

The other ten percent involved action; the implementation of what I'd learned and planned for.

The pair would split up, one taking the elevator, one the stairs. If they had intel—and they must have to know where I lived—they'd be aware of the fire escape outside my window, and a second team would be covering it.

I made an instant mental checklist, the things I needed in the order I needed them. Weapon, then shoes, then purse. The house was clean; nothing to burn me here. I wore sweats and an old tee. I pinched the waistband, felt the ever-present strip of wire. Then I leaned over the sink, reached behind the refrigerator, and yanked the Glock 19 off the Velcro strip that held it there.

The phone rang a final time, the answering machine picking up.

"*You've reached Carmen Sawyer's phone.*" That wasn't my real name either. "*I'm not available right now, so please leave a message.*"

"Hiya, babe. It's been a while." The voice on my machine was male, deep, predatory. A voice I'd hoped to never hear again. "Carmen, huh? That's cute. Well, *Carmen*, I got your buddy, Mr. Kaufmann, with me. If you don't do exactly what I say, he dies."

My concentration fizzled, interrupted by a mental picture of Kaufmann's kind face. That image was replaced by Cory's cruel sneer.

Somehow the bastard had found me.

"Pick up the phone, babe." The tone was soft, almost seductive. I could tell the bastard was grinning. "If you don't pick up within three seconds, I'm cutting Kaufmann's—"

His voice was drowned out by my proximity alarm, beeping like crazy on my countertop next to the Mr. Coffee. I hit the button, and the flat-screen TV—actually a video monitor—blinked on, my hallway camera showing a man with a shotgun at the door. Too soon for the duo from the sedan to have gotten up to the eighth floor, so this was someone new.

"One…" Cory said.

The door was reinforced, solid. But I no longer had time to grab my shoes and purse. I switched my encrypted cell to silent mode and clipped it to the inside of my panties, on my hip, then reached for the cordless handset, grabbing it with my palm, not my fingertips.

"Two…"

A shotgun blast, from the hall. I felt the vibration in the soles of my bare feet. The door held. I didn't stick around to see if it would withstand a second salvo.

"Three…"

I pressed the talk button while sprinting for the window.

"It's me." My breath was even, voice calm, though I could feel my pulse spiking. I smelled gunpowder and my own sweat. Background noise on the phone was standard static and hum. "Let me speak to Kaufmann."

My blinds were drawn. They always were. I put my back against the wall next to the window and twisted the rod, levering them open. A shot punched through the pane, making a small hole without shattering the glass. Sniper round, high velocity. The fire escape wasn't an option.

"What's the rush?" Cory said, his deep voice oozing. "We got a lot to catch up on. It's been twenty years."

"Put him on, Cory, or I swear I'm hanging up right now."

Kaufmann spoke, making my feelings temporarily override my brain. His words came out in a rush. "I'm near the lake he's not alone he has—"

A slapping sound. Kaufmann being hit. It was repeated, and I heard a grunt of pain.

I pushed back the emotion welling up in me, killed it before it could erupt, and pictured myself encased in a block of ice. Cold. Hard.

"You ready to talk to me now?" Cory said.

"Yes."

Another shotgun blast. The door shook and one of the hinges twisted off, shedding a screw onto the carpeting.

"What was that sound?" Cory demanded.

Focus. Stay focused. Too much happening at once.

I let out a slow breath, falling back on what I was taught. Process. Evaluate. Segregate. Then take control of the situation.

"I'm having phone problems. I may need to call you back."

"If you hang up this phone, bitch, I'll take some tin snips and—"

I tuned Cory out, crawling on my knees and elbows under the window, over to the front door, squatting alongside it.

A third shot rocked the apartment, making the wall shake. As the door fell inward I watched the vid monitor on my kitchen counter. The man was hiding on the right side of the doorway, opposite me, his back pressed to the wall. While the door was reinforced steel, the wall was plain old wood and plaster. Using the video monitor as a guide, I placed the barrel of my Glock an inch from the surface and fired twice. My loads were beryllium copper, and penetrated both the wall and the assassin's right knee. As he fell forward I was already aiming through the doorway where his head would appear.

My third shot ended him.

"—horrible pain. Do you understand?"

"Yes," I said into the phone.

I went through the doorway, low. My assailant was Caucasian, in his forties, muscular, dressed in a trench coat, jeans, and black leather gloves. His face was hard to make out under the damage my bullet had done, but I noticed a scar trailing from the right corner of his mouth down to his neck. I memorized it.

No use patting the guy down—he wouldn't be carrying ID. The shotgun wouldn't be traceable, either. I took it anyway, a Remington 11-87, tucking the warm stock under my armpit and moving in a crouch to the stairwell door. Underneath the gunpowder haze, the hallway smelled faintly of cigarettes. Mrs. Coursey in apartment 912. Someone, probably the elderly man in 914, had burned toast earlier. Animal scents, a dog, from the woman in the apartment above. The pungent stench of blood as the hit man soaked the floor.

"What the hell is going on?"

I whirled, aiming the Glock at my neighbor, Mr. Grant, sticking his head out of 907. This was Chicago, and most people knew when they heard gunfire to not open their doors.

He looked at me, looked at my gun, and slid back inside the imaginary safety of his home. I heard his lock snick into place. Then I held my breath, listening for other sounds. Mr. Knoll in 910 was watching CNN. I was able to make out the words *dramatic prison escape*. From the stairwell, muted sounds of footsteps nearing. One set, heavy, probably the man from the sedan. From behind me—

"Here are the instructions," Cory said. "I'll only give these to you once."

—the elevator reaching my floor.

I pinched the receiver between my ear and shoulder, freed the shotgun, and held it by the hot barrel.

The stairwell footsteps echoed closer, the man jogging up the last flight. Both of the assassins had to have heard the gunfire and would alter the strategy accordingly. That made me alter mine, and I ran to the right, out of the line of sight of the elevator.

"We want thirty thousand dollars in US currency. Hundred dollar bills, unmarked."

"Money? You want ransom for Kaufmann?"

"That's just for starters."

The lift doors opened and a familiar green pineapple shape arced out and rolled into the hallway. Which is what I would have done. Which is why I was ready.

I stretched the shotgun out. Using it like a mini-golf putter, I swung the stock, tapping the grenade and rolling it back into the elevator as the doors were closing.

I flipped the shotgun, grabbing the grip in the air just as the elevator exploded and the man came charging low out of the stairwell.

Ears ringing from the grenade, I didn't hear the next thing Cory said over the phone, nor did I hear the shotgun go off when I pulled the trigger.

The buckshot tore off much of the stairwell man's face. I never saw the woman in the elevator, but this one was dressed in blue coveralls and white latex gloves. His dead hand still clenched a semiauto with a suppressor screwed on.

I did a quick wipe down of the shotgun with my shirt, then discarded it. Spent gunpowder clogged my throat. I pinched my nose, held my lips closed, and tried to breathe out, forcing my ears to equalize. I still couldn't hear very well.

"This connection is terrible," I said into the phone. "You're breaking up."

My hip buzzed. I startled, whirling around, then remembered my encrypted cell. I dug it out of my panties.

Now I had no choice. I couldn't talk to Jacob while listening to Cory's ransom demands. And Jacob had priority over everything else. I squeezed my eyes shut, hands shaking, and hit the disconnect button on my landline with my knuckle. I'd know in a few seconds how Kaufmann suffered for my decision.

"Is Wanda there?" Jacob asked. I could barely hear him.

I'd already used the Milan code phrase, so I used the follow-up. "She's visiting her cousin in Nebraska. Can I take a message?"

"Are you out of the building yet? The Carmen Sawyer ID is burned. Word from the Chicago PD is that there are state and federal warrants out on you. I count at least ten squad cars heading toward your apartment. Two of them are pulling up right now."

Standard operating procedure. Someone higher-up trumped up some fake charges so the feds and local law enforcement would bring me in. But were they trying to save me or bury me?

I shook my head. Think. I needed to think. Kaufmann first.

"I need you to triangulate that call made to my home phone. It's a..." I groped for the word, "*friend's* cell. Cory kidnapped him.

I also need a DOD back door and a direct uplink to an ICU satellite in sync orbit over Chicago."

"Opening back door…now. *Diciassettesimo papa.* You don't have time to mess around with Cory right now, Chandler. Wait… what the hell?" Jacob paused, then said, "How did they find me?"

My heart rate jumped up an extra twenty beats per minute, and it was already hovering around 130. "Who found you? What's happening there?"

"Chandler, they're blowing the main…"

The phone went dead. *Jacob.* I let out a breath. Nothing I could do about it at the moment. I hopped over the corpse, tucked away the cell, and stepped into the hallway. My house handset rang. Cory.

"It wasn't my fault," I said, trying to keep my breathing steady. "This damn phone connection."

Kaufmann's voice was faint, and my hearing still hadn't fully returned, but his words felt as if they were fired into my head with a machine gun.

"He cut off one of my fingers."

Everything I've been taught—all of my training, all of my experience—slipped away. For a second, I couldn't breathe. I shuddered, rooted to the spot, alone and afraid. "Kaufmann? Talk to me!"

Cory came on. "Do your best not to lose the connection again, Carmen. Next time I'm not going to bother with a finger. I'll take the whole hand. You know I'll do it. Shit, I'll *enjoy* doing it."

Ice, I reminded myself. I was ice. So cool I had antifreeze for blood. I unbunched my jaw, forced back the tears, and looked around the stairwell.

Focus.

No heat in there, making it at least ten degrees cooler than the hallway. Brick walls, metal stairs, eight steps per flight, two flights between floors. Below, I heard footfalls. At least five sets, coming up in a hurry. "I'll give you the money. Whatever you want. Just don't hurt him again."

"Listen closely, babe. I'll only say this once."

If that many cops were coming in after me, they must have the exits covered. Getting arrested meant Kaufmann would die. No doubt Cory was planning on killing him even if I paid—Cory wasn't known for leaving survivors. But I couldn't help Kaufmann if I was in custody.

Assuming whoever set me up would let me live long enough to be taken into custody.

Down wasn't an option. So I had to go up.

"I'm listening," I said, controlling my breathing. The steps were cold under my feet, and I took them two at a time. I could smell stale beer and vomit, probably courtesy of the college kids from the floor below, and the lemon-scented bleach John the custodian used to clean it up. The footsteps got louder, more numerous. Eight cops...no, *nine*...coming up fast. I increased my pace.

"The sidewalk at eight seventy..."

The phone hissed static at me.

I'd gone out of range.

I stopped, went back down a few steps.

"Please repeat that. I couldn't hear you." My voice went up an octave, a little acting but also some real emotion getting out. "Please don't hurt him again, Cory. This goddamn phone—"

"Eight-seventy-five North Michigan Avenue," he said, irritation in his tone.

I didn't want Cory to be irritated. I knew what he was capable of.

The cops were less than three floors down from me. They'd check my apartment first. But it wouldn't take long to search, and when they didn't find me, they'd send a team upstairs. Could I kill innocent police officers to save Kaufmann?

"Got it," I whispered. "Eight-seventy-five North Michigan. What time?"

"You'll have the money in a yellow shoulder bag. Wait there for—"

Static again. I wanted to smash the phone against the wall, but instead crept down five more stairs until his voice returned.

"—exactly three hours from now. If you go to the police, I'll kill him."

Less than fifteen vertical feet separated me from the police. I could smell the aftershave on one of them—Lagerfeld—and their body heat and movement had raised the stairwell temperature two or three degrees.

"Don't hurt him again," I said, low and firm.

Yelling, from my floor below. They'd discovered the bodies.

"Miller! Casey! Check the stairwell!"

Their footsteps tap-tap-tapped up the stairs, about to round the corner and see me.

"That's up to you, babe." Cory disconnected.

I wiped the phone off with my shirt, dropped it, and bolted, moving fast as I could, bouncing on the balls of my feet, ascending four flights in seven seconds, coming to the roof access door. I tried the knob. Locked, as expected, and no time to pick it. On the wall was a fire alarm. I pulled it, the siren filling the stairwell, then fired my Glock three times at the lock mechanism.

The door swung outward. I lunged through. My foot snagged a cable—something that hadn't been there previously—and my body kept going. I pitched forward and threw out my hands, my gun skittering across the flat concrete rooftop just as a supersonic bullet parted my hair and dug a burning trail across my scalp: a shot that would have killed me a millisecond sooner.

I'd made a huge mistake. With everything going on, I'd forgotten about the sniper.

*"Use all of your senses, all the time," The Instructor said. "The brain is a parallel processor, but it dismisses most sensory input as redundant, irrelevant. You must teach your brain to stop ignoring what seems normal, obvious, or mundane. Hyperawareness can often be the difference between a live operative and a dead operative."*

I tucked my arms in to my chest and rolled sideways, coming to rest behind a metal chimney roughly the size and shape of a street corner mailbox. My Glock was ten feet away. Might as well have been a mile. The cable that saved my life snaked across the roof to a new satellite dish.

A bullet punched through the aluminum like a finger through soggy bread, making a hole only a few inches from my nose. I flattened myself against the tar paper, my cheek resting on dried pigeon droppings. Another shot, two seconds later, perforated the chimney five inches lower than the first, burying itself into the rooftop ten meters behind me. The wind whipped through my hair, but the short length kept it out of my face. These were Chicago winds, snaking around buildings, blowing eddies left, then up, then back.

"There's a sniper up here!" I yelled, hoping it would make the police stay back.

My breath came fast, my heart pumping like a cardio work-out, but my mind was focused and clear. The time between shots told me the sniper was using a bolt-action rifle. Calculating the hypotenuse of the trajectory told me he was in the apartment building to the west, roughly one floor above me. He'd either been on the fire escape facing my apartment or in one of the rooms. When the police arrived, he must have deduced my only way out was the roof, so he'd gone up as well. His building was seven stories taller than mine. The higher the sniper ascended, the better his angle, the easier his shot.

I needed to get off the roof.

Since the sniper was in motion, I assumed he hadn't any time to secure his mount. That meant each time he fired, he'd have to load another bullet, which would cause an unmoored rifle to jiggle a bit. On a telescopic lens, the slightest jiggle would force him to readjust after every shot. The high wind would make hitting a moving target even tougher.

"This is the Chicago Police Department! Put down your weapon and put your hands above your head!"

I glanced back at the doorway, saw the cops standing there like paper targets, and yelled, "There's a sniper on the opposite building!"

They followed my voice, training their guns my way. I got up on my fingers and toes, hopped to get my feet under me, and sprinted east.

I registered my mistake immediately, when the tar paper around my feet erupted in weapon fire. The sniper had a fully automatic rifle, not a bolt action as I'd assumed. He was a pro, and he'd played me.

But he'd underestimated how fast I could move and where I would go. I didn't bother zigzagging or backtracking, which were standard sniper countermeasures. I beelined for the roof's edge, feet slapping hard for maximum traction.

Ready or not...

Stretching out my hands, I dived off the side of the building.

I soared through the air, bullets cracking the sound barrier all around me. Heights weren't my strongest suit, and as I caught a glimpse of the street ten stories below—the cars and trees and people looking like toys—every part of me wanted to scream.

Use the adrenaline. Use the adrenaline.

Arms open and reaching, I waited for the fire escape I prayed was still there, the fire escape I hadn't checked since my long-ago roof reconnaissance when I first moved into the apartment.

My memory was a bit off.

The fire escape was still on the side of the building, but my angle was wrong by about a foot. The railing blurred as I passed over it and out into open sky.

*Shit shit shit.*

I adjusted, bending into a pike, reaching back around. My elbow hooked onto the iron railing, jerking me backward. I felt sharp pain and heard a *pop*—my shoulder had dislocated or broken. I clung to the side of the fire escape, my feet dangling above the alley two hundred feet below.

Pain ripped through my arm and down my side. No time to dwell on it now. I had precious few seconds to get my footing and get down to the ground level before the various people after me figured out where to look. I'd have to file the pain away, deal with it later. I reached up with my good hand, did a one-armed pull-up to disengage my elbow, and sought out the rusty iron grating with my toes. Then I flipped myself over the railing and scurried to the first ladder, trying to process my situation.

The sniper would be vacating. He'd seen the cops and given away his position. I had a whole building between him and me, so he was off my worry list for the moment. The cops were another story. The ones on the roof would take cover, radio for backup. Any units on the ground would be moving into position beneath me.

The breeze was considerable. I had to use my injured arm just to make sure I didn't blow off the ladder. My muscles screamed at me for relief, but I made them work anyway, pushing my way down the first three floors fast as I could. I chanced a look down, my mind swirling, vertigo tugging at me. A quick flash of memory invaded my brain, a training exercise where The Instructor had made me climb a forty-foot-high pole and traverse a rope leading to another pole. The height had paralyzed me until he'd drawn his sidearm and shot at me to force me to do it.

Goddamn heights.

I swallowed the dizziness and pressed onward. The scent of garbage drifted up from the alley, malted barley from a nearby brewpub, and now there were sirens in the distance, approaching fast.

I descended another ladder—only five more to go. The metal on the fire escape was old and sharpened by years of bad weather. My feet were starting to numb from the cold, but I could still feel the scrapes on the soles of my feet. I took a quick look. Some blood, but not enough to make me slip. I kept going.

The sirens had almost reached my building. The garbage stench grew stronger. I glanced down. The ground was about forty feet below, this part of the alley still clear of police vehicles. Roosting pigeons flapped into the air to my right, cooing their objections. My heart rate shot up at the surprise, and I lost precious seconds prying my fingers off the ladder to continue the descent.

With two floors left to go, a police truck pulled around the corner. A Chevy, white with blue trim, shaped like an ambulance. It moved slowly down the alley. I could see the driver through the windshield, which meant he could see me.

There were still twenty feet between my feet and the asphalt, a fatal distance, but the truck was at least eight feet high. A twelve-foot drop was dangerous but survivable. Dropping onto a moving truck would be tough. The high wind made the odds worse. My stomach clenched, fear and adrenaline, and I wondered if I'd be able to force myself to act.

*Just do it.*

I launched myself off the fire escape, calculating as I fell. Ankles pressed tight together, knees slightly bent, I figured I had a forty percent chance of surviving when I hit the truck's roof.

My feet struck hard enough to dent the aluminum, and I immediately bent my legs and dropped onto my back, both hands slapping down to disperse the energy of my fall as if I were on a judo mat.

The truck hadn't been moving fast, and I'd jumped in the direction of travel, so for a millisecond it seemed like I might actually stay on top.

Then the driver hit the brakes.

I tucked in best I could, rolling off the roof, bouncing off the hood, and spinning onto the alley as if an angry god had spat me out.

Someone said, "Holy shit." One of the cops from the truck.

I came to a stop on my side, perhaps ten feet in front of it. My one arm was worthless, and I instantly counted three more scrapes to add to my other injuries, but I was miraculously alive.

Should have given myself better odds.

I got a leg under me, did a trick with my ears to bring my balance back quicker, and then took four unsteady steps east before launching into a full sprint.

The alley let out onto Clybourn. I noted four police cars, two unmarked sedans that I ID'd as feds, and seven cops milling about on the sidewalk. The cops in the alley would be contacting others. But none had looked in my direction yet, and I chugged onto the sidewalk, sidestepping two gawkers and turning north onto Sheffield. My bare feet slapped the pavement, but I could barely feel them now due to cold and the pain of all my other injuries. I cut through another alley. When I reached the next street, I doubled back. The cops were certainly on my trail by now, but it would be a tough trail to follow.

Two blocks later, I slowed down to a walk. My heart rate was hovering around a hundred eighty beats per minute, and I got my breathing under control while triaging my body.

The shoulder was the worst injury, and now that I had time for examination, I determined it was dislocated, hanging two inches lower than it was supposed to. It felt hot to the touch, and the fingers of that arm were numb from the bone pressing against the axillary nerve.

I knew basic anatomy, knew combat medicine, knew where the ball of the humerus was supposed to connect to the socket of the scapula. Trying not to think too hard about what was coming, I grabbed my biceps, jerked upward as hard as I could, and felt it slip into place. A wave of agony took me, among the worst I'd ever felt.

I fought to focus past the pain and tune into my surroundings. The street was moderately busy, five cars heading north, seven going south. Two women waiting for the bus. A homeless guy sitting on the sidewalk, his back to a burger restaurant. I smelled exhaust, old vegetable oil, and pigeon shit. My tee was covered with bird poop, rust, and grime. After a few seconds, I managed to control my whimper. But nothing could stop the tears streaming down my face.

I continued to walk, slowing my heartbeat, managing my breathing. I tried not to think too hard about Kaufmann, about Jacob, about everything that had just gone down. I couldn't afford emotion. Not yet. Survival came first.

I inventoried the rest of my body. The gash in my scalp where the bullet had grazed me was already scabbing over, although my hair was sticky with blood. My feet were cut up, but superficially and not requiring immediate attention. Some tenderness in my right ankle, probably from when I landed on the truck. Both elbows scraped, and a sore spot on my hip. That made me reach for the spot and dig out the encrypted cell.

It turned on, no problem. I wasn't surprised. This thing was made to stop a bullet if it had to. I wondered if I actually needed it anymore. If Jacob had been compromised, the next call I received could be suspect, even if it came from him. But I'd been told, in no uncertain terms, that I was to never ditch the phone, not even in dire circumstances. I tucked it away again.

Again I steered my thoughts to more immediate matters. My beat-up state was certain to gain notice from passersby, and my description, including clothing, would be on the airwaves by now. I needed to change my appearance. I took a casual look around, didn't spot anyone paying attention, and ducked inside a discount store.

Like most dollar shops, this one sold discontinued junk that the owner bought by the pallet. Generic sundries, cheap foreign tools, no-name makeup and hair care supplies, sad-looking silk plants, and an astonishing variety of clocks featuring images of Jesus.

I walked past an aisle filled with obsolete magazines and worked at the seam on my tee, tugging it open and removing the rolled fifty-dollar bill. My sweatpants, underwear, bra, as well as every piece of clothing and every shoe I owned, each had a hidden fifty. That made my wardrobe worth several thousand dollars more than I paid for it. The hours of sewing proved worthwhile at that moment, and the two hundred dollars I had on me should be enough until I could reach one of my lockers.

I made quick work of the store, grabbing some cheap gym shoes, khakis, a dark green blouse, a box of baby wipes, a bottle of aspirin, a box of decongestant, and a straw sunhat. A three-dollar pair of sunglasses rounded out the ensemble. Since I couldn't purchase the decongestant without giving the clerk identification, I resorted to waiting until he wasn't looking and picking the lock of a glass case with the two metal wires hidden in the waistband of my pants. After paying for the rest of the items, I walked into the burger joint next door and spent four minutes in the washroom, cleaning away the dirt and blood with the wipes and dressing in my discount clothing. I threw away my tee and sweatpants, and used the drawstring to tie the two pieces of metal around my neck.

As my body recovered from fight-or-flight mode and the adrenaline ebbed, the pain started becoming a problem, interrupting my focus. I took three aspirin and three decongestants. The latter contained a stimulant, pseudoephedrine, which is used in the production of methamphetamine. It would keep me alert even though I felt like crashing. I tucked four more of each pill into my sports bra, then ditched the bottles.

I was nauseous—a side effect of adrenaline and pain. I waited in line and bought two double cheeseburgers and two bottles of water, not hungry but uncertain when I'd have a chance to eat again. I forced everything down while walking north and figuring out my priorities.

My disguise was fine for the moment, but it wouldn't hold up to close scrutiny. In order of importance, I needed a weapon, a safe house, a new disguise, and intel. Then I could start dealing with my problems, which were evading the police and FBI, figuring out who set me up and was trying to kill me, and rescuing Kaufmann. That meant confronting Cory.

Much as I wanted to, I couldn't forget I would have to deal with Cory.

I doubted Cory had anything to do with the hit out on me. First off, he didn't play well with anyone other than malleable young girls he'd trained to do whatever he asked. But even if Cory and I didn't have a history, I'd come to the same conclusion. If he'd been working with the people who wanted to kill me, he would have tried to keep me in my apartment. But he got off the phone too fast and didn't even seem to know I was being shot at. I'd believed Cory couldn't find me, but I'd forgotten how smart and observant he was. And although it had been almost twenty years since his trial, he obviously remembered seeing Kaufmann there the day I'd testified.

There wasn't a chance I would let Kaufmann's act of support and kindness lead to a horrible death at Cory's hands.

But first things first. A weapon and a safe house.

The gun would be relatively straightforward. The safe house would be tougher. Both the cops and the assassins had found my apartment when only Jacob was supposed to know where I lived. My name wasn't on the lease, my bills were paid through various dummy corporations, and if anyone traced the phone they'd get a fake address in Mundelein. That I'd been found meant a serious breach in security, and I had no idea how far it went.

The Carmen Sawyer ID was blown, and so were the bank account and credit cards associated with it. If the counter-intel went deep enough, my backup persona might also be compromised. Most hotels required a driver's license and credit card for incidentals, and both the good guys and the bad guys had systems in place to track check-ins.

I crossed the street and waited for the bus, the burgers' dead weight in my stomach, the aspirin doing shit. My focus cracked and splintered, leaving me aching, tired, and not thinking about my objectives as I should have been. Instead images of Kaufmann assaulted me, bleeding and scared with arguably only two hours and thirty-three minutes left to live.

*"Pain means you're alive," The Instructor said. "It's your body informing you of damage. Attend to the damage when you're able to. Then, forget the pain. It isn't helpful to you anymore. You're going to learn some techniques to work through pain, but I'd be lying if I said you'll become immune. We can teach you to cope with a lot of things. But we can't teach you to stop hurting. Hurt stops on its own, when you're either healed, or dead."*

The bus dropped me off a block from the Stretchers on Laramie. It was the nearest in a chain of women-only fitness clubs. I rented lockers at ten of their locations, four in the city, three in the suburbs, and three in other states. The padlocks I used were all a distinctive red color, making them easy to spot. I didn't have the key, but sewn into every pair of pants, skirt, and dress I owned was a lock pick and a tension wrench. I didn't invent this system, and rarely had to use it, but now that I was on the run, all of this prep work made me understand how smart it was.

I cased the place first, watching for three full minutes from across the street before approaching. Then I walked past, getting a good look inside the storefront window. The actual gym was deeper in the building, so I couldn't check it out. But the lobby was clear except for an employee I recognized as the one who signed me up. I doubled back, checking for tails. Finding none, I went in.

The interior was cool, the air conditioning humming. I heard faint rock music coming from the workout area. The Stones, "Paint it Black." I smelled lavender air freshener and cinnamon gum from the woman behind the desk.

"I'm sorry," I said, twisting my mouth into a smile I wasn't close to feeling. "I just realized I left my pass at home."

I'd cut up and thrown away the laminated member pass four minutes after receiving it.

"Your name and the last four digits of your social," the woman said without looking up from her magazine. No doubt half the membership regularly left their passes at home.

"Darla Thompson. Seven seven eight eight."

Darla Thompson wasn't my real name either. It was an unestablished ID used only for Stretchers. Darla didn't have any credit cards, no real address, and since I had gotten the driver's license out of state from a private dealer, it lacked the realism of my Carmen Sawyer and Betty Richards identities. I paid for the membership and the rental lockers by money order every six months.

The woman punched my data into her computer, then checked my face against the archived photo that appeared on her monitor. I didn't bother taking off my hat or sunglasses, and she didn't bother to ask. It made me wonder how much money this place lost from sisters or similar-looking friends sharing memberships.

"Welcome back, Darla," she smiled, her mouth crooked. "It's been a while."

I recognized her because I was trained to memorize faces. But for her to have remembered me out of thousands of members when I hadn't been there for months, *that* was impressive.

Then I realized my onscreen data probably listed the last time I'd been there, and I wasn't impressed anymore.

She pushed a button under the desk, buzzing me through the frosted glass doors. When I opened them, the music tripled in volume, pumping through speakers embedded in the ceiling. I walked past a Pilates class in progress, the free weight room, and the circuit training section, and stopped in front of the locker room.

It had no door—no men allowed, so one wasn't needed. For the sake of modesty, the entrance turned at a right angle after you walked in so no one could see inside. I inhaled, smelling citrus shampoo, sweat, and hairspray. Heard one of the showers running, but no other sounds.

I went in with heightened awareness. It was a long shot anyone knew about my locker here. Supposedly Jacob didn't even know. But it's impossible to be surprised if you're expecting something to happen.

When I walked around the privacy wall, I stopped again, letting my senses report. Warmer. Steamier. Bleach and disinfectant mingling with the previous odors. Other than the woman in the shower, it didn't feel like anyone else was around. A quick look confirmed my guess. No people. No open lockers. No unattended bags or clothes.

I circled twice to make sure, then discreetly peeked into the bathroom. Someone was in the shower stall, her feet visible beneath the plastic curtain. The shampoo scent was stronger and there were suds swirling down the drain between her toes.

I quietly found my locker and was taking the picks off my neck when the obvious hit me.

*Where were the showering woman's clothes?*

Some women arrive in their workout gear so they don't have to change. But those ladies don't shower here, because it would mean putting on their sweaty clothes when they finished. Those who changed here usually stripped out of their gear, showered, then dressed. But they didn't lock up their soiled clothes before showering. No one was going to steal a stinky tee and pair of yoga pants, and they were usually left in a heap on the bench or on the sink.

Maybe this woman was an exception, unlocking her locker, locking up her gear, showering, then unlocking her locker again.

But why bother locking up your gear in an empty locker room?

Movement to my right.

I dived left just as three shots punched into the wall behind me, catching a faint glimpse of a wet woman in a black swimsuit holding a suppressed semiauto.

Silencers are a myth. Gunpowder explodes, and explosions are loud; too loud for a metal tube to contain them. What lay-people call silencers are actually suppressors, which are able to reduce the sound considerably, but it's still louder than a person clapping their hands together. The rock music, however, coupled with the shower noise, effectively covered the shots.

Since I'd acted on instinct and not forethought, I'd rolled onto my bad shoulder. Agony stormed through my body, snatching away my breath. My vision blurred. Bright firefly motes darted and swirled in front of my eyes. I pushed myself onto all fours. Not able to hold weight, my arm gave way, leaving me to scurry on three limbs. Sight compromised, I used the shower sound as a compass, imagining the layout of the room in my head.

The hit woman was between me and the exit. An aisle of lockers was to my left. I guessed I was three yards away from them, and I crossed the distance in less than three seconds, scooting onto my butt with my back pressed against the cool metal, a handle jamming into my shoulder and bringing out fresh stars. I shook my head, willing my sight to return, and noticed peripheral movement on my right.

I pushed myself to my feet, half-staggering/half-sprinting into the shower, hearing two suppressed shots clang into lockers behind me. The temperature went up a few degrees, water vapor coating my face. My throat was closing up from fear, but I forced air through it, filling my lungs with steam. My heart rate was off the charts. I had nowhere else to go, and in a moment the assassin would corner and kill me.

Bathrooms don't offer much in the way of weapons. If this had been a private residence, I could have grabbed the porcelain toilet tank cover to use as a bludgeon, or smashed a mirror and attacked with a shard. But public toilets had no tank covers, and the mirrors were safety glass. The doors to the stalls hung on heavy-duty hinges, impossible for me to remove. Going hand-to-hand against someone with a gun was a last resort, and even then I only had a five percent chance of success. With my injured arm and my spotty vision, I cut those odds to two percent.

That left one alternative. And a weak one at that.

I sensed movement behind me but didn't bother to check. The tile floor was wet with soapy footprints, and I dived forward onto my belly, momentum taking me past the towel bin and into the shower stall. I snatched a fallen towel as I slid by, going under the shower curtain, the spurting nozzle drenching my head and back and compromising my hearing even further.

I flipped over, onto my butt, onto my knees, the towel getting soaked. Then I was back on my feet, swirling the towel in my good hand, bursting through the curtain and raising the dripping cloth like a whip.

I struck where I assumed the hit woman would be, at face level as she was coming around the corner. It was my best and only chance.

The towel snapped, cracking like a gunshot...on empty air. She had anticipated my attack and was already backing out of range, her gun up, the head shot inevitable.

But she hesitated.

Just what I needed. I whipped the towel around again, tossing it at her face and going in low. I jammed her in the chest with my good shoulder and drove with my legs.

Her shot went off over my head, the sound cracking loud in my ears despite the suppressor.

I kept moving, forcing her backward two steps—three, four— half on her feet, half falling. Blood rushed to my ears. I pushed harder, fighting not to slip on the tile floor.

Her backward movement shuddered to an abrupt stop. Her body went limp, sagging in my grasp. We hit the floor.

I wound up on top of her, my face pressed to her chest, my arm around her back. I shifted my arm, snaking her neck under my armpit, ready to lean back and snap her neck, but her head was surprisingly limp. I disengaged, staring at the wet towel still on her face, a towel that was quickly turning pink. Glancing up, I realized why—I'd bashed her head into the corner of the sink.

I kneeled, prying the gun out of her fingers, feeling her wrist as her pulse weakened and ceased. For a few seconds, I simply panted, waiting for my breathing to catch up, my heartbeat to slow down. The bright motes swimming in my vision faded, and I was able to study her body. She was about my height, my size. Her black bathing suit was a simple one piece, worn for function not flattery. Not that she needed fashion tricks to look thin and fit. Her body was as honed as mine.

I frisked her, locating a bulge that contained an extra clip for her weapon. I also found something else. Something both intriguing and disturbing. In her right shoulder strap, sewn into the seam, was a fifty-dollar bill. In her left strap, two pieces of wire that felt like lock picks.

Questions bombarded my mind. Questions I didn't have time to address. I removed the towel to look at her face, intending to memorize it.

I wouldn't have to.

Staring at her was like staring at my own reflection. The jaw, the haircut, the cheekbones, the nose, even the eyes were mine.

This woman looked so much like me she could have been my clone.

*"After a lethal encounter, cleanup is your first priority,"*
*The Instructor said. "If the area is still hot, leave imme-*
*diately. But if you can take a few seconds to hide the*
*body, that will buy you a few minutes or hours down the*
*line. If there's time to search the body, do so. However,*
*distinguish between gathering intel and processing it.*
*You can think about what you found after you're safe.*
*Dwelling on things while you're still in danger will slow*
*you down and get you killed."*

My breath caught, and I spent five useless seconds just gaping at her. *At me.* This was impossible.

Wasn't it?

I touched her hairline, looking for plastic surgery scars. Found none. No contact lenses either. I tugged down her suit, exposed her left breast. There, below the nipple, was a small, round mole.

*My* mole.

I felt dizzy, as if my thoughts were whirling around me. I was looking at myself, staring at my own face, my own body, dead. This couldn't be happening. I wasted three more seconds attempting to process what I was seeing, and then a bell went off in my head reminding me I had to get out of here.

Yanking out my phone, I took a quick full-body picture of the dead woman. Then I pressed her thumb to the phone's screen and took a second pic of her fingerprint.

After placing the bloody towel back over her face, I dragged her into the closest toilet. Hoisting her onto the seat brought the stars back, but I managed to get her balanced. Then I tore off the top portion of her bathing suit and tied it to the water pipe behind her so she'd stay in the sitting position. I locked the stall door, shimmied underneath it, and grabbed a fresh towel.

A quick walk around revealed the locker room was empty. I located locker 352. My fingers were shaking, my whole body was shaking, and it took me twice as long as my normal eight seconds to pick the padlock. After grabbing the duffel bag inside, I toweled off, stuck the suppressed .22 into my khakis against the small of my back, and forced myself to focus on my next move. The hit woman must have a locker, but there were hundreds here. I had no time to break into them all. Whoever was after me could send someone else, or someone might already be in place.

I needed to get to a safe house. Someplace I could absorb this, recover, plan my next move. I checked the clock on my encrypted cell. Only an hour and thirty-six minutes until my meeting with Cory.

It was also ten minutes past the time Jacob had said he'd call.

The tremor that had claimed my muscles delved deeper, centering in my chest. Jacob never missed a call. For the first time in almost a decade, I was on my own. With everything that had happened in the past hour, that made me feel the most off-balance.

I relocked my locker, shouldered my duffel, and left the locker room, getting my breathing under control. The Pilates class was still going on. The woman at the front desk still had her nose in her magazine and didn't bother glancing up when I approached.

"It's me again, Darla Thompson. Can you tell me when I first came in this morning?"

Her sigh was slight but intended to be heard.

"Last four digits of your social."

"Seven seven eight eight."

Another sigh. "You checked in at nine thirty, and again at ten twenty-six."

She looked at me now, raising an eyebrow at my wet shirt and pants.

"Thanks," I said, turning on my heels.

At least now I understood her earlier "It's been a while" comment. She was being sarcastic. The hit woman—my double—had checked in as me, fifty-six minutes before I checked in myself. So she must have been on her way here before Jacob called me at the apartment. As a backup, in case the op failed? And how had she even known about this place?

I stepped out onto the street. The wind was still up, raising gooseflesh all over my body, the wet clothes intensifying the chill. I headed west. Normally, after being ordered to go to ground, I would be on a bus out of town after picking up my duffel bag. But I had to meet with Cory and rescue Kaufmann, which meant I had to stay local.

In the bag, I had ID and credit cards for Carmen Sawyer and for Betty Richards. But if the people after me knew about Darla Thompson, Betty might also be compromised. Betty was surely compromised if the people chasing me had gotten to Jacob.

I needed someplace private, with Internet access, a bathroom, a kitchen, and a bed. Someplace that didn't require any sort of identification or interaction with strangers. And I thought I knew a place.

I hailed a cab, gave the driver the address. He was white, overweight, and his hack smelled like BO and onion breath. I dug through the duffel bag, made sure he wasn't looking, and opened the med kit. I filled a syringe with Demerol and discreetly injected my bad shoulder. Blessed numbness seeped into the area, and I had the urge to slump back in the seat and heave a long sigh. But I couldn't let my guard down, not yet. Instead I slipped on a silver Casio diver's watch from my bag and synced it to the time on my phone. Then I put two zip ties and my lock picks into my front pocket and stared out the rear window, checking for tails.

Twelve minutes later, the cab spit me out on Roosevelt. I paid with a fifty, got my change, and walked the last three blocks. There was a cool autumn breeze, but my hair was almost dry, my damp clothes warming up from the cab ride and my physical activity. I smelled car exhaust, sewage from a nearby drain, and cinnamon from a bakery up the street. The sky was overcast, but I sensed the barometric pressure, and it didn't feel like rain. My hearing had almost returned to normal, with only a faint ringing. I kept my bad arm against my side as I walked. The pain was gone, but I had no idea of the damage, didn't want to make it worse.

The apartment building was typical of the area, five stories, redbrick, built with the design acumen of a three-year-old playing with blocks. From the outside, I judged there were forty units, eight per floor.

I circled the building, didn't notice anything out of the ordinary. Then I slipped into a neighboring building's doorway and waited three minutes just to make sure no one was following, doing the isometric calf exercises I'd been taught to keep my muscles loose.

I was clear.

The front security door was cake, six seconds with my pick and tension wrench. No lobby, just a hall leading to the apartments on that floor, the elevator, and the stairwell. I smelled traces of mildew, roach poison, and fresh paint. Someone had cooked pancakes for breakfast. Voices and a jangle of music came from a TV on one of the upper floors. I took the stairs to apartment 304, listened at the door, then knocked. No one should have been home, so when I heard movement coming from inside, I stepped to the left of the doorway and tugged the .22 from my waistband.

Victor opened the door, looked around, and then saw me. He smiled in recognition, then confusion took over. "Carmen?"

I brought the gun up in a smooth arc. It caught him under the jaw even as he was flinching away. He backpedaled, and I followed him into the apartment. I cocked back my right leg and fired it into his gut.

Victor crumpled to the floor on all fours. I closed the door behind me and jammed the gun into his ear.

"On your face, arms out, palms up."

"Carmen?" His voice had a quaver in it. "What the hell—"

"If you make me ask again, I'll shoot you."

He eased himself down and splayed out his arms. He was wearing jeans, a blue polo shirt. I noted he'd shaved since I'd seen him on my computer monitor, and I could smell cologne. Claiborne for Men. I put my knee on the back of his neck, pinning his face to the carpeting, and frisked him. Wallet in his back pocket. Cell phone in his front. I took both.

"I have some cash," he said, the fear still in his timbre. "In a box in my closet. A few hundred dollars."

"Why aren't you at work?"

"What?"

"Work. You said you were on call."

"Last minute thing. A buddy phoned, wanted to trade shifts." He gave a strangled laugh. "Is this what you do, meet guys online then break into their homes when you think they're at work?"

He seemed genuine. But all operatives took acting lessons. I could go from laughter to tears in an eyeblink, just like Meryl Streep. But I doubted Meryl could kill a man eighteen ways using just her thumb.

"Hands behind your back. Cross them at the wrists."

I increased the pressure on his neck, digging a zip tie out of my pocket. It was a white plastic strip, eighteen inches long, made for bundling cable. In a quick motion, I stuck the .22 under my armpit and encircled his hands with the tie, snugging it tight.

"I didn't think I even gave you my address," he said.

"You didn't."

He made a sucking sound. "I think you knocked one of my teeth loose. This is a pretty awful first date, if I may say."

I took note of his attempt at humor but didn't acknowledge it. Nerves talking? Or cool under pressure? At this stage I couldn't tell. "Ankles together, then bend your knees so I can reach your feet."

He obeyed, and I cinched another zip tie around his feet, noting he had on socks with a White Sox logo.

"Now what? You kill me?"

"That depends on you, Victor. I'd like to trust you, but some things are happening in my life that make me incapable of that."

"If you'd like to talk about some of those things, I'm a captive audience."

The normal me might have smirked. The normal me liked this guy. But I couldn't afford to let the normal me do the thinking now. I unslung my duffel and fished out the med kit. It took a few seconds to find the vial of amobarbital. I judged his weight to be a hundred ninety, filled the syringe with an appropriate dose, and shoved it into his biceps as I pressed the plunger.

Victor bucked, throwing me onto my ass, but I'd managed to give him the full dose. He twisted to face me, the needle still sticking out of his arm.

"What did you do?"

"It's a sedative. You'll sleep for a few hours."

He blinked, his eyelids already getting heavy. "W…why?"

"I need your apartment for a little while. If you've been telling me the truth, when you wake up I'll be gone. If I discover you've been lying to me, about anything at all, you won't wake up."

"L…lousy first date."

Then his eyes fluttered shut, and his head hit the carpet.

My to-do list was growing exponentially. I needed to toss Victor's place to see if he was just an unlucky civilian or somehow part of this whole mess. I also had to tend to my injuries, find a shoulder bag like Cory had specified, figure out who that hit woman was, access the DOD database, try to contact Jacob, learn the extent of my frame-up, and form a plan to handle Cory and get Kaufmann back unharmed—a plan that was already way behind because my duffel bag only contained ten thousand and not the thirty thousand Cory had demanded.

I prioritized, doing a quick tour of the apartment to make sure it was empty. It was, except for an incredibly obese calico who meowed when she saw me.

"Hello, Mozart." I tickled her chin and she purred.

I found the bathroom, shedding my clothes and checking out the medicine cabinet. It was stocked full of bandages, first-aid supplies, and various professional equipment. Exactly what would be expected from a paramedic, which is what Victor supposedly was. I stripped off my bra, brushing away the remnants of the damp pills I'd stuffed inside earlier, and checked my injuries in the mirror over the sink.

I was a mess, cut up and bruised and swollen over much of my body. The worst was my shoulder, bright pink and puffy. I didn't have time to properly clean or tape any of my wounds, so I slathered on a whole tube of antibiotic ointment, gave myself a booster shot of Demerol, and swallowed four aspirin and some amphetamine salts from my kit. Then I shoved my clothing and gym shoes into the dryer in the closet near the kitchen.

My encrypted cell had a touch screen, but it didn't dial out like a regular phone. There was a nine-key sequence that changed according to the date, and entering a wrong number made it shut off for ten minutes. I pressed the buttons carefully, not hitting send, and waited for Jacob to answer.

Jacob's phone didn't ring. Instead, it played a recording that the number had been disconnected. I silently counted five seconds after the message ended and said, "This is Yolanda. I'm in Ontario."

I waited. Jacob didn't pick up.

I disconnected by pressing zero and tucked the phone away, walking to the bedroom closet. Among the men's shirts, sweaters, and suits, there was a small selection of female clothes. Jeans, culottes, some shirts and blouses, a sweater, a pants suit, and a jacket. All size six. I took the jeans and a long-sleeved shirt. They smelled like L'Air du Temps and fit me perfectly.

Then I headed for the second bedroom. Sure enough, Victor had transformed it into an office of sorts. I recognized the beige sofa I'd seen on the webcam. Some free weights cluttered the floor under a small window. I sat at his desk in front of his computer. Windows 7 and IE were already running. While I downloaded Google Earth, I accessed the back door for the Department of Defense, which almost certainly wasn't aware it had a back door. Jacob changed the passwords several times a day to make sure no one else could use his entry route. He'd told me *Diciassettesimo papa*. I knew Italian but hadn't brushed up on my Catholic history in a while. Wikipedia informed me the seventeenth pope was St. Urban I. That password got me in.

For one of the most encrypted, expensive websites on the planet, the DOD database was a bitch to navigate. It took me a minute to access their facial recognition software, and six more to create an adequate likeness for the scarred hit man who had knocked on my door.

I had to give our government some credit, though, because it only took seven thousandths of a second to get me a match.

Alex Sokolov. Ex-KGB. Records reported he died seven years ago, but most Russian records said that. I didn't have time to go through the whole dossier, so I saved it as a text file, named it Alex, and buried it on the C drive.

In a separate window, I accessed www.NBC5.com for local news. There was a link about the two-week manhunt after the prison break at Stateville, but that wasn't what I clicked on. Instead, I fixated on the lead story.

# 3 DEAD
# IN NORTH SIDE KILLING SPREE

I quickly skimmed the details about the three assassins I'd retired at my apartment. It didn't give out names, but there were the obligatory pictures of the corpses, sanitized for the public, low resolution, no gory details. In the case of the two men, just bodies, no faces. The woman in the elevator must have had a lot of her body torn up by the grenade, too gross for the website. But I was sure someone had taken a photo of her.

I logged onto Usenet, and after downloading an NZB reader, I quickly located a pirated FTP program with a keygen. I snatched it, installed it, and accessed the FTP URL for Channel 5 News. It was a site I'd hacked before, and the passwords were still the same. Their FTP address was where the www.NBC5.com server was located and all their online data was stored, and it took me less than a minute to open the file locker with the full-size unused PNG photographs of the death scene.

I found what I was looking for on the fifth photo I viewed: a close-up of the woman from the elevator. Her lower body was a mangled mess, but her face was largely untouched.

Like the hit woman at Stretchers, she had short, dark hair and blue eyes. And like the woman at Stretchers, she was a dead ringer for me.

*"My job is to train you," The Instructor said, "but I don't know what I'm training you for. I can guarantee you'll be told to do things you do not want to do. Things that violate your principles, your humanity, even your patriotism. But a weapon doesn't question why it was*

*fired, or what it was fired at. You're a weapon, a tool to be used by the government or the military. I pray your handler has enough principles, humanity, and patriotism for the both of you."*

Two hit women, both with my face and body. A former KGB assassin. Jacob compromised. Stretchers compromised. My ID blown. Cory on the loose. Kaufmann kidnapped.

I had no idea what it all meant and which facts were related to each other. Nor did I have time to dwell on it. Protocol dictated I establish a perimeter, interrogate my unwilling host, then evaluate the intel.

Kaufmann threw a wrench into normal operating procedure. If I were on a mission, things would be different. But the only bright spot in the fact that I was operating on my own, not under any direct orders, was that I could make saving him my first priority.

Whether Uncle Sam approved or not.

The ICU—a spook acronym that wasn't actually an acronym at all but rather a literal meaning—was a net of spy satellites that could be aimed by field operatives. Any agent with a laptop computer and the required longitude and latitude could zoom in on almost any area on the planet within two minutes of giving the command.

Unfortunately, Jacob was cut off before I could get the latest ICU uplink data. But Google Earth wasn't a bad substitute.

I loaded the program, which began by filling the screen with the familiar round and blue view of the earth from space, conveniently facing North America. I used the mouse scroll wheel to zoom in, each revolution bringing the world closer and closer, first over Illinois, then over Chicago, streets and buildings and eventually cars and people coming into detailed focus.

Instead of degrees, I punched in the street address and got a close-up satellite picture of 875 N. Michigan, revealing a familiar Chicago landmark. Google Earth also let me superimpose street names and store locations over the picture. Then I clicked on a camera icon at street level and got a full, 360-degree panoramic view of the whole area, dated from ten minutes ago. I quickly figured out a route, entry and exit points, and visualized how Cory would run it.

If his plan followed my assumptions, and I knew him well enough to be sure it would, neither Kaufmann nor I would live through this.

Steering my thoughts away from Kaufmann's fate for a moment, I pinged Victor's router, got the URL, and quickly synced my phone to his Wi-Fi. A minute later, I was uploading my doppelganger's fingerprint to Jacob's database. I wasn't at all surprised I didn't get a hit. I saved the search offline, then spent two minutes erasing all of my tracks from Victor's hard drive.

I checked my watch, saw I only had fifty-two minutes remaining, and went to the dryer for my shoes and socks. I locked the door behind me when I left the apartment, using the keys I'd found on Victor's kitchen table. I took the alley exit, pausing for a moment to get my bearings. I smelled garbage and car exhaust. The wind had picked up a bit, chilling my still-damp gym shoes. The alley was quiet, vacant, and I took it south, holding the duffel bag full of ten thousand dollars in my bad arm, keeping my right thumb hitched in my rear pocket, near the weapon nestled against the small of my back.

Fourteen steps out of the alley, I spotted a tail.

She was standing at a bus stop, a stylish wool cap on her head, staring intently at a tablet PC no bigger than a paperback novel. Her large sunglasses broke up the contour of her face, making her anonymous and unidentifiable as an agent.

Except to me.

The woman was doing isometric calf exercises. First flexing the left calf, then the right, then lifting the left toes, then the right.

I knew she'd lift the left heel next, then slightly bend the knee. I knew this because it was the same exercise The Instructor had taught me during training.

This woman proved me correct, following the sequence exactly. I was too far away to tell if this was another lookalike. But I would know soon enough.

I crossed the street quickly, keeping an eye on her, then approaching from the side at an angle beyond her peripheral vision. She kept her nose in the tablet, legs still twitching, oblivious to my presence.

I wanted to interrogate her, to know how she'd found me so quickly, to learn who she was and what she wanted. But I was short on time, and leaving her here to try my luck later could lead to her interfering with the Cory meeting. Contrary to the movies, subduing and capturing someone was incredibly difficult, especially without preparation and the proper equipment. A thousand things could go wrong.

Murder, however, was pretty straightforward.

My best bet was a quick shot right behind the ear. I did a discreet check for cops, then reached for my weapon.

The move was so fast I almost missed it. While keeping both eyes on the computer screen, she yanked a pistol from under her sweater and pointed it right at me. I jerked sideways, two shots zipping through the space I'd occupied a nanosecond ago, bringing my suppressed .22 around and catching her in the chest.

Unlike the jacketed rounds for my Glock, which were for penetration, the .22 was loaded with star frags—special bullets shaped like a pointed king's crown. When they hit a target, the crown opened up like flower petals, allowing for maximum energy transfer and creating an internal wound up to three inches in diameter. For a small caliber, they packed a big punch.

So big, my stalker went down instantly, glasses spinning off her face, dropping both her gun and the tablet, then slumping to the sidewalk like a length of cut rope.

The whole thing was over in less than a second, all the shots fired blending together like a car backfiring. Once again I checked the street for any witnesses, then hurried to the body, keeping my weapon alongside my thigh.

When I got close enough, several things struck me at once. The first was her face. Eyes closed, lips parted, undeniably my features. While her chest didn't seem to be moving, there also wasn't any blood. Her blouse and bra beneath were shredded by the star frags, and there wasn't a vest under them. Rather, her skin showing between the fabric tears was brownish and lumpy, almost as if it had been slathered with peanut butter.

Bringing up my gun again, I pressed it under her neck while I touched her sternum. The brown goop was moist and sticky, and her heart thrummed under my fingertips.

I pulled the trigger the moment I realized what the paste on her skin was. But my doppelganger had anticipated the move. She swept my gun to the side. My round hit the sidewalk. She brought up the heel of her hand and clipped me clean under the jaw.

I toppled backward, my teeth crunching together so hard it rattled my brain, the sparkly motes in my vision quadrupling in size when my coccyx hit the street. I blindly brought the gun up, reflex squeezing the trigger even as I felt a foot connect with my knuckles, knowing I hit her somewhere in the legs, knowing it didn't matter if she had that stuff smeared all over her body. Liquid body armor. I might as well have been shooting case-hardened steel.

My gun went flying—a testament to the power of her kick. During training, I'd had to hold onto a gun for a week straight without ever putting it down, but she knew right where to hit me to make me lose my grip.

Then I was on my back, and she was on me, and I knew she'd had the same training I'd had, meaning I'd likely be dead within the next two seconds.

*"Your body is a weapon," The Instructor said. "Hands, feet, elbows, knees, head. In close combat, commit immediately and fully, aim for your opponent's vital points and nerve points, and hit and stick to deliver maximum damage. Strike fast, strike hard, and try to strike first."*

I struck, going for her eyes. My fingers hit their target, jabbing the cheekbones and sliding upward into the soft tissue. I could feel her grunt of pain in my own chest. I thrust harder, trying to gouge her eyes out, or better yet, penetrate the thin bone behind the optic nerve and plunge into her brain.

I wasn't so lucky.

She moved her head to the side and brought the edge of her hand hard against the front of my good shoulder, connecting with the large bundle of nerves that passes in front of the joint. My fingers buckled. My arm slumped, numb and useless.

She brought her hands to my throat, her thumbs pressing right below my larynx, aiming to crush my trachea. I clawed at her with my other hand, still tingly from the Demerol. My vision blurred. But through the motes I could see her eyes were half closed, tears and some blood glistening on her cheeks.

Flexing my stomach muscles, I lunged upward, smacking my forehead straight into her nose. She released her grip, stunned for a moment, reflex bringing her hands to her face.

A moment was all I needed. I bucked my body, tossing her to the sidewalk. One move and I was on my feet. My balance lagged behind, and I had to pause half a second to adjust.

Too long. Barely a moment passed and she was up too, striking fast and hard with a cut to the jaw.

I blocked her blow and drove my elbow into the side of her head. Still unsteady on my feet, I couldn't muster enough force to do real damage, and she came back at me with a palm-heel strike to my solar plexus.

Breath fled from my lungs. I gasped, sucking in air. I managed to block her next blow, still wheezing when she landed a knee jab to the stomach that doubled me over.

She grabbed my hair and yanked my head back, searing pain ripping along the cut in my scalp. I struggled to twist to the side, throw her off balance. No good. She shoved my head down, smacking my forehead hard against her knee.

Flashes of light exploded in front of my eyes. I staggered to the side, somehow keeping myself from going down.

My injuries were making me sluggish. After the morning I'd had, she was faster, fitter. If I hadn't impaired her vision, there would be no way I could keep up. I wasn't sure I could now. I needed to end this. Quickly.

Before she ended me.

She struck again, fast, as I knew she would, coming in too close, too certain of my defeat. She attacked from the right, trying for a strike to my carotid artery.

I managed to block with my left elbow then straighten, bringing my right elbow up under her jaw. I clipped her hard, driving her head back. I followed with a strike to her throat from the other side.

As she staggered back, I grabbed her, my right arm over her chest, my left under her thighs. I straightened my legs, pressing her against my torso and lifting her like a barbell.

She wasn't ready to give up yet. She found my face with her hand, trying to land a stunning blow to the sensitive spots behind my ear and the base of my skull, and failing that, jabbing for my eyes.

I tucked in my chin, keeping my balance. A grunt rasped in my throat, an aggressive and guttural sound. I managed a short lunge forward with my right foot. Using that momentum, I brought her body down hard and smashed her back against my knee.

I felt her spine break just as I collapsed forward, my legs crumbling, unable to hold her any longer. Both of us hit the sidewalk.

For a second, I half-expected her to throw another move at me, a move I wouldn't be able to handle.

But she didn't stir, didn't even twitch.

Witnesses? I could feel people watching, no doubt calling 911. A guy across the street. A taxi parked on the corner. But no one was stupid enough to approach. Tuning in to sounds, I heard traffic, a bus, the distant cry of a siren, the crackling of leaves blowing across the sidewalk.

I willed my mind clear. I had to move.

I struggled upright and started frisking my dead double. I didn't find anything compromising, didn't expect to, but the job took only seconds, since I knew precisely where to look. Like the woman at the health club, she had cash and wires sewn into her clothing precisely the way I did.

I took her weapon, her sunglasses, her tablet computer, and stuffed them into my duffel alongside the money. Hands shaking, I tugged out my cell phone, took a quick picture of her thumbprint, and sent it to a secure Internet drop box where Jacob could access it, if he was still able.

I left her body on the sidewalk, not bothering to hide it. With the police on their way and with eyewitnesses peppering the street, the extra time and energy it would cost to conceal her corpse wouldn't get me much.

My stomach roiling, I staggered away, taking fifteen steps before I was able to balance enough to break into a jog. I rounded the corner with my fist pressed to my stomach so I didn't throw up—the nausea, as well as the almost uncontrollable trembling of nearly every muscle in my body, was a side effect of too much adrenaline.

I'd put two blocks between me and my lifeless double before I was able to calm my jitters, settle my thoughts, and fully focus on what I had to do next. It took another two to locate a drugstore. The scream of a siren pierced the ambient traffic sounds just before I ducked inside the revolving door.

Inside I could still hear the cop car's wail mixed with the hum of voices, the whir of the register printing out a receipt, and background music, a bland rendition of a Simon and Garfunkel classic. Perfume tinged the air, something cheap that carried a harsh citrus note. A woman behind the cosmetics counter eyed me as if she thought I could desperately use the Shimmer Face Primer on display.

Fighting techniques were only one of my trained skills. I had also studied facial expressions and body language, and I could read the intentions of others as well as I could disguise my own. The woman seemed to be what she appeared, an employee trying to sell makeup, but after all the surprises I'd had, I couldn't be too sure. And even a well-meaning employee could cause me problems if she noticed my injuries and decided it was her business to help.

I gave her a fleeting don't-try-to-sell-me smile and hurried past like a normal busy woman doing errands on my lunch hour. She offered a polite nod and turned to an older woman in a tracksuit.

I scanned the rest of the store, including the wide-angle mirrors positioned around the ceiling's perimeter, keeping my head low so my face didn't register on the cameras behind them. I didn't see any other Walgreens shoppers who flagged my attention. And miraculously, for what seemed like the first time all day, I was the only one in the store bearing my exact features.

I made quick work of my shopping, picking up a yellow canvas book bag (which sat next to a display of eReaders—who really needed a book bag anymore?), a bottle of niacin, a utility knife, and a blue knit cap. Once out the door, I pulled on the cap and the sunglasses I'd taken off my double and continued down the street. The only sirens were distant now, their screams partially drowned by the rumble of the El several blocks away, the usual traffic noise, and the whoosh of wind. The breeze carried the snap of fall and scent of pizza—oregano and cooked sausage—from a nearby deep-dish restaurant.

I turned my head to the side as I walked, as if simply taking in the day. Several people dotted the sidewalk behind me, the foot traffic picking up as people stepped out to get a bite to eat. I took a right turn, ducked into a doorway for a moment, transferred the cash from my duffel to the yellow bag, then stepped back out onto the street. After crossing the side street, I rejoined the first street I'd been walking and noted the traffic patterns of those behind. No one appeared to be following.

I stopped on the next corner and hailed a cab. I collapsed into the backseat. "The Shedd Aquarium, please."

The odor of stale menthol cigarettes hovered around the driver. "Sure thing." He accelerated and blended into traffic.

We headed in the direction of the lake. I cracked the window and let exhaust dilute the smoke stench. A few minutes later, we swung onto Michigan Avenue's Magnificent Mile. I glanced out the window and pretended to take in the glitzy stores, the Tribune Tower, the ornate architecture of the Wrigley Building, all the while checking for tails. We crossed the Chicago River and moved south. By the time my cab had reached Millennium Park, I was as certain as I could be that I was alone.

We took Roosevelt Drive to Lake Shore, turned at Soldier Field, and wound past the Field Museum. As we approached the aquarium, I made a visual sweep of the area. School busses clogged the parking lot. A mother dragged two dawdling children up the steps to the main entrance. Wind whipped flags and raised whitecaps on the lake.

"We're here," the cabbie said, reaching for the meter.

"No, wait."

His hand stopped midair. "This is the Shedd Aquarium."

"I know. I'm waiting for someone. Can you sit here and let the meter run for now?"

"Sure thing." He sounded less than enthused.

I pulled the tablet computer I had taken from my most recent dead doppelganger out of the duffel. If there was anything on the woman that might give me a clue who she was and what was going on, this was it. The problem was getting past whatever security measures were in place.

Three minutes later, I hadn't made much progress. The computer was encrypted. I would need more time to work on it. Time I didn't have. "I've changed my mind. Take me to Macy's on State Street."

The cabbie glanced in the rearview and arched his brows. "Whatever you want." He was an older guy with a square face, salt-and-pepper hair, and an expression that plainly said he didn't care about anything. He wove his way out of the parking area and started retracing the route we'd just traveled. I looked down at my watch.

Soon I would be face-to-face with Cory again.

I spotted the black SUV a block from Macy's. It turned out from Pearson and fell into traffic four cars behind my cab. It was a slick move. One executed by someone with experience, and at first I wasn't sure why it drew my attention. But I'd been taught to trust my instincts, and right now they were jumping. "Can you drive around the block? I'd like to see if my friend is here."

A disinterested grunt from the front seat, but the driver took the next right.

Four cars behind us, the SUV did the same. The next turn brought similar results. By the time my cabbie had orbited the entire block, I'd long since gotten the confirmation I needed and was working on figuring out who was behind the wheel.

It wasn't Cory. I couldn't see the driver well, but I could see enough to know it wasn't a face I knew. So who was it? And how did they find me?

No one had followed me from the drugstore. No one had tailed my cab to the aquarium. And except for the last few blocks, no one had picked us up on the drive to Macy's. That left only one explanation.

I was being tracked.

I felt for the slight bulge at my waist. A cell phone signal could be tracked by different service towers and then triangulated to find its location. I'd turned my encrypted phone off. No one should be able to pick up a signal that wasn't there, but maybe with this phone, on or off didn't matter. Jacob was compromised. Maybe that meant my phone had been compromised as well.

I fought the urge to toss the damn thing out the window. The phone was vital. Jacob had stressed that more times than I could remember. I couldn't simply ditch the thing. I had to figure out some other solution.

And whatever it was, I had to come up with it fast.

"Take me to 875 North Michigan."

"You sure about that? Or you gonna change your mind again?"

"The meter is running, right?"

He held up a hand. "Yeah, yeah, I get it. Shut up and drive."

I twisted in my seat and looked straight at the SUV.

It took the next right turn, as I had guessed it would. The driver realized I'd gone around the block for a reason and knew he'd been made. Not that it really mattered. If they were tracking my cell phone, and that was the only thing that made sense, the SUV didn't have to be riding the cab's bumper in order to keep tabs on me. He'd catch up soon enough.

But maybe I could use this opportunity to make his job a little more complicated.

A few blocks later, the cab came to a stop at the curb. This time the driver made no move to turn off the meter, as if waiting for the next destination. "Here you go. 875 North Michigan Avenue. Hancock Center."

I peeled some cash off the stack in the yellow bag and thrust it at the cabbie. "Keep the change. Maybe buy yourself some cigarettes."

I stepped out onto the curb and looked up at the hundred-story building. Black and slightly tapered, with the two iconic white antennas on its roof forking into the sky and the crisscross pattern of girders running up all four sides. It was so tall that it seemed to sway and tilt, and I felt my stomach do a little dip.

I glanced at my Casio and checked the time.

Eleven minutes before my meeting with Cory.

And not a second to waste.

*"Often, you'll have to ditch items. Garbage cans are best. A mailbox can work in a pinch. But if you want to return for the item later, you need to be able to hide things in public places where they won't be easily found. That requires a bit more thought and an understanding of human behavior."*

The lobby of the John Hancock Center smelled like marble, a vaguely dusty scent that reminded me of the halls of government. People passed me, heels clicking on hard floors, emerging from their condominiums or shopping at one of the retail spots in the center. It was a beautiful building, a Chicago landmark, but it was a wasteland when it came to hiding places.

Unlike some other city skyscrapers, there weren't any metal detectors, but I noted the security cameras peering down from the ceiling. I wasn't too worried about the authorities. I was sure they were looking for me, but by the time they noticed the woman on the security footage was of interest, I'd be long gone.

If they noticed at all.

I worked my way deeper into the building. Planters would be too obvious, and since many of the plants were real, the chance of pots being swapped out with fresh greenery before I could retrieve the phone was too high. Not that I wanted to ditch the phone on the main floor anyway. Lobbies had too much traffic.

I spied two women crossing the lobby. About twenty years apart in age, they had the same long, narrow nose and brown eyes. I guessed mother and daughter out for a day lunch or shopping.

Neither one was paying much attention to anything but their own conversation, a good sign they were exactly what they seemed. Civilians. They strolled toward a bank of elevators. I fell in twenty paces behind them, close enough to hear their voices but back far enough for my eavesdropping to escape notice.

A woman wearing dark pants and ill-fitting jacket stood near the elevator doors. She stepped out, blocking the women's trajectory. "Can I help you find something?"

The one I'd pegged as the daughter took the lead. "We have lunch reservations at the Signature Room."

"That's on the ninety-fifth floor. It's accessed by a different bank of elevators." The woman pointed the way.

Surmising the elevators likely served the forty-nine residential floors in the building, I followed the lunching women. A restaurant would work well. Not only was it public, making it easy for me to come and go without attracting notice, the more elaborate décor should provide many hiding spots. In addition, the high floor offered a unique twist. Whoever was tracking my phone would see that I was in the building, but triangulation didn't show on which floor the signal was originating. I was a blip on a two-dimensional map. It would take a bit of time for my pursuers to cover ninety-five floors.

I followed the two women through a narrow hall to another elevator bank. They stepped into the lift. I hung back and waited for the next.

The car I finally caught was smaller than many apartment closets. I punched the button for the Signature Room, and the doors closed before anyone had the chance to follow me inside.

The elevator car lurched upward, then settled into a rumbling acceleration. The door rattled. I opened the back of my throat as if in a closed-mouth yawn, allowing my ears to equalize pressure. Forty seconds and the door slid open.

Rimmed with walls of glass overlooking the city, the restaurant felt open and airy and smelled of parsley and steak and garlic, with a hint of floral, coming from the roses at the maître d' stand. The low hum of voices mixed with clinking silver and a background of easy listening music. A waiter passed by, dark pants, dark gray shirt, and a tie. The rest of the staff was dressed in similar shades of black and gray.

"Do you have a reservation?" A black-suited maître d' asked, glancing down at his seating chart.

"I'm just looking for a friend." My theme for the day.

"No one mentioned waiting for another in their party. Perhaps your friend is upstairs in the lounge?" He gestured to the wide, carpeted staircase to his left.

"Yes, thanks."

I gave the restaurant a quick scan while crossing to the steps. I noted wine racks behind glass doors, planters filled with silk flowers, a heat register rimming the room at shin level. All places I could stash a phone, although all might be disturbed.

Or a little too obvious for anyone searching.

I climbed the steps, trying to focus on finding hiding spots and not the breathtaking view of Chicago and Lake Michigan unfolding around me. Floor-to-ceiling windows boxed the restaurant. I glanced east, toward the lake, and saw cables trailing down the glass, a sign of window washers at work on floors below.

The staircase doubled back and met another bank of elevators, another maître d' stand, and a pair of private dining rooms flanking either side. I passed one of the dining areas and started down a long hallway that opened into one of the private dining areas. A spectacular panorama of the city stretched out to the south, and if it hadn't been overcast I'm sure I could have seen Indiana. It was like a view from an airplane.

Not spotting any better hiding places than I had in the larger dining room a floor below, I continued down the hall toward the main lounge. A short line of people waited for a chance at a table. No time to join the wait, I ducked into the women's bathroom.

Public restrooms always offered a large variety of hiding places, and this one was no different in that respect. What I didn't expect was the glass wall overlooking the city, giving the ladies' room a view equally jaw-dropping as those in the dining areas. I pulled my attention from Navy Pier and the white-capped lake and concentrated on the interior.

The bathroom smelled of lemon disinfectant and eucalyptus from the floral arrangement on the marble vanity. I logged possible hiding places with a glance. Under the lip of the vanity. Behind the toilets. The recessed lighting in the ceiling. But again, those spots felt too obvious. The people I was dealing with had more than my face, they had my training as well. And if there was a Looking for Hidden Shit 101, the spots I'd found so far would be covered in the first lesson.

I had to come up with something better. I checked my watch. Only a few minutes until Cory would be expecting me out on the sidewalk.

I left the restroom and continued down the hall to the lounge. The host was leading the group I'd noticed to a table. I took the opportunity to breeze past, as if I was a tourist just wanting a peek at the view to the building's east. The room presented the same assortment of hiding spots, planters, radiators, and recessed lighting, along with cocktail tables and some possibilities in the lighting above the bar itself. Often people focused on everything eye level and below when looking for something. They rarely thought to look up. But still…I glanced back down the hall.

I had a better idea.

*"It's all about control," The Instructor said. "You must keep as much control as possible, at all times. An agent should always have choices, always do things on her terms. Sometimes, options will be taken away from you. If that happens, make new options. An operative with no choices is a dead operative."*

I took care of the cell phone and made it back to the street with sixty-three seconds to spare. The John Hancock building itself sat back from Michigan Avenue. In front, the sidewalk opened up to display a half-moon-shaped array of shops one story below. Steps funneled to the lower level on both sides. Steel rail and glass rimmed the edge of the depression, stretching the length of the block parallel to the street. I stepped out on the bare stretch of sidewalk between guardrail and curb and tried to quell the nervous trill in my stomach. I felt exposed, no cover other than a light pole, a trash can, and a few spindly trees.

I scanned the street.

No sign of the black SUV.

No sign of Cory.

Wait.

Half a block away, a white four-door sat idling along the curb. Sun reflected off the windshield, making it difficult to see inside, but I managed to make out two silhouettes. The car's passenger door opened, and Cory stepped out onto the street.

He was a little more buff, chest broader, arms straining the long sleeves of the T-shirt he wore. He'd been lifting, no doubt taking advantage of the weights in the prison yard. A jacket draped over his right arm, one sleeve flapping in the wind. He'd always had a habit of squinting his eyes, but now crow's feet fanned out from their corners, and creases slashed his forehead and dug between his brows. Gray sparkled among the stubble on his head. But despite changes in his appearance, his walk was the same, half-amble, half-prowl, and for a second memory overwhelmed me.

My palms felt damp, my chest tight, and just like when I was fourteen, my vision seemed to narrow and all my senses focused on him. I knew exactly how he would smell. How his voice would sound. How his lips would thin when angry. I knew the feel of his skin, and the sounds he made, when fucking…when killing.

I wanted to run, to just get away. From the memories, from the past, from my own weakness. But I'd learned long ago that running didn't change a damn thing. There was no way to undo all he'd done to me. Besides, I wasn't that naive teenager anymore. I'd killed more men than Cory had.

I was better than he ever was.

Harnessing that thought, I pulled in a deep breath, car exhaust and a whiff of hot dogs from a nearby vendor. A car honked in the street behind me. People shuffled past; snips of their conversations swirled and scattered in the wind. The concrete was firm under my feet. My arms hung still by my sides, the yellow bag and duffel slung over my weak shoulder. My 9mm felt comfortable and familiar, pressed against the small of my back.

"Hiya, babe." He stopped three feet away and scanned me up and down. "Time's been good to you."

His familiar scent reached me, a mix of cigarette smoke, leather, and sweat. I braced myself against the answering memories.

I was ice. Cold. Calculating. "Is Kaufmann in the car?"

"Maybe. And maybe he's got a gun pointed at him right now. Just like you do." He pulled a corner of the jacket back with his left hand to show me the handgun.

As if that was supposed to surprise me.

Tracking his hands with my peripheral vision, I kept my main focus on his eyes.

His brows shifted. His eyes searched mine, as if realizing he couldn't read me the way he used to. "Before you go and do something stupid, I got one of those Bluetooth earpieces on. Anything happens to me, my partner ices Kaufmann."

I hadn't done anything truly stupid since the last time I'd believed a word Cory said. I held out my hands, palms up and nonthreatening. "I want to see him."

Cory watched me for a moment, then nodded. "Make him sit up," he muttered.

In the car, the driver's silhouette moved. A second figure rose from the backseat.

"How do I know that's him?"

"You'll just have to trust me." He nodded to the yellow book bag on my shoulder. "The money in there?"

I nodded. Not all the money he wanted, but I figured we'd get to that later.

"Good girl. Now give it to me or he loses another finger." Judging from his smile, he not only meant the threat, he enjoyed the prospect of cutting off body parts just as much as he always had.

I took the bag's strap in one hand and held it out a few inches, as if I barely had the strength to offer it. "Don't hurt him. Please."

He stepped toward me and laughed, a derisive snort of a sound that used to make me feel small and stupid. "I always liked it when you begged. Let's hear it again, babe."

"Please, Cory." I let a tremor seep into my voice, a tremor that wasn't entirely acting. "Please."

He took another step closer. Reaching out his left hand, he grasped the bag. His right hand snaked out from under the jacket, the pistol aimed at my chest.

I released the strap. In the same motion, I swung my right hand down hard and seized his wrist above the gun. I pivoted my body sideways, out of the way of a bullet.

He didn't have a chance to fire.

Holding his arm, I grabbed the pistol with my left hand and forced the weapon backward. At the same time, I thrust my knee hard into his groin.

He grunted and pitched forward. His hand released the gun.

I heard a shuffle of feet and surprised voices. I sensed people's heads snap around, looking for the source of the commotion, but at this point, I was beyond caring what they saw. I fitted the pistol into my right hand and dropped the barrel in line with his crotch. "Tell your partner to let Kaufmann go, now, or I shoot off your pitiful little dick."

Tires screeched on pavement.

I glanced up, expecting to see Cory's ride taking off. But the white car sat in the same spot.

The black SUV that had followed me earlier had whipped around the corner and was barreling up the street toward us. The passenger window lowered.

*Shit shit shit.*

I released Cory and spun away, the book bag hooked in my elbow. Automatic weapon fire peppered the sidewalk behind me. People screamed. Three strides and I leaped for the rail. My hands hit the top, and I vaulted the barrier. My feet landed on two different steps, and I lurched forward into the far rail before I could regain my balance.

Glass shattered above under a rain of lead.

Holding Cory's pistol at the ready, I started up the staircase. People cascaded down, screaming and stumbling, threatening to sweep me with them. Glass crunched under my shoes. Finally I shoved my way back to street level. I slipped behind a sign for the self park ramp. The SUV rounded the corner. I trained Cory's gun on it, but it was too far away and moving too fast. A stray shot would be more likely to strike a panicked civilian than my intended target. But they had to know there was a good probability they'd missed me. In just a few seconds, I'd get another chance.

I spotted the white car. It had pulled away from the curb and was moving toward me, still half in the parking lane. I wasn't sure where Cory had gone, but I was dead sure of one thing: I wouldn't let his partner get away with Kaufmann. I leveled my barrel and took my shot, going for the tires.

The car skidded to the side then overcorrected and bounced up on the curb. The driver's door flew open.

I lined up my next shot, ready to take out Cory's partner before he could retaliate against Kaufmann.

Wait. Not *he*.

*She.*

A girl jumped from the driver's seat, tall and slim and so young she'd probably only sprouted breasts in the last week. Long brown hair hung in her eyes. She took a few steps in my direction, then skidded to a stop and stared at my gun, her mouth forming an O and her eyes going wide. Her hands hung empty at her sides.

Just a kid…

*Like I had been.*

Another scream of rubber on pavement. The SUV roared around the corner, coming back the way it had gone.

It would be on us in seconds.

I grabbed a glance at the car, noted the engine was still running, and looked back at the girl. "Run."

She did, and so did I.

I reached the open driver's door of the white car just as the shooting resumed. Slamming it into drive, I gunned the engine. The car shot forward on the sidewalk, bucking on the deflating tire. The SUV roared straight at me, bearing down in a game of chicken I'd never survive. "Kaufmann. Keep your head down."

I heard a mumble from the backseat. It was Kaufmann's voice, all right, but I couldn't make out the words.

In front of me, the SUV jumped the curb as smoothly as running over a seam in the highway. Up ahead, a truck idled in the parking lane, the driver either gone or dead or paralyzed with fear.

I spun the wheel toward the street. The car flew over the curb and hit hard, the impact jarring up my spine. I swerved around the idling truck and glanced off the back bumper. Metal screamed against metal. I skidded onto Michigan Avenue, just missing oncoming traffic.

The SUV was still on the sidewalk, blocked by the truck, but that would buy me no more than a few seconds. If Kaufmann and I stayed out on the street, we were dead. I had to get out of the line of fire. And I had to do it now. I spied the self park sign and pushed the pedal to the floor. "Hold on."

The car skidded around the corner, the tire I'd shot flopping. I spotted the ramp's entrance and the two security guards manning it. One hunkered in the booth, a phone to his ear. The other stood at the entrance.

I drove straight for him.

He stared at me for a second, as if he couldn't believe what he was seeing, as if he couldn't comprehend what I was about to do. Finally self-preservation kicked in. He half-dashed, half-leaped to the side. I crashed through the flimsy wooden gate and kept going. The parking ramp corkscrewed upward, a tight curlicue of poured cement. I followed, pushing the car as fast as I could negotiate the turn. My passenger side mirror kissed the edge of the half-wall and broke off with a crunch. The tire I'd shot was useless now. The bare rim shrieked against concrete. Sparks flashed in the dim light.

The SUV would follow, of that I had little doubt. But for a few seconds, the barrage of bullets had stopped.

"Kaufmann? Talk to me." The odor of blood and sweat and fear filled the car. I did my best to glance over my shoulder while watching the tight spiral ahead.

A rustle of movement from the backseat.

Had Kaufmann been hit? I hadn't seen any holes in the car, but I could have easily missed them. "Kaufmann? Are you OK?"

"Don't worry about me."

My throat tightened. I'd been scared for Kaufmann since Cory's call, but at that moment, I realized how much. I pushed the emotion back. This wasn't over. I had to fully focus on what was happening now.

The spiral opened up, and the car thunked onto the ramp's top level. I swung into a handicapped spot next to the elevator and jumped out, shucking the duffel and shoulder bag. I grabbed a glance of Kaufmann through a shattered back window.

He lay on his side in the backseat. His hands were bound in front of him with handcuffs, and he clutched a bloody rag around his injured fingers. Duct tape wrapped his ankles. He looked small, pale, the lines bracketing his mouth and digging across his forehead etched deep. I was sure the past few hours had taken their toll, but at least he was alive.

Now I had to keep him that way. "Stay down."

He hitched himself up on one elbow. "We need to call the—"

"You need to lay your ass back down."

He didn't move, damn fool. Probably thought he was going to save me. Again. He didn't realize it was my turn to pay him back.

I checked Cory's gun and handed it to Kaufmann. He grasped it in his uninjured hand. I pulled my semiautomatic from the back of my waistband. "Stay down. If anyone comes looking for you, kill them."

"Carmen, I—"

"Just listen to me. Cory isn't as bad as the ones we've got coming after us now. Shoot first, and shoot to kill."

I pulled away from his bewildered expression and took position behind a concrete support. I fitted my weapon tightly into the web between thumb and forefinger and wrapped my second hand around the first. I moved my index finger to the trigger. The odors of exhaust and burned rubber coated the back of my throat. The roar of an approaching engine reverberated off concrete, the sound amplified by the corkscrew shape of the ramp.

The music goes round and round...ohhh...and it comes out here.

I could see the SUV winding toward me. It emerged on the sixth floor. The moment I saw the driver's eyes, I squeezed the trigger.

The report cracked in my ears. I let my wrists move with the kick of the first shot. When it settled back, I gave him a second tap.

The windshield cracked, splintering into hundreds of tiny lines, obscuring the driver's face. The SUV kept hurtling forward across the parking level. It hit the half wall hard, reared up as the concrete crumbled, and plunged over the edge. The loud crash of vehicle and pavement shuddered up my spine.

When I got back to the car, Kaufmann was sitting upright in the seat, Cory's pistol in his bound hands. He stared at me for a moment before he finally spoke. "I'm pretty sure you haven't been entirely honest with me."

A typical Kaufmann understatement. "I'll explain. Later. As much as I can."

To his credit, he didn't say a word, just let me help him out of the car. I cut the duct tape around his ankles with the utility knife I'd bought. I picked the handcuffs binding his wrists and stashed the cuffs in the duffel. We ducked into the elevator. He sagged against the wall as I hit the button to take us to the lobby.

The elevator car started down, moving much more smoothly than the high-speed car I'd taken to the ninety-fifth floor. The cramped quarters smelled strongly of sweat and stress and even more strongly of blood.

I eyed the rag wrapping Kaufmann's fingers. "Let me see your hand."

He unpeeled what looked like a girl's T-shirt and held out three fingers. I examined the bloody stump, and my stomach did a little flip. I'd seen many injuries worse than this, but this was Kaufmann and he was hurt because of me. I needed a second to regain my balance.

"You killed the driver. You caused..." His lips thinned into a line.

I pulled my gaze up to his eyes. "It's what I do. What I *really* do."

I wasn't sure what I expected. Shock. Disbelief. Repulsion. Instead, Kaufmann offered a simple nod. "Later?"

I wanted to hug him. "Yes. Later."

As much as I needed to explain things to Kaufmann, to take care of his hand, we didn't have time. At worst, more of the people who were after me waited outside the lobby door. At best, the police would be looking to arrest whoever had taken out the SUV driver and caused it to hurtle six floors to the pavement below. Dealing with the bad guys was uncomplicated. They were trying to kill me. I would try to kill them. The cops presented a more complex problem, especially where Kaufmann was concerned.

The elevator's movement slowed and settled. "Kaufmann," I said. "We can't go to the police."

Kaufmann stared at me as if I were speaking gibberish. "People died. Maybe more than we know."

"And I can't explain that now."

"I'll explain it, what I know, anyway."

"You can't."

"I'm an agent of the court. I have to."

I shook my head. I wasn't worried about his ethics. "You won't be safe."

"The police can protect me from Cory."

I also wasn't worried about Cory. I looked Kaufmann square in the eye. I had to convince him to follow my lead before the elevator doors opened. "Those guys in the SUV, there are more of them, and I don't know who they are. But if they can reach me, they can reach you."

Kaufmann shook his head.

The elevator's bell chimed. I could hear the shriek of sirens even before the door opened. "Years ago I trusted you, Kaufmann, and you saved me. Now you have to trust me. If you don't do what I say, we both will likely die. Now tuck your hand in your pocket and follow me."

The door slid open. I heard the clatter of running footsteps, the bark of voices. Outside the lobby doors, a circus of flashing lights exploded red and blue. Blue-uniformed police officers blocked the exit, trying to control the crowd. Two officers pushed through the revolving door and into the lobby.

I scanned the area, stopping on the yellow-and-black Best Buy sign just off the lobby. I started in that direction, willing Kaufmann to come along.

For a second, his body physically swayed toward the cops. Then he focused on me, and we walked into the electronics shop. We blended with shoppers and minutes later made it out the exit, swept by the crowd. A block away, we managed to flag a cab, leaving Hancock Center behind.

*"Debriefing is essential,"* The Instructor said. *"It's not called the intelligence business because people are smart. Knowledge is power. When debriefing, think like a reporter. Who, what, where, when, how, and why. And learn to know when a subject is lying. Everybody lies."*

Settling into the cab, I got my first good look at Kaufmann. In the bright sunlight, he looked even paler than he had in the parking ramp. His gray hair stuck to his forehead. He smelled of blood and the slightly metallic scent that accompanied fear. I cupped my hands over his, cradled in his lap. His skin felt cold and clammy, his pulse disturbingly fast.

For a second, I thought about risking a hospital. I discarded the idea before we had traveled a block. I had to go with my training, not my emotion. And my training was telling me whoever had gotten to Jacob wouldn't let police or hospital security get in his way. After my rescue of Kaufmann, they knew where I was vulnerable, and they would use him to reach me, just as Cory had. My only chance to keep him alive was protecting him myself.

I gave the cabbie an address about a block from Victor's apartment. Normally I would double back, change cabs, or do some other countersurveillance moves, ending up several blocks from my destination and walking the remainder of the distance. But Kaufmann had lost a lot of blood. I needed to get him to a safe place where he could rest and I could get my hands on first aid supplies. My friendly neighborhood EMT could provide both.

"How are you feeling?" I asked, nodding to his hand.

"I've had better days."

The cab took a right turn, and the shifting sunlight brought out the depth of shadows under his eyes.

"It's later," Kaufmann said, his kind eyes meeting mine.

I nodded, knowing he was referencing the promise I'd made in the parking ramp to explain what I could.

"Cory escaped from Stateville two weeks ago. He must have noticed you at his trial, figured out you were important to me."

Of course Cory had. Back then, he could read me like a billboard. I should have thought of that. The moment I heard of Cory's escape, I should have made sure Kaufmann had some kind of protection.

"I'm not asking about Cory. I could figure that one out on my own." He glanced at the cabbie, then back at me. "Who were the men in the SUV?"

I looked Kaufmann straight in the eye. At least I could answer this question truthfully. "I don't know."

"But they have something to do with your job?"

"Yes."

"What is your job exactly?"

I wished I could tell him. But while spilling my guts would make me feel better and less alone, it would only put Kaufmann in more danger.

His brows dipped low. "You're not going to tell me."

"I can't."

"Will more of them be after us?"

"I don't know. Maybe. Hopefully, not for a while." At least with my phone stashed at the John Hancock Center, they wouldn't be able to find me so easily. And I doubted they'd foresee me returning to Victor's. That move was decidedly not by the book.

"Does Cory have anything to do with them?"

"I don't know." I'd been over and over it. I couldn't see a connection no matter how I tried, but maybe Kaufmann could help shed some light on that. "How did Cory manage to abduct you?"

"There was a knock on my apartment door. I opened it."

"When?"

"About twenty minutes before he called you this morning. I opened the door, and he pushed inside." He glanced out the window as if unwilling to meet my eyes. Or ashamed.

I wanted to ask why he'd answered some random knock, but I held my tongue. Kaufmann was a smart man, but smart people could do stupid things when unaware of their surroundings. He obviously knew he shouldn't have opened the door. The last thing I wanted to do was rub it in his face. "Did he hold you in your apartment?"

Kaufmann nodded. "Until we left to meet you."

I hadn't seen that coming. I'd assumed Cory would take him somewhere else, somewhere tougher for me to locate. Not that it mattered, since I hadn't had much opportunity to storm Kaufmann's apartment this morning. Maybe Cory didn't really care where I caught up with him, just so long as I did. "Did Cory seem to be working with someone? Taking orders over the phone or in person?"

"He wasn't taking orders. And he never talked on the phone except when he called you." Kaufmann turned away from me and faced the window. "You haven't asked how he got your number."

"That wasn't your fault, Kaufmann."

He faced me again, his eyes intent. "I didn't give it to him."

"I believe you."

"He knocked me around, but I didn't."

"You don't have to do this, Kaufmann."

"He would have killed me. And I would have let him before I gave you up. But the girl found my cell phone. Found your number. It had your real name, not Carmen, or Judy, or Emma, or any of the ones you've used over the years. Stupid old man making stupid mistakes…"

His eyes glassed over. I gripped his good hand, squeezing hard. "This isn't your fault."

He sniffled, trying on a pathetic grin. "Sure as hell doesn't feel that way."

"The only one to blame here is Cory." I pictured the teenager who had run from the car after I'd shot out the tire. "Tell me about the girl."

Kaufmann's voice grew hushed, the kind of tone reserved for disturbing tragedies. "She was the reason I opened the door. She said she needed help. Fourteen years old, the poor, misguided thing."

My stomach felt queasy, and I knew it had nothing to do with the adrenaline now ebbing from my system. A bad taste rose in the back of my throat. "She's fourteen?"

"Same age you were."

"Let me guess. She's from a lousy background, thinks she's finally found someone who cares, is there for her. Her soul mate."

"Don't know the details, but I'm sure you're right."

I followed his gaze to the bloody T-shirt wrapping his hand. Emotion battered at the edges of my self-control. I'd found a way to move beyond all Cory had done to me, but the thought of him doing the same to another, the thought of him hurting Kaufmann to punish me…I heaved a long, cold breath. "As soon as I can, I'll take care of Cory, don't worry."

"I don't care about Cory. I'm just worried about you."

If Kaufmann were anyone else, I would hate that he knew I once was that fourteen-year-old girl, that he could see the vulnerability in me now. But while I'd deluded myself into believing Cory was there for me all those years ago, over the years Kaufmann had proven he actually was. If not for him, I'd be nothing but a broken shell. "Don't worry about me. I can handle Cory."

He tilted his head in acknowledgement. "And the girl?"

"I just hope she ends up with a parole officer like you, old man. I'm just afraid you're one of a kind."

Kaufmann pressed his lips into a tight smile.

For a few blocks, he stared out the window and said nothing. The whisper of breath through his nostrils came faster. His blood loss over the last few hours was catching up with him. I watched the street behind us, looking for tails. I thought of asking the cabbie to circle the block once before dropping us off but decided against it. I needed to stop Kaufmann's bleeding and get fluids into him. I couldn't have him going into shock.

"You're a spy, aren't you?" he whispered.

I shot a look at the cabbie, saw he was fiddling with the radio. "Sort of."

Kaufmann nodded. "I always suspected. No job, yet money to spare. Always moving. Changing names every few months. Then once in a while disappearing for a few weeks at a time."

"Maybe I'm a bank robber."

He shook his head. "No. Not after what you went through with Cory. You wouldn't do anything like that again."

I had a mini flashback. Being young and stupid, falling for the bad boy twice my age because my stepfather didn't give two shits what I did. Cory broke me in slowly. First sex. Then drugs. Then some petty crime. Busting open a vending machine. Robbing a bum. Snatching a purse from an old lady.

Then it got worse. Then people starting dying.

At the trial, I played the innocent, brainwashed victim. Forced to participate in a four-state crime wave. I never pulled a single trigger, never cut a single throat.

But I never tried to stop Cory, either. I'd done everything he'd told me to do all because of my misguided, girlish crush. Whatever love I thought I'd had for him died the moment he shot that first bartender.

I hadn't tried to stop him. I hadn't even tried to run away. I had just gone along, like I had before. Not for love any longer, but because I was scared out of my goddamn mind. And when it finally all ended—in a police car chase that wound up being broadcast on *World's Most Dangerous Criminals*, with our car flipped over in a lake and sinking fast—I was still so afraid I couldn't move. Not even as the water seeped in and inched up my body. Not even as it covered my face.

Not even when the police pulled me out of the lake and brought me back to life.

I didn't make a sound for three days after they saved me. My first utterance was sobbing, and that went on for two more days.

I would have been thrown in the loony bin if it weren't for Murray Kaufmann, juvenile probation officer extraordinaire. Kaufmann had brought me back. Helped me get my head on straight. Helped me testify. I wound up getting two years in juvie hall, but Kaufmann saw me through that, too. He never gave up on me.

And I'd be damned if I was going to give up on him.

The cabbie stopped at the address I'd given. I paid him with cash from the yellow bag and helped Kaufmann out onto the sidewalk. Beyond the usual traffic noises, a dog yapped from a parked car and the thump of woofers rattled the windows of an apartment across the street. I detected no unusual scents, either, aside from the odors of blood, stress, and the faint whiff of the wintergreen lifesavers Kaufmann favored. No one seemed to be following. From what I could tell, ditching the phone had done the trick.

I took Kaufmann's arm. "Lean on me."

He shook his head. "I'll be OK. Really."

Half a block later, I slipped my arm around his back, and he let me prop him up. It wasn't easy, as I was coping with injuries of my own along with my duffel and the yellow bag. But we managed without falling.

We approached Victor's building from the opposite direction and limped into the back entrance. By the time we reached the apartment, I couldn't help noticing Kaufmann's lean was heavier, his steps growing more unsure.

Victor was still unconscious when we entered. He lay in an awkward position on the floor, his wrists still bound behind his back with the zip tie, his knees bent, ankles similarly hitched together. For a moment I felt guilty for what I'd done to him. Then I stashed the emotion away. If Victor was the mild-mannered Sox fan EMT he said he was, I would have time to regret drugging and binding him later.

"Who is he?" Kaufmann asked.

"A friend."

Kaufmann's brows arched.

If he was rethinking his friendship with me right about now, I wouldn't blame him. "It's complicated."

"Obviously."

A low trilling sound came from the hall.

I spun in time to see Mozart rub against the door molding. She wound between Kaufmann's legs and rubbed her fat, calico body against me from whiskers to tail.

At least Victor's cat thought I was all right. Somehow that pleased me more than it should.

I ushered Kaufmann into the kitchen. The room was cramped, barely big enough for a small table slid against one wall. I smelled the faint odor of fried eggs, dish soap, and sour milk coming from the sink. Victor's jacket hung on the back of the only chair. I guided Kaufmann to sit, and after checking the jacket's pockets and finding them empty, I threw it around his shoulders.

A search of the refrigerator turned up a bottle of orange juice. I opened the twist top and gave it a sniff. Satisfied it was fresh, I gave it to Kaufmann and ordered him to drink. At least that would hydrate him and raise his blood sugar while I focused on stopping the bleeding. "Let me take a look at that hand."

He set the bottle of juice on the table. Steadying himself with his good hand, he nodded and held out the other. "Go ahead."

I unwound the bloody T-shirt, trying to steel myself against the tight expression of pain pinching his face and the sweat beading along his hairline. His skin looked like wax.

The strong, copper-sweet odor of blood oozed over me, making my stomach hitch. I clamped my bottom lip between my teeth and forced myself to look at the damage I'd caused. Where his index finger should have been, there was only a stub. Blood surged from the wound in time with his pulse. But as bad as it looked, I let out a breath of relief. At least Cory had taken the finger off at the joint and not severed the bone.

"What are you going to do?" Kaufmann's voice was weak, his words forced out between clenched teeth.

"I'm going to disinfect it and put in a few sutures. I should be able to slow the bleeding, help it clot."

He took a long drink then set the bottle of juice on the table. Swiping his good hand over his face, he let out a sigh. "Got a bullet for me to bite?"

"I was thinking of something more pharmaceutical...and effective."

"Thank God."

I led him into Victor's bedroom. Once Kaufmann was comfortable on the bed, I dumped the yellow bag filled with money in the closet and pulled a clean syringe from my duffel along with the amobarbital I'd used on Victor. There was no need for Kaufmann to be clear-headed. Better to send him into a haze where the pain would be more bearable. Even better if he could sleep. And one of the best side effects of the amobarbital was the touch of amnesia it left behind. I couldn't erase the trauma Cory had put Kaufmann through, couldn't restore his finger, but at least he wouldn't have to remember the next few hours.

"Care to hurry with that?" He gave me a little smile, but I could tell the gesture had taken a good amount of effort.

"By the time you wake up fully, the worst of this will have passed." I rolled up his sleeve and gave him the shot. "I'm so sorry, Kaufmann. For your finger. For Cory. For all of it."

He shook his head. Raising his good hand, he brushed my words from the air. "No reason to be sorry. You saved me, just like you said you would. But even more, you saved yourself."

I narrowed my eyes on him, not following.

"When I first met you, you were on a bad path."

"An understatement."

"You changed, turned your life around, made something of yourself. I don't know the details of your job, and I don't think I want to. But I can tell what you're doing, it's important."

A flush of heat pooled in my cheeks. I thought about the many men I'd killed. Bad men, every one, according to their dossiers. I could refuse jobs and had in the past. The only people I'd sanctioned had it coming.

But still, a contract killer is a contract killer. Even one who worked for Uncle Sam. "Kaufmann, I'm not exactly a Girl Scout. I've…"

"Hush. I've been a parole officer for a lot of years. I've seen a lot of young people get caught by bad choices. Very few can pull themselves out. You did." His words were a little slurred now, the amobarbital taking effect.

I put my hand on his shoulder and guided him back on the bed. "Just relax."

"I just want you to know…" His eyes became hooded, as if he was fighting to keep them open.

"Know what?"

"Couldn't be prouder if you were my own daughter." Kaufmann's eyelids dropped lower. "Just want you to know that."

I blinked and tried to swallow the tightness in my throat. I'd gotten him into this. All of it. And instead of blaming me, he'd given me what had to be the best words anyone had ever said to me.

I opened my mouth to explain what he meant to me, how much I loved him like I loved my own parents who had died when I was too, too young, but then I shut it without speaking, watching his breath settle into the steady rhythm of sleep. I replayed what he'd said in my mind, feeling the history, the emotion, the texture of each word, and then I folded and tucked them in the most private place in my heart. When he woke, I'd tell him all he meant to me, not that anything I could say would suffice.

For now, I just had to hope he knew.

I pushed up from the side of the bed and tossed the syringe into a wastebasket. I had some basic supplies in my duffel, but from my earlier search of the place, I knew Victor had more. I rummaged through the bathroom medicine cabinet, collecting items I might need. When I stepped into the hall, I heard the stir of movement in the apartment's main room.

"I can help with that."

I jumped at Victor's voice, my heartbeat launching into double time. Pulling the pistol from my waistband, I slid into the room.

Victor lay in the same spot, still tied. No one else was in the room but Mozart, curled on the back of an overstuffed chair, giving herself a bath. I detected a whiff of cat box I hadn't noticed earlier. The theme music for Jeopardy wafted through the walls from next door.

Satisfied the apartment was still secure, I put my weapon away.

"I can help. Really." His voice carried a hint of slur and his eyelids hovered at half-mast, making him sound and look as if he'd had a bit too much to drink. He gave me a little smile that completed the picture. "I don't know what's going on, and I get the feeling you're not going to tell me. But I saw you bring in the old man."

He'd recovered from the amobarbital quickly. A little too quickly for my comfort. "So why did you pretend to be unconscious?"

"Would you find me less attractive if I admitted I wasn't feeling exactly brave after all that happened earlier?"

Less attractive? Not likely. Whether Victor was friend or foe, he was certainly attractive.

But then, my taste in men tended to be suspect.

"So who is he?" Victor asked.

"A friend."

"That's how you referred to me."

"In his case, it's not a lie."

"Ouch." He gave me a puppy dog look, as if his feelings were genuinely hurt. "It's the Sox fan thing, isn't it? Be honest."

I couldn't keep from exhaling a half-stifled laugh.

"See? You think I'm funny. That's a good basis for a friendship."

I let out a long breath and narrowed my eyes on him. "You're pretty cool under pressure, aren't you, Victor?"

"I don't know. I guess. Have to be for my job."

I supposed he was right. Facing life-and-death situations on a daily basis taught a person to compartmentalize their emotions. He wasn't that different from me, in that regard. Except where he tried to save lives, I was more apt to take them.

"I know I'm not in the greatest shape right now, but he looked like he was close to going into shock. You need to stop his bleeding and stabilize him. I see you found what was in the bathroom. There are more supplies in the spare room's closet."

"Thanks." I turned and started back to the kitchen.

"You could also use my help."

I could. And I had to admit, everything about Victor felt sincere. But as much as I would like to have an EMT help me stop Kaufmann's bleeding, I couldn't cut Victor's ties. Not until I was sure about him. "I can handle it."

"I'll bet you can." A small smile curved the corners of his lips. "You're a fascinating woman, Carmen. Scary, but fascinating. Are you planning on hurting me?"

"Not if I don't have to."

"Let's hope you don't."

I walked away from my lie, back down the hall to tend Kaufmann's wounds. Once I was sure I'd done all I could to stop his bleeding, I'd be back.

And unfortunately for Victor, he wasn't going to like what was coming next.

*"Like debriefing, interrogation is about obtaining intelligence. But often the subject is hostile and not willing to part with the information. Persuasion to cooperate is essential. First, you must gauge a subject's suggestibility. Then, various means can be used to elicit information, including the Reid technique, good cop/bad cop, pride and ego manipulation, drugs, fear, and pain. While the effectiveness of torture remains unclear, I have no doubt you'll eventually have to hurt a subject in order to get him to talk. Everyone has a breaking point. Find it."*

Kaufmann was unconscious when I returned to the bedroom. Using a zip tie like the ones I had used to bind Victor, I secured his wrist to the headboard. I didn't want him to move while I worked on his finger. I gave him several shots of local anesthetic and cleaned the stump of his finger with alcohol. Then it was time to stitch.

Even with him sedated and loaded with painkiller, I found myself flinching as I worked. Tending to my own wounds was one thing. Tending to another operative, or enemy, easier. But someone I cared about? The thought of causing Kaufmann pain, even though it was for his own good, set my teeth on edge and made my hands shake.

I knew the technique, but the forceps felt awkward in my hand, the action of penetrating the skin at a ninety-degree angle with the curved needle nearly impossible. I went with simple, interrupted sutures, tying off each stitch of skin individually with a square knot. The technique took longer than I wanted, but it was strong and afforded a novice like me a chance to realign the skin between each stitch. Kaufmann would have a nasty scar, but I doubted that mattered when it came to a finger stub.

By the time I finished the sutures, cut Kaufmann free, and wrapped his hand in antibacterial cream and gauze, I was exhausted. The adrenaline and amphetamines that had kept me going all day had ebbed, and the weight of my responsibility for Kaufmann bore down. My body ached from the scrapes on my feet to the slash in my scalp, and I'd give just about anything to shoot myself up with the amobarbital and slide into sleep.

But first I had to deal with Victor.

I didn't hear a sound from the apartment's main room. The odor of the disinfectant I'd used on Kaufmann's wound still hung in my nostrils, making it difficult to detect scents. Suturing Kaufmann's finger had taken more time than I liked. Victor would be out of his fog by now, but with any luck, the amobarbital still in his system would lower his guard. A barbiturate, amobarbital, or sodium amytal was an effective sedative, but it also acted as a truth serum, similar to its relative sodium pentothal. Of course, the drug's power as a truth serum was largely exaggerated. And if Victor actually was working with my doubles, he'd be trained to resist the effects.

But if he wasn't…

I clamped down hard on that hope. I had to forget I liked this guy and focus on only the reality in front of me. If he was who he said he was, he would have the chance to prove it. If not, I'd end him.

I rummaged through my duffel, fishing out the supplies I needed. From the kitchen, I collected a mortar and pestle I'd noticed on my first search of the place, opened a bottle, and spilled half a dozen tablets into the mortar. After grinding them to powder, I mixed in enough water to make a solution and filled a large syringe. A second syringe I filled with plain water.

The syringes and a pair of handcuffs in hand, and my pistol in my waistband, I walked down the hall for my rendezvous.

When I entered the room, Victor's gaze skimmed my face then focused on my hands. "Again? Do you have some kinky thing for needles?"

I didn't answer. Instead I made a show of laying out the syringes on the coffee table. I wanted to give him time to think about them, obsess on them, wonder what I was going to do next. An interrogation is a delicate thing, a balance of power. Normally I'd like to have more knowledge on my side. Facts to convince him I knew the truth, so he might as well come clean. Then all I would have to provide was the incentive. With Victor, I had no facts tying him to the women who were trying to kill me and no hint of who in the hell they were. With Victor, I would have to bluff like a master poker player.

When I finished placing my tools on the table, I sized up Victor, not saying a word.

"Is this where you tell me to talk? Look, I'll talk about anything you want me to. Ask me anything."

He looked small, lying on the floor, bound as he was. Much smaller than the man who'd answered the door earlier, fit and strong. Being tied and drugged and powerless, even for just a few hours, took a toll. It would help me get what I needed from him, but seeing him this way was a little like watching a magnificent bird with clipped wings or a Bengal tiger pacing bars of a concrete cage.

I took a long, deep breath and willed ice to envelope me. Getting the truth from Victor was all I could allow to matter. Since I was so bereft of knowledge, I'd start with the basics. "What is your name?"

"Come on, Carmen. You know my name."

Exactly the response I'd expect from a regular person, one who couldn't begin to believe he was being interrogated. Score one point for Victor the regular guy. Not that I planned to stop there. "You said you'd answer my questions."

"Victor. Victor Cormack."

"How did you find me online?"

"Find you? We met in the IRC chat. We hit it off. You know that, too. You were there."

Of course I knew that much. I also knew it wasn't too hard to clandestinely monitor someone's Internet service provider and follow their Internet trail, even as careful as I had been to conceal mine. With plenty of time and planning, Victor could have discovered the Internet relay chats I preferred and entered the same chat room under various names until he started up a dialogue I liked.

The thought that a guy I met and liked would go to such lengths to set me up was a bit paranoid, perhaps, but being paranoid had kept me alive more than once. "Who helped you find out what IRCs I liked to frequent?"

"What?" He narrowed his eyes to blue slits and shook his head. "I don't understand what you're getting at."

Time to be more direct. "Who do you work for?"

"The Chicago Fire Department. You know that, too." He let out a frustrated sigh. "I'd like to think this is some kind of game or joke, but I'm not sure that would be better."

"No joke, Victor. Why didn't you go to work today?"

"I told you—"

"That's just the problem. You told me a lie." I delivered the line with a certainty I grabbed out of thin air.

"I didn't. I switched shifts." He answered without pause, then gave a laugh flavored with a hint of bitterness. "Shifts can run long. I wanted to make sure I'd be free for our date tonight."

I let my expression soften. I'd gotten nowhere so far, and I wanted to try another tack, one not so confrontational. But I had to admit, acting as if my feelings toward him had warmed wasn't a tough trick after his last comment.

"Listen Victor, I know you didn't expect me to show up here. I understand why you felt you had to lie. I also realize you weren't aware of what went down at my apartment this morning."

"This morning? What happened?" He actually appeared concerned.

Either he liked me too, or he was one hell of an actor. I ignored his query. "I know you didn't have anything to do with that. I know you were just supposed to find me. And believe me, I understand about needing a little extra money, God knows. I'm not going to hold that against you. What I need to know is if they told you why."

"Told me? Who? What did they tell me? I don't know what you're talking about."

"Come on, Victor. I'm not the one playing games now. I already know how it went down. I can even believe whoever approached you didn't give you a name. I just want to know why they were looking for me. You tell me that much, and your worries are over. I'll give you another sleep shot, take my friend, and be out of your life forever."

"I don't know who you're talking about. How can I tell you anything?"

I studied him for signs of lying—an averted gaze, fidgeting, sweating, blinking too little or too much—and came up empty. He was showing some signs of stress, his voice was pitched a bit higher than it would be if he was relaxed and his pupils were slightly dilated, but that was to be expected. He'd had a rough day.

I picked up the first syringe and slipped off the plastic guard.

"Carmen, please. You don't have to do this."

I shook my head. "Apparently, I do. I have to admit, I thought you'd help me with this. I'm disappointed." The truth was, I was far from disappointed. Not only did Victor's body language suggest he was telling the truth, he was also sticking by his claims of ignorance instead of jumping at the easy explanations and excuses I offered. Unfortunately that didn't mean I could trust him yet. I had to test him over higher heat. I stepped toward him.

He eyed the needle in my hands. "What are you shooting me up with this time?"

"Something to help you remember."

"Some sort of truth juice?"

"Something more effective." I knelt by his side. Before he could brace himself, I stuck the needle into his muscle and delivered the dose.

"Ouch." He shifted his weight, his movement limited to rocking a little back and forth on the floor. "Now what?"

Now it was time to wait. And watch. "I need you to answer my questions."

"I told you. I can't help you. I don't have a clue what you're talking about." He shifted again as if growing uncomfortable. After a few minutes, I noticed a little flush starting to bloom in his cheeks. "What was that stuff?" he asked.

I smiled. "A little something the US government developed using the toxin of the cone shell snail."

"Toxin?" He stared at me as if I'd changed colors. "You poisoned me?"

"You aren't going to die right away. It's a slow-acting poison."

"Well, I guess that's OK, then." He shook his head. "Are you out of your goddamn mind?" Fear spiked his words, driving his voice higher, louder.

Just the effect I was after. "Let me tell you a little about what you're feeling."

"Why are you doing this? What did I ever do to you besides think you're hot?"

I tried not to hear the last part. "You're experiencing a tightening in your chest, aren't you? Next your face and neck will flush. You'll start sweating."

"That was how you made me feel before I found out you were some sort of sadistic maniac."

I continued. "Your skin will become blotchy, your fingers tingly. You'll feel sharp heat, like a sunburn. And then your body will begin to shut down."

"So you're killing me, why?"

"I told you. We need to talk."

"And women wonder why men hate hearing those words."

I turned away from him and paced across the small room, buying a few seconds of time to compose myself. I'd observed different defense mechanisms from people I'd interrogated. None had unnerved me as much as Victor's flirty humor. It had been his humor that had first drawn me to him in the chat room. It had kept me coming back for more in our Internet conversations since. But today, the way he still joked even while staring fear and death in the face?

It was an unspeakable turn-on.

There was no more powerful aphrodisiac than facing death, and after the day I'd had, I'd probably feel turned on by half the male population. But that didn't excuse my ever-growing crush on this man. Wanting to fuck Victor didn't make him easier to read.

I moved to the window and looked out at the afternoon sun casting angles of light and shadow on the street below, taking a moment to harden my resolve and let the dose I'd administered catch up to him. With the amount I'd injected, it shouldn't take long for him to feel all the symptoms I'd described. If the fear I sensed under his jokes was real, actually feeling the symptoms I'd described should make him eager to tell me everything I wanted to know.

Red blotches started showing on his neck. His forehead carried a sheen of moisture, his blond hair sticking in dark fringes. His breathing grew faster, bordering on a pant.

Finally I spoke. "How are you feeling, Victor?"

"At the moment, I'm leaning toward scared shitless."

Just the effect I was after. I dipped a hand into my duffel and pulled the picture of the Russian hit man that I'd printed from his computer. I held it in front of his face.

"Let me guess, you're expecting me to know who this guy is." He canted his gaze up to my face and looked directly into my eyes, unwavering. "I've never seen him before."

Again, I wanted to believe him. Even though giving me a name would save his life, he hadn't. Every test I'd given suggested he was telling the truth. But was I missing signs because I wanted him to be an EMT from Chicago and not a spy out to kill me? I had to be sure. I had to push him further. "Then why have you been in contact with him?"

He stared at me, his lips open, breathing through his mouth. "What?"

He hadn't been in contact with the Russian. Not that I knew. But I hoped watching his reaction to the accusation would let me get an accurate read on him. Right now, I was reading genuine bafflement.

Or an excellent actor.

I decided to press it. "Your arms are burning, aren't they? Like a bad sunburn. And I'll bet your fingers and toes feel like they're being stuck with needles. Does your chest feel tight?"

His shallow breaths told me it did.

"I don't know what you want me to say. Tell me, and I'll say it."

"I want the truth."

"I'm telling you the truth."

I held up the second syringe and spoke, this time in Russian.

He shook his head. "I don't know what the hell you're saying…"

"Come on, Victor. If you want to live, you'd better quit fucking around." I repeated my Russian statement, watching for some kind of acknowledgment in his eyes, some kind of reaction to my words.

He stared at me with wide eyes, on the verge of panic. "I don't know what you want from me. You're insane."

This time I spoke in English. "You know that toxin I gave you?"

"How could I forget?"

I directed his attention to the second syringe with a shake of my hand. "This is the antidote. I'll give it to you, but first, you have to help me. You have to give me the truth. Are you a spy?"

"Are you joking?"

"Are you a spy?" I asked again and watched him closely.

"Of course not. What the hell is going on, Carmen? Spies? Is this for real? Who talks about spies?"

"I'm not giving you this shot until you come clean."

"And if I don't tell you I'm a spy, I'll die. I get it. But I've been honest. You're not listening." He gasped in a breath.

If he were anyone else, someone I didn't give a shit about, I might believe him. But I just wasn't sure I could trust my own instincts. Not where he was concerned. Still, every objective test I'd given him had suggested Victor was on the up-and-up. And in light of that, I'd taken this interrogation as far as I was willing to go.

At least for now.

I set the syringe back on the table and picked up my razor. I crossed to him, knelt by his side, and sliced the zip tie binding his feet. I took a step back, pulled up the tail of my shirt, and flashed him my gun. "Get up."

It took some effort, but eventually he scrambled to his feet, his hands still bound behind him with the other zip tie. "Where are you taking me?" Judging from the tight line of his lips, he was expecting a firing squad or a wood chipper.

"Over to the couch. Walk."

He hobbled across the floor in the gait of a man whose feet had gone too long without decent blood circulation. "What about the antidote?"

"You won't need that."

He reached the sofa and twisted to face me. "So that's it? I can't answer your questions because I don't have a clue what you're talking about, so you're going to let me die? Or are you planning to shoot me and get it over with?"

"Neither." I circled back behind him and pulled out my razor. A couple of slashes and his hands were free. I drew my gun, just in case he tried something stupid, and motioned to the couch. "Sit." I indicated the spot.

He did as I ordered, rubbing the angry red lines ringing his wrists.

I grabbed the handcuffs I'd taken off of Kaufmann from my back pocket and tossed them to Victor. "Put one of the cuffs on your right wrist."

"You've got to be kidding."

I brought my weapon up and slid my finger to the trigger.

"OK, not kidding. I should have known better." He circled his wrist with one of the bracelets.

I moved my index finger back alongside the trigger guard. "Now close the other cuff around the radiator."

He hooked the handcuffs over a rib of the radiator and locked it into place. Even though he was still showing fear, now that he was upright, he looked like the Victor who had opened the door to me a few hours before, the one who'd smiled and joked on the webcam earlier this morning. And for a moment, I couldn't help acknowledging that little flutter up under my rib cage.

"Now what happens?" Victor asked. "You watch me die?"

"You're not going to die."

He narrowed his eyes as if trying to figure me out. "You didn't give me poison, did you? What was it? I feel like I'm burning up."

"Niacin." I shrugged. "Vitamin B3. It's water soluble. The effects will wear off, and as a bonus you won't have to worry about pellagra." My turn at a joke, if a quip about a nasty skin, nervous system, and digestive disease caused by niacin deficiency could be considered joking.

His lips flattened to something short of a smile. "And you did this…why?"

"I needed to know if you were telling the truth."

He closed his eyes and shook his head. "You have some serious trust issues."

I couldn't argue. I did. But only because I preferred to remain breathing. At least that's what I liked to tell myself.

Victor shifted on the cushion, the handcuffs clanking against the radiator. "Wouldn't you know it," he muttered under his breath.

I raised my eyebrows in a silent question.

"I always get turned on by the strange ones."

I almost smiled. "Is that supposed to be a compliment?"

He shrugged and leaned against the sofa's arm. The move was a relaxed one, and I couldn't help feeling relieved to see his fear fade and the Victor I'd known before take over. "Tell me something. After all our chats online, did you ever feel anything, or were you just looking for an apartment to use or a cheap stash of first aid supplies?"

That was a question I shouldn't answer. I didn't regret what I'd done. Although I hadn't been thinking of Victor in a tactical sense in the time I'd spent chatting with him online, once my cover identity had been blown, using him was an easy decision, one I wouldn't hesitate to make again. I should walk away and let him curse me or hate me or whatever he pleased. It would be easier that way. But after putting him through all I had, I couldn't do it.

Or maybe, I just didn't want to. "I felt something."

"Funny, you hide it well." He tilted his chin down and looked up at me, a smile tilting one side of his lips. "Unless you're just into handcuffs."

The warmth of that smile pulled at me, made me want to reciprocate, made me want things I shouldn't. I'd just finished interrogating this man, telling him I'd poisoned him, leading him to believe he was going to die. How could he forgive me so suddenly? "Is that your way of trying to convince me to release you?"

"That would be nice."

"Not happening."

"So you *are* into handcuffs. Or are you just into control?"

"Today I am." I tilted my head, watching him. "You're a little forward for what you just went through. You aren't trying pull one over on me, are you Victor?"

"You really do have trust issues, don't you?"

I didn't see the need to answer.

"So I'm that obvious?"

"That depends on what you're trying to do."

He laughed, a sound not harsh or even at my expense, but one of simple amusement. "I don't know if you really did feel something in our chats online, Carmen, but I did. And I'll forgive all that other stuff if I can just get what I've wanted from you all along. What I was hoping you wanted from me."

"Sex?"

"A chance."

I forced myself to focus on my surroundings. The rumble of an El train passing outside of the apartment. Mozart pawing through kitty litter in the bathroom. The thrum of my pulse.

*I am ice.*

It didn't work. I'd had a feeling about Victor since we'd first bantered in that chat room. That he was unlike the men I'd met online or in bars. That as different as our lives were, we operated on the same wavelength.

That maybe, between us, there could be something real.

I'd kept the feeling at bay, kept myself from hoping for something I could never have. I didn't work in an office from nine to five. I wasn't even something as normal as an EMT. In my profession, relationships weren't an option.

But that didn't mean I didn't want to be with a special man. That didn't mean I didn't dream of it at night when my subconscious broke free.

Which was why I walked the hell out of there.

My steps were shaky at first, but I made it out of the living room without turning around. I continued down the hall and checked on Kaufmann. He was sleeping fitfully. I went into the kitchen and opened the fridge.

"Carmen? You're not afraid of me, are you? I'm the one with the handcuffs on."

My stomach was in knots, but it wasn't from hunger.

Well, not *that* kind of hunger.

I reminded myself that life-or-death situations often played hell with a person's libido. That after coming close to death, nothing reaffirmed life more than sex.

Perhaps Victor was feeling the same way right now.

Or perhaps Victor was a spy who wanted me dead.

Nothing looked good in the fridge. I slammed the door shut.

"Can we at least talk about this? I'll forget about you pretending to poison me. I'll even forget about you hitting me and tying me up. But it would mean a lot for me if you came back here and we talked."

*Shit shit shit.*

Despite my better judgment, my feet brought me back into the living room. I stood in front of him, my hands on my hips.

"This is probably inappropriate," Victor said, "and I can't imagine the kind of day you had. But, *damn*, you really are one beautiful lady."

My heart gave a little jump in my chest. I took a step toward him, then another. I must be out of my mind. I most certainly was, but I didn't care. After this day, I wanted to give that chance Victor had asked for and take one for myself. I wanted to know I was alive, to lose myself in a kiss, to feel the warm friction of skin on skin.

I wanted to look at a man and have him look back at me the way Victor was now.

I leaned over him and brought my lips down on his. The kiss was effortless, all hunger and heat. He tasted like he'd been drugged and unconscious for half the day, but I didn't care. My senses, so trained, so honed, clamored and blended until I couldn't tell one from another, like voices in a chanting crowd, like a symphony where all the instruments blended into one transcendent music. I wanted to get closer, to feel more, to lose myself in sensation.

He brought his free hand up my cheek and buried his fingers in my hair. He cradled the side of my face, urging my mouth closer, my lips harder on his.

Finally I ended the kiss and pulled the T-shirt over my head. My bra hit the floor next.

I could feel Victor watching me, his gaze skimming over my breasts and down my belly, sexier than a caress. He cleared his throat. "Is it hot in here?"

"That's just the niacin talking." I pushed the jeans down my legs.

"And the old man?"

"He's sleeping." I kicked off denim and slid my thumbs into the waistband of my panties and inched them down.

"Who is he, anyway? I mean really? Your father?"

His assumption made me hesitate, my panties halfway down my thighs. Earlier his questions had been easy to brush off. But things had changed. Even though I still had him cuffed to the radiator, I realized I'd crossed a threshold. I trusted Victor. And more than that, impossible or not, I wanted there to be more between us, more than I'd hoped with any man in a long time.

But this question felt more intimate than the skin I'd revealed, more intimate than any sex act could.

I thought about the gift Kaufmann had given me before the amobarbital had dragged him under. Except for my very different bond with Kaufmann, relationships with men had always been elusive for me. Thanks to Cory, I'd lost any semblance of naïveté about the subject of love before I was fifteen. But I'd never wanted sex to be all about scratching an itch. I'd always sensed there was more, beyond my grasp. I just hadn't had the courage to reach for it.

Not until now.

I let my panties drop to the floor and stood naked in front of Victor. For a long time, I was still, letting him look at me, letting him see me. Finally I worked up the courage to step over the edge. "Yes. The man I brought here, he is my father. In every way that counts."

Victor nodded, as if he understood, as if he sensed how much of myself I'd just exposed, the chance I'd just offered. He skimmed my body with his gaze, then focused on my face, and for the first time with any man, I felt like he was really seeing me. "Thank you."

My throat felt thick. "For what?"

"Trusting me."

I had his pants around his ankles before he could say another word. He was miraculously quiet while I peeled his briefs over his hips and pulled them down his legs. He was half erect, and as I sized him up, his cock flexed toward me as if giving some kind of come hither.

I leaned over him, kissing him again and using my knees to nudge open his thighs. I knelt between his splayed legs and took him in my mouth. He was hard with one stroke of my tongue up the underside of his shaft. Harder still when I encircled him with my lips and took him full into my mouth.

He tasted lightly salty and smelled of Dial soap and Claiborne for Men and his own unique scent. The hair on his legs rasped against my breasts and teased my nipples. I opened my throat and made his whole body shake in a moan.

I wanted him at my mercy, every nerve in his body focused on what I was doing to him, the sensations I was creating. I wanted him to turn himself inside out for me. With each lick, each nibble, each rasp of my teeth, I wanted to make him willing to do anything for me, be anything, anytime I needed him.

I don't know if I felt guilty for what I'd put him through, but I doubted that was it. I'd done worse things to men and had never felt the need to make it up to them afterward, even if they were still alive. With Victor, I wanted him to want me, to need me, to be loyal to me. I wanted the touch of my hands and mouth to sear him like a brand.

His hand moved through my hair, over my cheek. "Let me loose."

I shook my head.

"I hope you've figured out even if you let me loose, I'm not going anywhere."

"Maybe I just have a thing for handcuffs." I flicked him with my tongue and watched his forehead buckle with the effort to stay in control.

"I want to use my hands on you. My mouth."

I circled his tip with my tongue and then took him into my throat again. I could imagine his hands moving over me, caressing my breasts, delving between my legs. Shivers worked over my skin at the thought of his warm mouth suckling at my nipples and scattering kisses over my belly. A small shudder took me, and I could feel his tongue delving between my legs as clearly as what I was doing to him now.

I moved deeper between his legs and took his balls in my mouth. A shudder moved through him and another moan. I looked up at him, past the tower of his erection. His eyes were laser sights on me, drinking in what I was doing, and I felt more satisfied than I had in years. He really wasn't going anywhere.

"My turn," he grunted. "Please."

With one last stroke of my tongue, I skimmed my body up his, his cock leaving a moist trail between my breasts and down my belly. I claimed his mouth for a moment in a rough kiss, my tongue delving into his mouth and tangling with his. Then I rose over him and positioned myself against his lips.

His free hand snaked behind me, grabbing my ass, pressing me to his face. The first touch of his lips turned my legs into rubber. But his strong arm kept me on my feet, kept me trapped against his probing tongue. At first, it was just gentle licks, never staying in one spot too long, never allowing a rhythm to build. Then stroking became softer, quicker, darting in and out of me, gently taking my lips in his own, sucking softly.

I grunted, deep in my chest. I felt the orgasm welling up inside me, the pressure building. I wanted more friction. More contact. I moved closer, trying to capture his flickering tongue, but he kept pulling away, kept teasing me, even as I ground against him.

"Please," I urged. "*Please.*"

He slipped his hand between my legs, his finger penetrating me, and he began to give my clit the slow, fat licks that I needed, that I *craved*.

Shudders wracked my body, doubling and redoubling. I heard a scream and somehow recognized the sound was coming from my throat. Pure sensation crashed over me, waves of pleasure ripping me to pieces and rebuilding me again. My legs shook so badly I couldn't stand up anymore.

I sank down. Spreading my thighs to sit astride him, I let him enter, crying out again at the delicious pressure. So full. Too full. It was almost pain, almost too much. And then he began moving, thrusting upward with his hips, filling me further, pushing me toward the edge of another crest.

Pressure built, my body squeezing. I could smell our mingling sweat, sharp and clean, mixing with the salty tang of sex.

His hand circled to my buttocks, grasping me, lifting me, driving upward into me. I arched my back, and he buried his face in my breasts and captured a nipple in his mouth, coaxing me, urging me to another climax.

I shuddered, spasms tightening my body. He drove harder, faster, and I moved with him. Heat built to burning. Our flesh slapped a rhythm. Our breathing blended into one.

I couldn't say how long we moved like that, thrusting into each other, yet one. Dizziness spun over me. Something like happiness. I felt drugged, no longer in control, no longer even wanting to be.

I shuddered again, and he gripped my hips, pushing me down onto him, filling the hollow inside me. He cried out then, a feeling more than a sound. A tremor shook him and held, held us both.

The spasms slowed, then stopped. I sat still, his face in my chest, my arms wrapped around his shoulders, his neck, cradling his head, clinging to him. I wanted to soak in the feeling as long as I could, the tangible sensation of skin on skin, his cock still inside me, the certainty of our connection. But all too soon, the fighting flutter of pigeon wings erupted outside the window. The scent of a neighbor's slow-cooked roast beef dinner teased the air. And I could feel the heat and connection and certainty ebb like a retreating tide.

*"You're human, so you'll want to form attachments. Once you do, it's time to get out of the game. If you care about people, you can be manipulated and compromised. Field agents have to keep relationships superficial. Love kills."*

I climbed off Victor's lap. Without a word, I picked up my clothing and padded out of the room alone. I could feel him watching me, sense his unspoken questions hanging in the air, but I didn't turn back. I needed to think about what had happened, what I wanted, what I'd felt. But my mind wouldn't cooperate. Whatever bond might be growing between Victor and me, it was a fragile one, slight as the remnants of a dream, and I couldn't shake the feeling that if I examined it too closely, it would cease to exist.

I took a shower and then studied my injuries in the steamy bathroom mirror. I'd picked up new bruises thanks to the steps outside the John Hancock Center. My shoulder had resumed its throbbing, and I gave myself another shot to deaden the pain. A vague nausea claimed my stomach, and I wasn't sure if the cause was physical or emotional. Or maybe it was just exhaustion. Not that it mattered. I couldn't afford to rest. If my stomach settled, the best I could do was raid Victor's fridge and hope a rise in blood sugar would do the trick.

I threw on the robe hanging on the bathroom door. Slipping into the master bedroom, I checked on Kaufmann and rifled through Victor's closet. I pulled out a pair of silk blouses, one teal, one royal blue. I selected the blue along with another pair of jeans from Victor's lady friend's collection of clothing. Pulling them on, I had the urge to ask Victor about her. Were they exclusive? If he had a woman who stayed here, keeping clothing in his closet as if marking her territory, why was he flirting with me online, asking me to dinner, having sex with me on the living room sofa?

I got dressed, finger-combed my hair, and let it air dry. Instead of returning to the kitchen, I headed for Victor's office.

I sat down at Victor's computer and pushed thoughts of him from my mind. If I wanted to stay alive, like it or not, I had to concentrate on more than my sex life. I accessed the Internet drop box and retrieved the fingerprint I'd taken from the double I'd killed on my way to recover Kaufmann. I doubted I'd get any closer to an identification than I had with the print from the woman at the health club, but it was worth a shot. I had very few leads. I had to work them all.

I wasn't shocked when the database failed to provide a name. Then the computer showed a record that I'd already scanned the fingerprint.

Something must have gone wrong. I entered the first fingerprint again.

Again the website failed to give me a match, and it reported the same print had been entered three times.

I stared at the screen, quieting the questions pinging through my mind. I asked the site to compare fingerprints from the first woman I'd killed with the second.

A match. An exact match. According to the database, not only did the two hit women look the same, they were the same.

Not possible.

I'd killed the woman in the health club. I'd stake my life on it. And that was no zombie who had almost killed me outside Victor's apartment. So how could they have the same fingerprints? Two people never had the same whorls, loops, and arches.

Even identical twins each had their own prints. Theoretically, even clones should.

I stared at the pad of my thumb. I was conscious of time passing, a clock ticking in the apartment. The hum of the refrigerator. Mozart's low purr as she rubbed against my leg. Finally I scanned my own print. I hit enter and waited for the result.

An exact match.

The background sounds of the apartment rose like a buzz in my ears. I checked the results. I made a new scan and checked it again.

Not only were the two women I'd killed the same person, but I was that person, too.

I forced myself to breathe. In and out. Slow. Calm. The buzzing started to fade, and I heard traffic on the street below and water rushing through pipes. I reached down and scratched Mozart under the collar.

The phone rang.

Victor's answering machine picked up on the third ring. "Probably at work. Leave a message."

Trying not to notice the little jolt of pleasure I took from the sound of his recorded voice, I pushed up from the chair. There had to be an explanation for the fingerprints. I needed to focus on finding it.

The answering machine beeped. "Chandler, it's me."

My heartbeat stuttered, and for a second, I couldn't breathe. I hadn't seen him since I'd finished training, but his voice was always in my head.

*The Instructor.*

"Chandler, I'm in a car parked out front. We need to talk."

# SOME TIME AGO...

*"You've been specifically chosen for Project Hydra based on a specific set of criteria," The Instructor said. "Training will be challenging. Once you begin, you will not be able to quit. The only way you're leaving the training facility is in a body bag."*

DAY 1

My room is small, unfurnished except for a bed, a clock, and a dresser for clothing, which has been provided for me. Fatigues, socks, a belt, combat boots, green cotton underwear. I read somewhere that the military never issued any white clothing because it could be used as a flag to surrender. There was also a shower, a sink, a toilet. No windows.

I just arrived from Fort Knox, where I received infantry training after completing basic. A man met with me the day before graduation. He had no rank on his uniform and didn't mention what branch of the military he worked for. Only that I was picked out of ten thousand possible candidates for a special branch of service, and if accepted I'd be earning over a hundred thousand dollars a year.

Ten minutes after graduation, I was on a helicopter. We flew for sixteen hours, stopping to refuel twice. I noticed we were heading north, but wasn't told of our final destination. When I landed late in the evening, a man I knew only as The Instructor met me, took my personal belongings, and showed me my room.

There is no TV, no radio, no phone. I'm not allowed any contact with the outside world. The Instructor gave me a pad of paper and a pen, and I was told to write a journal, even though I won't be allowed to keep it when I leave here.

So far, The Instructor is the only other person I've seen. He said I wasn't allowed to tour the compound without permission, and when he left me for the night, he locked me in.

Day 2

When I woke up, I was ordered on a ten-kilometer run on a trail around the camp grounds. Judging from the flat terrain and cool air, I think I'm in the Midwest, maybe southern Illinois, or Ohio. There are barracks, a mess hall, and a few other buildings, all empty and in disrepair. The compound is split into two parts, a fence between the halves. The Instructor and I seem to be the only two people here.

After the run, I was told I'll be issued a television and required to watch various videos. After each video, tests will be given.

I made my own breakfast in the mess hall: powdered eggs, reheated sausage, and standard army coffee. Only a few parts of the camp have electricity, powered by a gas generator.

The first class of the day was bladed weapons. The Instructor and I sparred for eight hours, and I learned how to wield and conceal common weapons such as folding knives and bayonets, along with uncommon ones, such as how to turn a plastic safety razor into a lethal device. If I still had parents, they'd be proud.

That night, after dinner of a sandwich and more coffee, I helped set up a TV and VCR in my room and was ordered to watch a lesson on speaking Russian.

Day 3

Weight training. Another run. Knife and axe throwing. Another Russian video. It's like being at Rambo camp.

Day 4

Six excruciating hours on picking locks. The Instructor seems to have no personality, no sense of humor. But unlike previous teachers I've had, he has an infinite amount of patience. I have yet to see him get emotional about anything.

Maybe he's a robot.

Another Russian video, plus a video on Zen Buddhism, of all things.

### Day 7

Too exhausted to write for the last few days. Running 15 km now daily, plus weight training. Practiced hand-to-hand combat with The Instructor, took a test on speaking Russian, getting more Russian video lessons.

The food is subpar, and it's rather lonely, but I've grown used to that.

I like it here.

### Day 12

Finally met someone new. A short man, older, only spoke Russian. He didn't give his name. He spent the day teaching me long-range sniper techniques. After many hours, I was able to hit a melon from a kilometer away.

I wonder what they're training me for.

### Day 14

Haven't seen The Instructor in a few days, and all of my training is indoors. Once again I wonder if I'm the only trainee at this camp. If there are others, why aren't I allowed to see them?

### Day 17

No more Russian videos. Now it's Mandarin Chinese. Been practicing karate for the past few days. The Instructor is very good, but I managed to knock him down twice. He's still all business, completely unemotional.

I've lost weight but am gaining muscle. My stomach is ripped. I don't think big biceps on women are sexy, but I can do a hundred pull-ups without breaking a sweat.

## DAY 18

I almost died today.

The Instructor had been putting me through some balance exercises, and I was told to climb a pole and walk across a rope strung to an opposite pole. The pole wasn't very high, only five meters, but once I was up there, vertigo kicked in and I couldn't move.

After a minute of being frozen, I asked to come back down. The Instructor pulled his sidearm and said he would shoot me if I didn't get across that rope within the next ten seconds.

I took four steps, fell off the rope, and hung onto it.

The Instructor fired five rounds at me while I crossed to the other pole, hand over hand. It scared me to the bone. I've never had live rounds fired at me before. One bullet actually went through my pants cuff.

When I got to the other side, I couldn't help it. I was crying.

He calmly reloaded his pistol and ordered me to do it again.

I went back and forth between those two poles nineteen times before I could finally walk the rope.

I think The Instructor might be psychotic.

## DAY 19

No mention was made of him shooting at me. The Russian came back and showed me how to field strip and reassemble a ridiculous number of guns. We worked for twelve hours, and then I had two hours of Mandarin lessons.

I'm wondering if I'll ever get a day off.

DAY 22

Still no day off, and when I asked The Instructor how long this training will last, he told me, "As long as it takes."

A new teacher arrived. This one spoke only Mandarin. No name offered. I knew enough to understand much of what he said. We spent the day meditating, and he showed me how to isolate my senses. That night, more Buddhism videos.

DAY 29

After a week of espionage and surveillance techniques, I got a new teacher. A woman, older, lacking personality just like The Instructor, whom I haven't seen in a few days.

The woman is a pilot. I was put in a flight simulator and taught how to fly a helicopter.

Again I'm wondering what I'm being trained for.

DAY 36

I finally took a Huey up. A real live chopper! I flew over the camp, and for the first time saw how isolated it was. Nothing but plains for miles in all directions.

DAY 59

Haven't written in a while. Too tired, too busy.

I've learned so many martial arts they've begun to blend together, though I can regularly beat The Instructor in most of our hand-to-hand combat sessions.

I'm an expert sniper now and can shoot a baseball from a mile away in a crosswind.

My Russian and Mandarin are improving, and I'm learning French and Arabic.

DAY 65

Instead of a 20 km run this morning, I was taken to a field, given a handgun, and told to shoot a cow, lying in the nearby field. It had a broken leg and was wailing in pain.

I put two rounds in its head.

Now I'm wondering how its leg got broken.

## DAY 70

Along with weight training, I've begun to meditate every day. I've learned to slow down my heart rate and put my mind into a theta rhythm. This enables me to hold my breath for over two minutes.

It also has helped me to really focus my senses, so I have a better idea of what is going on around me. I'm using my ears more. My nose. It's weird, like being both tuned in and detached at the same time. I feel more aware of everything.

## DAY 76

Skydiving fucking rocks!

## DAY 78

Another cow. This one was healthy. I was told to kill it, and refused.

Using an iron rod, The Instructor broke the cow's leg.

When it began to scream, I put two rounds in the poor creature's head.

## DAY 85

I've been having nightmares about the cow. Other than that, training is going well. Got a new teacher, this one a Saudi. He taught me how to make IEDs—improvised explosive devices—out of various materials. Also taught me how to disarm them.

## DAY 91

Another cow. Completely healthy.

I shot it dead two seconds after being ordered to.

DAY 101

Balance is improving. I can get through an obstacle course while walking on my hands. I stood on top of a pole on one leg for six hours in a strong breeze. I can walk fifty meters on a high wire.

The other day, I was taken to one of the closed-off rooms of the compound and shown an autopsy in progress. I had to participate, putting on gloves, using the scalpel.

It didn't bother me like I felt it should have.

Later, I had to take a test on various organs and bodily systems. I learned eight different killing blows and why they worked. Human beings are more fragile than I thought.

DAY 121

I think I'm starting to crack.

I'm learning so much, so fast. I feel parts of my personality slipping away. Who I am. Who I want to be. Instead, they're being replaced by cold, impersonal training.

Maybe I'm becoming a robot, like The Instructor.

DAY 130

Another cow.

This time, I wasn't ordered to shoot it. I was given the iron bar and ordered to beat it to death.

I followed orders, but I cried the whole time.

DAY 135

I flew an ultralight today. Very cool. And much simpler than the Huey.

DAY 145

I miss people. Men, mostly.

I find myself thinking of Cory. Not sexually, though for all of his psychotic tendencies, the sex was good. I'm thinking about him because I'm such a different person than the little girl he took advantage of. If I met him again, I'd kill him.

Or maybe I'd fuck him first. I'm that horny.

## DAY 146

The Instructor acknowledged something I've known all along: that he's been reading my journal. He said that a healthy sex drive is natural in both men and women, and he offered, in that flat, emotionless way of his, to have sex with me.

Like he was asking if I wanted a cup of coffee.

I almost agreed to it.

## DAY 150

I was forced to watch a snuff video.

It was in Arabic. A fat, one-eyed man was interrogating a bound Pakistani. He tortured him with electricity, a knife, and finally a blowtorch, all the while asking him inane, unanswerable questions.

It lasted for three hours. I wasn't allowed to turn away.

I threw up twice.

Afterward, The Instructor brought me to a part of the compound I hadn't been to before. The brig.

Sitting in the cell was the one-eyed torturer.

I was ordered to shoot him.

I did it, quicker than it took me to shoot the cow.

## DAY 151

After the day's training, terrible thoughts swirling in my head, I told The Instructor I wanted to take him up on his offer.

We didn't kiss. The sex was passionless, perfunctory. But the orgasms brought me back from the brink of insanity I felt I'd been heading toward.

The Instructor didn't ejaculate. When I tried to make him come, he dismissed me.

DAY 152

No talk about the sex. Business as usual.

I vow I'll never sleep with the cold, heartless bastard ever again.

DAY 175

This was the worst day of training, and maybe the worst day of my life.

For the past week, I've been taught to resist interrogation. It started off harmless enough, with verbal sparring. Techniques to avoid giving away anything with body language. Psychological tests, stress tests, biofeedback while being questioned.

I was given a number. Six. I was ordered not to reveal that number if asked, no matter what.

Then I was forcibly abducted from my room while I slept—something I almost escaped from by resisting until The Instructor told me to stand down. I was stripped naked and thrown into a brightly lit, barren cell. It was cold, and a loud, piercing tone was played at random intervals. It hurt my ears and made it impossible to sleep. I had a bucket for the bathroom. No food or water.

I wasn't sure how long they kept me there. I stayed sane by reminding myself this was training. But after what could have been ten hours, could have been fifty, they pulled me out and strapped me to a table.

It's called *waterboarding*, and according to the government it was considered an *enhanced interrogation technique*, not torture.

Bullshit. It's torture.

They asked me my number. I didn't reply. So they put a cloth over my face and poured water on it.

They kept pouring until I couldn't hold my breath anymore. Until I had to breathe in the water.

Suddenly I was in the car with Cory again, and the water was over my head, and I was choking, dying. The sense of panic, of helplessness, of pure fear, was enough to drive me mad.

I lasted less than three minutes, then I gave up the number.

But they didn't stop.

I wasn't sure how long it went on. They hit me in the stomach while it was happening, to make me gasp for air. I passed out too many times to count, drowning, possibly even dying once or twice only to be brought back so they could do it again. Finally I didn't wake up.

The next time I opened my eyes I was back in my bed. My stomach still aches. My throat and lungs feel like they've been scrubbed with steel wool.

The Instructor came in to check on me an hour ago. He brought hot tea, some cookies.

I told him to get the fuck out or I'd kill him.

I meant it.

DAY 177

I understand why it was done to me. At some point, I may be required to interrogate someone. I needed to know what it was like.

But the waterboarding changed me. I'm harder now. Less sympathetic.

I'm also through with doing everything I'm told to do, unless I agree with it. If they ever try to grab me in my sleep again, I'll fight to the death before I let them take me.

DAY 203

I finally understand what I'm being trained for.

Instead of the usual 25 km run, I was given a file.

It includes a dossier of a man named Dalton Wick. He's white, forty-six years old, single, a day trader. He lives in Peru, Illinois, in a gated community with a state-of-the-art burglar alarm.

It also includes over a dozen pictures of Wick engaged in sexual relations with a crying, hysterical five-year-old boy.

I'm ordered to kill Wick by tomorrow night. Whatever equipment I need will be provided for me.

I've spent all day thinking about it.

Planning it.

## DAY 205

Everything went off without a hitch. I drove to Peru, bypassed his alarm, broke into his home, and shot him with a suppressed pistol while he slept.

When I got back to the compound, I thought I was OK. But during the debriefing, I began to cry, and the next thing I knew I was on top of The Instructor, tugging off his belt, pressing my lips to his.

This time I rode him so hard he had no choice but to come.

## DAY 345

Long time between journal entries.

I'm an assassin now. I've killed four people. All of them deserved it—murderers, molesters, torturers, psychopaths. I was told I could refuse taking jobs if I wanted to. One case I passed up was a pimp named Deevon. He was an asshole who got his whores hooked on smack and regularly beat them when they didn't obey. A true piece of human garbage, but I didn't think he was worthy of death. So I turned it down.

The next day the morning paper was handed to me, with an article about Deevon being shot and killed.

Apparently, I wasn't the only killer Project Hydra had trained.

I'm close to leaving this place, which I never thought of as home, but I feel I might miss. I'll be assigned a handler, given a new identity, and a new life as an undercover black ops hitter.

I have to cut off all ties with the past. That's fine, since I don't have a family. But I refuse to give up Kaufmann. The Instructor says I'm allowed to keep him as a friend, as long as I never reveal what I do or who I am.

I'm told I'm the second-best student that Project Hydra has ever had.

My code name is Chandler.

I haven't slept with The Instructor again. And if I never see him again, I'm OK with that.

*"It was an honor training you," The Instructor said. "It's doubtful we'll ever cross paths. If we do, it might very well mean I've been compromised. Don't hesitate to kill me if you have to. I won't hesitate to do the same."*

I dug through my duffel and readied another syringe of amobarbital with trembling fingers. I wasn't nervous, exactly, but along with hearing the sound of The Instructor's voice and its accompanying memories came another upswing of adrenaline, and after so many of these swings in the past hours, my system was struggling to cope.

I found a woman's jacket in Victor's closet, pulled it on, and concealed the syringe in the right sleeve. Noticing Victor's wallet on the dresser, I stuffed it into my pocket, along with his keys. My gun slipped neatly into the back waistband of my jeans. I checked on Kaufmann, still sleeping, and then walked down the hall and passed through the living room without sparing Victor a glance.

I paused at the door, listening to check if the hall outside was clear. Victor called to me, "Going somewhere?"

"Out."

I wanted to tell him more, but I knew the urge was selfish on my part. I had no idea what The Instructor had in mind. If something went wrong, the less Victor knew about me and where I'd gone, the better off he'd be.

But despite my better judgment, I turned and looked at Victor over my shoulder.

He sat on the edge of the couch, pants pulled up over his hips but fly gaping open, hand still cuffed to the radiator. But while some men might be annoyed that I'd left them naked and without use of the two hands necessary to zip and button, Victor appeared slightly amused. He gave me a questioning lift of the brows that was more than a little sexy. "You'll be back?"

I probably shouldn't have felt so pleased that he cared, but I managed to keep the smile off my lips. "Yeah, I'll be back."

I turned to the door, checked the peephole, and listened for movement outside. Sensing nothing, I slipped out to face my past.

I took the stairs to the street level then kept on going. The Instructor had said he was parked out front, but I wasn't about to take the direct route. I doubted anything I did would truly surprise him, but at least I wouldn't be obviously predictable.

I emerged in the belowground parking garage. It reeked of oil, stale exhaust, and damp concrete. The space was small, with room for just a handful of cars. I moved at a fast clip, senses tuned for movement, detecting none.

Striding up the short ramp, I emerged from a side door into an alley. The air outside was brisk, cool, and wind kicked a Starbucks cup across the sidewalk in front of me. I moved to the corner of the building and peered down the intersecting street that passed in front of the building.

It was easy to pick out the car, a black sedan that practically screamed *government issue*. I noted the silhouette of a man in the driver's seat. Both of his hands clutched the wheel, showing me he wasn't holding a weapon. A good sign.

The distance to the vehicle wasn't far, but I wouldn't be able to cross the gap unseen. As soon as I stepped out from behind the corner of the building, I would be vulnerable.

What could The Instructor possibly want? I didn't know how he'd found me, but it didn't surprise me he had. It also wouldn't surprise me if he'd been the one to call the police to my apartment in an effort to take me in.

Then again, he might also have been the one to call the assassins.

I could walk away. Disappear. But that would be the same as putting a bullet into Kaufmann and Victor myself. And if I did run, not only would I have to run the rest of my life, but I'd never know what the hell was going on.

I watched the street, the cars, the doorways, the rhythm of pedestrian traffic. Nothing seemed out of the ordinary. I did a quick circle around the block, looking for the backup unit, the second team, or anything else that indicated The Instructor wasn't acting alone. Everything appeared to be clear.

I was about to take a chance with a direct approach when the sound of a truck downshifting caught my attention. A semi hauling produce slowed and sidled up to the curb a couple of car lengths behind The Instructor's.

The opportunity I was waiting for.

I darted across the sidewalk and stepped into the truck's shadow. Circling the vehicle, I walked between the parking lane and traffic. I pulled my gun as I reached the sedan.

I stopped behind the driver's door and slipped into the back-seat. The Instructor leveled his eyes at me in the rearview mirror, as if he wasn't surprised. "Hello, Chandler."

I held my gun to the back of his neck, alongside the head-rest. "Slowly take the key out of the ignition, and drop it at your feet."

He followed orders.

"Keep both hands on the wheel. If you take them off for any reason, I shoot."

Again, The Instructor complied. His face had grown harder, the wrinkles deeper. But his expression, or rather his non-expression, was exactly as I'd remembered. I wondered, fleetingly, how many more he'd trained since me. Also, shameful as it was, I wondered if he'd slept with any of them.

I pushed the unbidden memories back, then gave him a little prod with the barrel of my gun. Afternoon sun slanted through the back window. He squinted into the glare.

"Project Hydra," he said, "began in 1982. An unusual group of septuplets were born to a mother who died during childbirth. These sisters were truly unique, because they shared a trait that had never been seen before. They all shared the same fingerprints."

*Sisters.*

My gun hand twitched, and my stomach lurched.

*Oh, Jesus…those women I killed…*

"The Cold War was at its height," he went on. "Espionage was essential to our nation's security, and the advantage of seven identical covert operatives in infiltration, undercover, intelligence gathering, and assassination scenarios was obvious. These sisters, if properly trained, could be used against foreign powers in a myriad of ways, causing massive confusion and loss of morale in our enemies. So, naturally, the government stepped in."

I knew The Instructor was talking about me. But I couldn't let this be about me. I had to treat this like any other op and keep my emotions at bay. Because if I let myself dwell, even for a second, on the fact that I'd killed three of my—

I jerked my thoughts away and focused on his words.

"A special branch of the National Security Agency was created expressly to oversee the upbringing of the sisters. They were put into separate, specially chosen homes with military families who knew the importance of the children they were raising."

I was grateful for the dry, almost textbook nature of his narrative. Listening to his recitation, I could almost pretend it was one of those boring history lessons I had ignored in school.

I could almost pretend that it had nothing to do with me.

But it was impossible to distance myself from this. My parents? The couple who raised me, the loving mother and father who died in a car crash shortly before my tenth birthday, they weren't my real parents? They were chosen for me by the government?

"And were my foster families chosen, too?" I said, my hand tightening on my weapon. After my parents died, I was bounced around from one uncaring home to another and wound up the sole child of a sixty-five-year-old retired businessman who confused love with discipline. I could count the number of hugs he'd given me on one hand. The number of beatings—too many to remember. "And the bastard who adopted me? Was his abuse part of my training?"

"Of course we regret the abuse, Chandler. When the Cold War ended and Clinton took office, many of those in charge of Project Hydra were repurposed. You, and your sisters, were no longer considered a priority, funding was cut, mistakes were made. William Rector, the man who cared for you—"

"*Cared* isn't the term I'd use."

"—was former NSA. We only found out about his treatment of you after your arrest."

I thought back to Cory. How sexy and dangerous and exciting he was. But the biggest attraction for me might have been that deep down, I knew Cory was a psycho. Which was the best way to strike back at my straitlaced, unloving, surrogate father. The best way to say *fuck you* to a bad parent is to sleep with a criminal.

"If it matters at all," The Instructor said, "some of the others had a worse time than you did. Rector wasn't the best choice. But in his own way, he set you on the path to what you have become."

"A killer," I stated flatly.

"One of the best in the world. It wasn't accidental all seven of you wound up working for your country. As all of you grew, you were groomed by your families, teachers, and college recruiters, for military service. That's how you came to me."

"Tell me about my..." I felt the word stick in my throat. "*Sisters.*"

The Instructor had no way of knowing what my life had been like after my parents died, going to live with Rector. I wasn't allowed to ever have friends over, in the chance they might mess up his precious house. And I wasn't allowed to visit anyone because he kept me a virtual prisoner, doing chores, studying constantly, making me take extra classes on top of regular schoolwork.

My one dream, my only wish, was to have a sister, to be able to share some of those lonely, miserable times with someone else, someone like me.

To find out now that I had six of them, and that three were already dead by my hand…

"You were all given code names," The Instructor said. "Chandler, Hammett, Fleming, Ludlam, Follett, Clancy, Forsyth."

"Those are all writers."

"Spy novelists. Reagan was a fan. Of these, you dispatched Follett in your elevator, Ludlam at the health club, and Forsyth on the street not far from here."

He didn't have to remind me. I could still feel Ludlam go limp after I rammed her head into the sink, still hear the pop as I snapped Forsyth's spine. I pushed thoughts of my three dead sisters away and focused on the rest. "So besides me, there are three still alive?"

"Two. Fleming died during a mission overseas several years ago. The remaining Hydra members are Clancy and Hammett. Hammett is the reason your cover was blown. She's the one who orchestrated this effort to eliminate you."

My throat grew tight, my skin hot. When I'd learned the hit women were my sisters, I'd assumed they were following orders. I understood that. I could rationalize that. But to discover the orders were given by one of them? That I had no idea how to process. "Why?" I whispered.

"Because your sister is a psychopath and the most dangerous person I've met in thirty-eight years with the military."

*"Your ability to survive is based on how well you react,"*
*The Instructor said. "But your ability to thrive is based*
*on how well you can act first. You cannot fully trust*

*anyone, ever. So what road shall you walk? The one
paved for you? Or the one you pave yourself?"*

Hammett stares at the blips on the screen, then presses the
button to make her computer tablet sleep. She's tired, but at the
same time, exhilarated.

It took almost a year of planning to get to this point. And
though she took every variable and contingency into account, the
death toll is higher than expected.

Three of the Hydra sisters, dead.

That is an incalculable loss. The time, the money it took to
train them. The personal investment Hammett made to recruit
them. All for nothing.

*Chandler is good. Very good.*

*But not as good as I am.*

Hammett tucks the computer away and stretches, arching her
back like a cat. Soon Chandler will be under her control, at her
mercy.

Hammett smiles at the thought.

*And I have no mercy.*

She starts up the stairs, remembering an op from two years
ago. A French diplomat, some low-level power broker in the confusing, interconnected spider web of international espionage. By
all accounts, he was one of the good guys who just happened to
have an agenda at cross-purposes with those who gave Hammett
orders.

Hammett sneaked into his suite, to his bed, and did what
she'd grown accustomed to doing. She woke him up before she
killed him.

This began as a game for Hammett. She enjoyed watching them squirm. Watching them beg. Sometimes they offered
her things. Sometimes they offered her everything. Once she
fucked a particularly handsome Arabian prince, riding him

even as he trembled with fear, shooting him at the peak of her orgasm.

Though sadism is one of the baser emotions, that didn't make it any less of a rush.

But with the last few jobs, right before she went rogue, Hammett began asking her marks questions. Questions about life, and what they thought the purpose was.

Profound shit. Especially for those who were about to die. And it interested Hammett, because at that time, she had yet to figure out her ultimate purpose.

The Frenchman babbled on about love, being a good son to his parents, a good husband to his wife, a good father to his children—Hammett even allowed the poor sap to show her pictures of the little brats while he cried all over them. But she pressed him, pushing further, asking him why, if his precious family was so important, he'd taken a job where he was away from them two hundred days out of each year.

And that's when he gave her the real reason for his existence. The real reason for *everyone's* existence.

He said, with elegant simplicity, "I'm trying to get to the top of the food chain."

That resonated with Hammett, long after she put the bullet through his eye.

She smiles with the memory of this epiphany. Human beings are creatures forged by evolution. We exist because natural selection deemed us the strongest. So it makes perfect sense for each of us to attain as much power as we can, to be the strongest of all.

Hammett has almost everything she wants. A job that pays well and lets her indulge her sadistic streak, nice clothing to wear, expensive toys to play with, and any man she desires, whether he is willing or not.

But she doesn't have true power. The power only felt by the heads of state. The power over entire countries, deciding who lives and who dies.

That is the pinnacle of Darwinian evolution. That's what drives kings and dictators and presidents. That's what forges nations and shapes history.

That's what Hammett wants.

And very soon, she'll have it. The transceiver is the key to ultimate power. All that stands in her way is her sister. A sister who is weaker than Hammett in every possible way.

Hammett climbs the last few stairs and reaches the door to the apartment. She slips inside, silent as death. Almost immediately, she sees the man on the sofa, his pants undone, his arm handcuffed to the radiator.

The sight makes her laugh out loud.

"Well…what do we have here?"

*"At some time, you may encounter intel that is so big, so important, it will be difficult to act," The Instructor said. "You need to file that away, process it later. Don't let anything impede your ability to function. If you do, you're dead."*

The Instructor studied my reflection in the rear view mirror. "Remember when I said you were my second-best student? Hammett was number one."

I shifted in my seat. His voice held a note of awe, something I found almost more disturbing than his words.

"She's the perfect operative, the perfect assassin, because she lacks something that you have." He paused, as if allowing me to soak in what he was saying, or to ask him to continue.

I didn't bite. Instead I focused on the whoosh of passing cars, the odor of the sedan's worn leather seats, a woman strolling by talking on her cell phone.

"Do you remember the cows?" he eventually asked.

I offered a slight nod. A day didn't go by when I didn't remember those poor cows.

"The first time I ordered Hammett to kill one, she didn't shoot it in the head. She shot its legs out, then used my knife to slit its throat."

I filed those images away, not letting myself absorb them, not allowing my emotions to react.

"Hammett isn't held back by the trappings of humanity. Because of that, she's willing to do things you're unable to. She lacks the conscience you have, which makes her a very dangerous opponent. She has all of your training and none of your boundaries." His eyes bored into mine. "Whatever she's after, we can't let her get it. Even if it means our deaths."

I watched The Instructor through narrowed eyes. When I was in training, he'd known the answer to every question, understood every motivation, seen through every defense. Where Hammett was concerned, he seemed to be at a loss, as if he was struggling to catch up, like me.

"So how do I stop her when I don't even know what she's after? Kill her?"

"If you have the opportunity, take it. But she's smart, and she's been planning for a long time. She's also persuasive. When Hammett went rogue, she was able to recruit her sisters to help her. So far, her only mistake has been underestimating you. But she's learning, fast. Chandler… where is the phone your handler gave you?"

"My phone?" I had a guess why he was asking. "Can she track it?"

"No. The transceiver can't be tracked or traced."

I gave my head a little shake and thought back to the many times the assassins were able to locate me. There had to be an explanation. "Hammett has been one step ahead of me the whole time. If she isn't able to track the phone, how does she keep finding me?"

"I need to reach into the case on the passenger seat and remove a computer. Will you let me?"

"Nice and slow."

He moved at half-speed, carefully opening up a leather computer satchel and removing a touch screen tablet PC, like the one I'd taken from the assassin up the street after I'd killed her.

"Each of the Hydra sisters has a tracking chip, attached to the lining of their stomachs. It was implanted to make sure we knew where you were, so we could extract you from a dangerous situation if needed."

"Yeah, I bet that was the reason." I resisted the urge to wrap an arm around my middle. "I've got one in me?"

"All of you do."

The only way something could be planted in a person's stomach lining was through surgery. Yet I didn't remember having any surgical procedures done. "How?"

"During the interrogation training. While you were being waterboarded. We implanted it through your belly button when you drowned."

I remember the sharp pain in my stomach when I woke up from that hell, being told it was from the punching. The bastards had chipped me like I was a family pet.

He switched on the screen, and I noticed five blips superimposed over a map of Chicago, condensing the city into the size of a handprint. It looked like a satellite photo, similar to the interface Google Earth used.

"Why five, not seven?" I asked.

The Instructor paused, then said, "Fleming died years ago. The other is probably two blips that are close together, reading as one."

As outlandish as all of what he was saying seemed, it made a warped kind of sense. But one inconsistency kept nagging at the back of my mind. "Why didn't Hammett try to recruit me?" I asked. "She recruited the others."

"All of you had intensive psychological profiles done. Everything you did at the training camp was recorded. Your journals were studied, scrutinized by professionals. Out of all your living sisters, you were the one who tested the highest for ethics. You were the most trustworthy."

"Hold on," I said. Back in training, I'd never been given that kind of information, even about myself. "How did Hammett know that?"

The Instructor paused for a moment, then said. "The same way Hammett was able to find your sisters. She learned about the tracking devices and read all of your files."

"How did she do that?" Even as the words left my mouth, I knew. The clincher was when The Instructor glanced away.

"Hammett found me," he said, his voice getting softer. "After training, she smuggled out a spent bullet casing with my fingerprint on it. She was able to find out my name, where I lived. When she went rogue, she sought me out. She...was able to make me talk."

I narrowed my eyes. "You gave me up."

"Everyone has a breaking point. She found mine. She... tortured my wife...my children...in front of me. I told her everything I knew."

His tone was still flat, but I didn't need hysterics to recognize how broken the experience had left him, and I could guess how it ended. "She killed them anyway."

"I didn't talk to save them. I talked to spare them any more pain."

He hadn't shown half this much emotion in all the time I'd spent with him. I should probably feel more for him, for his family, but something held me back. "So why didn't she kill you?"

"I don't know. Maybe because she thought I might still be useful. Maybe she knew how much it would hurt me to leave me alive." He dropped his gaze. He looked tired and much older than I'd previously guessed. "I'm...sorry, Chandler."

I knew I was being cold, hard, but after all he'd told me, keeping my emotion at bay was the only way I could continue to function. The Instructor had taught me well. "Is Jacob compromised?"

"I think so. This blip here," he pointed to the screen, "is Clancy. She's an expert sniper. Even better than you. She's camped outside Jacob's compound. No doubt she's cut the power and is jamming communications. Eventually she'll find a way in."

I nodded. Keeping my eyes riveted to his, I dropped my left hand low and shifted my wrist. The syringe slid down to the jacket's cuff, then stopped.

"Where's the phone, Chandler?" he asked.

Instead of answering, I concentrated on shifting my arm, trying to shake the needle free without moving the rest of my body. The Instructor was sharp. Any hint that I wasn't fully listening, any tilt of my shoulders, and he would sense my plan. The syringe didn't move.

"This is important. We have to make sure it's safe."

"Why?"

Another shake, and the needle slipped into my palm.

"There's information on it. Information that can be used to compromise the security of the United States. There are only two transceivers in existence. The president has one. Based on your Hydra profile, you were entrusted with the other."

"Hammett wants the phone."

"That might be what she's after. With the proper encryption decoder, she—"

I flicked my eyes to the right, out the front windshield, and forced my pupils to widen as if I saw something surprising. He was watching me in the rearview mirror, and his eyes followed mine. In that brief moment, I brought my hand up and jabbed the hypo into his neck. He dropped the PC and reached both hands back. I managed to depress the plunger halfway before I was forced to release it and focus on blocking his flailing wrists.

It only took a few seconds for the amobarbital to take effect, and The Instructor's efforts to grab me became slower, sloppier. His head tilted, and he reached to the side, trying to get the car door open. I grabbed him by the collar, pulling him back against the seat. My mind swirled with everything I'd just learned, yet I was still in the moment enough to be disappointed at how easy he was to subdue.

He slid to the side, his face visible through the space between the bucket seats. Finally he stopped struggling, and his glassy eyes met mine with a look of…fear? Anger?

No, it was softer than that. In fact, it reminded me of the look Kaufmann had when he said he was proud of me.

Then his lids closed, and he was asleep.

I checked his pulse to make sure, giving him a harsh pinch on the side to see if he flinched or his heart rate jumped. I needed for him to be out of commission for a few hours, until I could process everything I'd just learned. A large part of me wondered if I could trust him, and if it would be better just to kill him right now.

But he'd given me vital intel, and so far was acting like an ally. And I had to face the truth of the matter: my allies were few and far between.

I climbed out of the backseat and opened the driver's door. Shoving The Instructor over, I slipped behind the wheel. If I had a locator chip in me, Hammett knew where I was right now. Which meant she could already be on her way to Victor's. I needed to get Kaufmann to a safe house.

And The Instructor had provided a convenient way to do that.

I pulled out from the curb and drove to the parking garage entrance, my senses on high alert. A woman emerged from Victor's building, and I nearly reached for my gun before she made it to the curb and raised her hand to hail a cab. It wasn't Hammett. She was too old, too plump.

A truck's brakes squealed. Somewhere, a dog barked. Rifling through Victor's wallet, I located a card with a real estate management company logo emblazoned on the front. I lowered the window, swiped the card, and the garage door opened.

I found a vacant space near the stairwell. It wouldn't take me long to wake Kaufmann with something from Victor's personal pharmacy and help him down to the car. We would be gone long before Victor's neighbors were likely to arrive home from work.

I finished hefting The Instructor into the passenger seat. His computer fell off his lap and bounced onto the floor, and I slid it under the seat along with the sedan's keys. I had given him a big enough dose for him to sleep at least an hour or two. It was doubtful he would wake up, find the keys, and drive away in the time I'd be gone. But if he did, I still had Victor's car keys in my pocket.

I got out of the car and scanned the area. I smelled nothing besides the ordinary exhaust fumes and concrete. Nothing, that is, but a faint whiff of stress coming from my own body.

I closed the door quietly to keep the sound from echoing through the garage and took the stairs to the third floor, bouncing on the balls of my feet, my footfalls like kitten steps on deep carpeting, not making a sound.

When I finally made it to Victor's door, I brought up the key and hesitated. Holding my breath, I placed an ear to the wood and listened for any sounds from within. I listened for a whole two minutes, and then let the air leak slowly out of my nose as I turned the doorknob.

A moment after stepping inside, I sensed something wrong. Movement, to my right, alongside the doorway. I turned but not fast enough.

I'd been electrocuted before, so I knew a stun gun when I felt it. The pain was instant and agonizing, locking my muscles, forward momentum dropping me to the floor.

The jolt went on for several seconds, and I was unable to see my attacker, but I felt a knee drive down on my back and hands quickly relieve me of my gun, Victor's wallet, and his keys. Over the merciless, ongoing jolt of electricity, I heard a familiar male voice purr to me in perfect Russian.

"You should have gone with your instincts and not trusted me."

*Victor.*

The pain reached a crescendo, my whole body feeling as if I was being burned alive, and even though I fought it with everything I had, I passed out.

> *"Knowing how to interrogate a subject means knowing how to withstand interrogation," The Instructor said. "Be aware of your body, and what it is revealing. The pain will likely become unbearable, but once you give up the information they're after, you will be killed. It will be a fine line between how much you want to live versus how much agony you can endure. Also know that if you give up any secrets related to Project Hydra, past missions, or the US Government, you will be considered an enemy of the State, tried for treason, and executed."*

When I woke up, I was on my back, secured to a table.

No, not a table. A backboard, like the ones used by lifeguards on the beach. My wrists were bound to the hand-holes with zip ties, my legs and body secured by Velcro straps. My head was similarly strapped down and held in place by a plastic cervical collar.

Glancing left, I saw cabinets and realized I was on Victor's kitchen counter.

I blinked a few times, trying to determine if I'd been drugged. My head was swimming. My heart rate was also accelerated, unusual for just waking up. Victor must have given me something.

"Good morning, sunshine," said a female voice, so recognizable it made me gasp.

Because it was *mine.*

I let my eyes follow it and saw one of my sisters standing next to me. She wore the teal silk blouse from Victor's closet, the one I'd almost picked out for myself. Her hair was short, like mine.

The only difference between looking at her and peering at myself in the mirror was a tiny scar on her chin.

"You know what's going to happen," Hammett said. "Don't you?"

I did. There was only one reason to have me trussed up this way. But I refused to let my mind dwell on what she intended to do. Letting my fear build would do nothing to help me. Instead I focused on observing as much as I could around me.

"You've been through it before. Twice, actually. The first time with that psycho you were fucking when you were a kid." She gave me a knowing smile, rubbing in the fact that she knew all about my past, all about me. "Must have been scary, trapped in the car, the water rushing in on all sides. Let me be honest with you, Chandler, during training I didn't like drowning at all. I'll bet you hated it even more."

I didn't say anything. I worked on trying to control my breathing, my heart rate, listening to the flap of pigeons outside the window, and breathing in the neighbor's slow-cooked beef. So far, I'd managed to keep panic at bay despite Hammett's mind games and whatever drug I had in my system. But once I sucked that first bit of water into my lungs, I'd lose control over my body. The sensation of drowning is so frightening, and it works on such a base, reptile-brain level, that no amount of meditation was going to stop me from freaking out.

No one could resist waterboarding. That's why it was such an ineffective method of gathering intel. Victims would lie like devils, agree to anything, make up insane stories, just to get it to stop. There was no way to be sure if what they were spilling was truth or what they thought the interrogator wanted to hear.

I looked my sister straight in the eye. "I'll tell you everything you want to know," I said, working to keep my voice even.

"I know," cooed Hammett, rubbing her index knuckle cross my cheek. "But let's have a bit of fun first."

She reached behind me, and I heard the sink go on. I closed my eyes and felt a towel dropped over my face. I wondered if Kaufmann was dead. If not, maybe there was a slim chance they'd leave him out of this. At least I could tell myself that and hope that they didn't realize how much he meant to me.

I thought of how much I wanted to say to him, how I'd failed to form the words before he'd slipped into drug-induced unconsciousness, how I might never have the opportunity now.

I heard footsteps, someone else coming in.

"I thought you were going to wait for me."

*Victor.*

"How's the old man?" Hammett asked.

"Just gave him something to wake him up. He'll be around soon."

My throat closed. I'd told Victor that Kaufmann was like a father to me. In my need to open up, to trust Victor, to forge what I thought might grow into some kind of bond, I'd betrayed the only person I had in the world.

I felt Victor's hand on my thigh, traveling up between my legs. I flinched, trying to twist away. Except for a small twitch, I couldn't move.

He chuckled. "Wow, you go from hot to cold pretty quick. A little while ago, you couldn't get enough of me."

I thought I might be sick.

"How was she?" Hammett asked.

"Adequate," he said, pinching my left breast. "But too needy."

"What I needed was a bigger cock," I said. "Rather than child-size."

I sensed the punch before it came and was able to clench my stomach muscles as his fist hit. Even so, the blow shuddered through my body and made me gasp for air. Before I had a chance to recover, I was slid, table and all, under the kitchen faucet. My hips lifted, tilting my shoulders downward, making blood rush to my head. Tepid water soaked the towel. Victor punched my belly again and again, and I fought not to breathe, squeezing my eyes shut, keeping my air passages closed.

I lasted maybe a minute before my body betrayed me, and I had to take a breath. The water rushed into my lungs. I coughed and gasped and choked on more water. A roar rose in my ears, blotting out all sound. My body convulsed against the restraints.

Then I went away. No more Chandler. No more memories. No more humanity. I was a blind, panicked animal, struggling for survival. The fear of dying, the pain of my lungs sucking in liquid, the blackness of death clawing at me, reduced me to nothing but pure, terrible sensation.

When they finally pulled off the towel, I couldn't stop coughing. My nose and throat were raw. My lungs felt like I'd inhaled fire. My whole body trembled. I couldn't control my weeping, but managed through raw, brute force not to beg.

Not that begging would do any good.

"Do you know what we're looking for, Chandler?" Hammett asked.

I continued to cough, gasping in air like I'd never get enough.

"This must be so terrible for you. The memories it brings back. I'd really hate to be you right now, dear sister. Your pain and fear must be unimaginable."

"Nice…scar," I sputtered. "Your pimp do that to you?"

Hammett's eyes got big, and she cracked a smile. "You're feisty. You'll be fun to break."

I went under the faucet once more, no towel this time, the water running directly up my nostrils. I coughed and gagged and eventually retched all over myself before they pulled me back.

Victor leered down at me. "What, no more jokes about my cock?"

"What…cock?" I managed. "I thought you…finger-banged me."

He jammed the wet towel against my face and shoved me under the water again. This time, rather than punches raining down on my stomach, the stun gun zapped my side.

I really had a lousy track record when it came to men.

The pain went on until I couldn't take any more. And then it kept going.

Choking, gasping, and then drowning. The water pulling me down, closing over my head, filling my lungs, like I was in the car again with Cory. No…not with Cory…with Kaufmann. And this time, I was the one who had driven into the water. It was my fault. All my goddamn fault. And yet there he was anyway, kind, beautiful Kaufmann, looking at me with that softness in his eyes, saying he was proud of me, that he cared for me, giving me more than any human being ever had.

And it still wasn't enough.

I must have died, because next thing I knew, warm lips were on mine, blowing air into me. I tried to bite down, but they pulled away too fast. Coughing took hold of me, vomiting, spitting out water. Bile seared the back of my throat. But the rest of me felt like I was floating.

"Bitch," Victor said, jolting me back to earth.

"Easy!" Hammett commanded. "You want to kill her again? We need information, dumb ass."

A light slapping on my cheeks.

"Chandler! Where is your phone? The one Jacob gave you?"

"It's…" My words gave way to more hacking. I thought my throat would shred, my lungs erupt from my body.

"Where is the phone, Chandler?"

Somehow I managed to laugh between coughing fits. So The Instructor was telling the truth. She wanted my cell phone. "It's… up your fat ass," I said. "With your head."

I felt the stun gun press against me, then abruptly pull away.

"We're wasting time," Hammett said. "Bring the old man in."

A pain descended over me, worse than anything physical. I thought about begging. Not for me, for Kaufmann. But I knew it wouldn't make any difference. All I had left was the truth, and I knew that wouldn't help either of us. The Instructor's orders to die rather than give my psychotic sister what she wanted raced through my mind.

So when they brought him in—my friend, my only friend, the only person in this whole cruel, terrible world that I cared about—the only thing I could do was apologize.

"I'm sorry, Kaufmann. I'm so, so, very sorry."

His eyes found mine. "Don't tell them shit," Kaufmann said. His hands were shackled in front of him, wearing the cuffs I'd last used on Victor.

Victor shoved him into the kitchen chair and held up a remote control. "My neighbors won't be home for a few more hours. But just in case." He pressed the button, and the stereo began to blast. AC/DC, "You Shook Me All Night Long," the volume cranked up to the max.

Then Victor went at Kaufmann with the stun gun.

Kaufmann managed to hold it together, at first. Stoic grunts. Minimal tears.

When Victor applied the stun gun to his more sensitive areas, the screaming began.

"You can stop it at any time," Hammett shouted close to my ear. "Just tell me where the phone is."

Tears blurred my vision and streamed down the sides of my face. "I threw it away."

"Where?"

My body shook in a sob. I had to tell her something. Anything. "The Hancock building. Lobby entrance, first bank of elevators. The can under the ashtray. Make Victor stop."

Victor didn't stop.

"Make him stop!"

Hammett patted my cheek and made a *tsk*ing sound with her tongue that I could see more than hear. "Dear sister, I was trained in identifying microexpressions, just like you were. Your face tells me you're lying."

Kaufmann's cries grew louder, more uncontrolled.

"I'm not lying! Make him stop!"

"He'll stop," Hammett cooed, "when you tell me the truth."

Out of the corner of my eye, I could see my old friend's face, a rictus of agony. He let out a long, keening howl that wasn't even identifiable as human.

Something inside me broke.

"It's on the ninety-sixth floor!" I screamed. "Above the restaurant! It's above the restaurant!"

Kaufmann stopped screaming. Victor cut the music off.

"I swear to Christ it's above the restaurant on the ninety-sixth floor of the Hancock building," I said. "The bar above the Signature Room."

Hammett was studying my face. "She's telling the truth. Where in the bar, Chandler?"

"Kaufmann…" I could see him in my peripheral vision. He slumped between the wall and the chair, his face turned away from me. "Kaufmann…"

"Where in the bar is the phone?" Hammett leaned close to my face and spoke slowly and clearly, as if talking to a small child or an idiot.

Victor gave Kaufmann a shove. His head lolled against the back of the chair, eyes staring into mine. But Kaufmann wasn't there anymore.

"He's…not…breathing," I heard myself say.

Victor brought his fingers to Kaufmann's throat, feeling for a pulse. "Must have had a heart condition." He made a face of fake concern. "Oops."

*No. No-no-no-no-no-no-no-no…*

The towel again. The faucet. I kept repeating the ninety-sixth floor, over and over, but after all that had just happened, I was willing to die before I gave them any more than that.

"We're not getting anything else out of her now," Hammett said, stepping away and wiping the sweat from her brow with the sleeve of her silk blouse. "How long will it take to get your team together?"

"An hour. Perhaps less."

"You all have credentials?"

"Of course."

"We'll call in a bomb threat. Clear the room, give us time to find the transceiver."

"What about her?" Victor said, pointing his chin at me.

"We may still need her. She's not going anywhere. Besides," Hammett smiled and turned away from me. "I'll bet she wants some alone time with her dear friend."

Victor chuckled. "He was like a father to her, I hear." He gave Kaufmann a shove, and his body slumped off the chair and fell to the floor, his dead eyes accusing me.

*"Emotions are a liability. Despair is a slippery slope. Keep your emotions in check, and remember your training. You can function at a higher level than other people. Use your logic, your reason, your senses. Bury your emotion. If you're crying, you're not in control. If you're not in control, you're dead."*

Hammett left the kitchen, Victor following. I heard them stirring elsewhere in the apartment for a minute or less, then the door opened and closed, and I was alone.

"Kaufmann?" His name rasped from my throat half-whisper, half-plea.

He didn't make a sound, but then I had known he wouldn't.

"I'm so sorry. Oh God, I'm so sorry." A sob shook my chest. I tried my best to choke it back.

*I am ice.*

*I am ice.*

*I am ice, goddamnit.*

Another sob came then another. They took control of my body, like dry heaves, ripping my guts out, tearing me in half. I wanted to curl up, to forget.

More than anything in the world, I wanted to die.

For a while, I let the flood of emotion carry me. I didn't cry, not in the normal sense of tears rushing down my face. But I didn't think, either. I didn't try to control the flood of pain. Wave after wave shook me, and I did nothing to stop them.

Even after the worst subsided, I couldn't regain control. Emotionally I was a mess, and my focus wasn't helped by whatever shit Victor had injected me with. My heart was beating so damn fast I could feel it in my throat. My whole body quaked, and even though my hair and blouse were wet and I was freezing cold, sweat slicked my skin. I guessed he'd given me norepinephrine or noradrenaline, fight-or-flight hormones administered to make the waterboarding even more intense.

As if that needed any enhancement at all.

When the sound reached me, coming from the living room, I almost jumped out of my skin.

There it was again, the doorknob rattling.

It was too soon for Hammett and Victor to be back. And a cop called to investigate the earlier screaming would identify himself.

The door opened and shut again. A soft shuffle of footsteps moved across the living room floor, slow, tentative. Two sets, one heavy, one light.

A scent reached me, almost too faint to discern. But even though it was light as a whisper, I could tell it wasn't Claiborne for Men. It wasn't cologne at all.

It was a scent I had known far longer, a mix of cigarettes, leather, and sweat.

The scent of a very bad man.

*"At some point you might believe that death is inevitable. Once that thought enters your head, you cease fighting. Once you cease fighting, death* will *be inevitable. The only way to stay alive is to never give up."*

"Looking good, babe," the familiar voice said.

I probably should have felt something, but after all that had happened in the last hour, I had nothing left to feel. "Hello, Cory."

He must have followed me from the John Hancock building. I'd been more focused on Kaufmann's health than avoiding tails. Careless of me, but at this point it didn't really matter.

The second set of footsteps apparently belonged to the girl. Cory's replacement for me.

"Don't tell me the two who just left did this to you," Cory said in an amused tone. His face loomed into my field of vision. The girl lingered like a shadow behind him.

Even in the midst of my despair, I couldn't help noticing the irony of the moment. If I'd been free, I would have had little to fear from Cory. He was insane, certainly, but of the two-bit variety, not the highly-trained, I'm-going-to-dominate-the-world type, like Hammett. He'd controlled me as a vulnerable girl, but that had been a long time ago.

Yet, here I was, once again at his mercy.

Cory's thin lips widened in a grin. "Why didn't you tell me you had a twin?"

I didn't particularly feel like talking about my sister, so I kept my mouth shut.

"I see your precious Kaufmann didn't come to your rescue." A fleshy thud reached me, the unmistakable sound of Cory's boot striking Kaufmann's body.

I closed my eyes.

"It's too bad. It really is. I was looking forward to cutting off the rest of his body parts while you watched."

My throat felt thick. I couldn't summon the energy or the will to answer.

"Don't tell me your sister did this to him. You must have pissed her off."

"Cory?" The girl's voice wasn't much more than a whisper. She hovered near the kitchen entrance, her big brown eyes darting around like those of a hunted animal expecting an ambush. "What if her sister comes back?"

Cory grinned and winked at me. "Then I'll fuck her, too. I've never done twins before."

"Cory, I'm serious." A touch of whine worked around the edges of her voice, reminding me what Kaufmann had told me, that even with the makeup and short skirt, she was only fourteen.

Twenty years had passed since I'd been in her place, but I still remembered the feelings that had driven me to Cory and convinced me to stay. Still, I could muster no pity for this girl, no understanding. If anything, I wanted to shake her, slap her, punish her for staying with Cory, for folding to his will, for being afraid of him.

Like I had been.

"Why don't you go outside for a bit, Di? Have a smoke or something. Let me get reacquainted with my old friend, here."

"Come on, Cory. You said—"

"Shut the hell up and let the grownups talk."

The girl flinched, as if Cory had physically hit her. She pressed her lips together and focused a look of pure hatred on me. "Cory, you said you were going to kill her."

"I am."

"Why don't you then, so we can leave?"

He gave me a look full of swagger. "After I'm done having some fun."

"But, Cory…"

"Go watch the door. I won't be long."

Normally I would have gone for the obvious insult, but I was too busy watching the girl. When I'd been in Di's place, I'd never questioned Cory. At first I'd been too afraid of his disapproval. Later I'd been too afraid of him.

"What am I supposed to do if someone comes in?"

Cory rolled his eyes. He glanced around the room and then focused a glare on me. "Where's my gun?"

"How the hell do I know?" I answered.

"You took it. Where is it?"

I'd never realized how dim Cory actually was. "If I had a gun, do you think I'd be in this position right now?"

He turned away from me and stepped to the kitchen table. When he returned, he was holding the stun gun Victor had used to…

I swallowed into a dry throat.

"Use this." He handed it to the girl. "Now get out of here."

She grasped the stun gun and took a few steps before pausing in the kitchen doorway and glancing back. Jealousy was written all over her face, an emotion common to teen girls, especially when they'd convinced themselves a manipulative psycho was the man of their dreams.

Cory didn't wait until she was out of the door before he grabbed my blouse and yanked. Buttons popped. He gave me a grin, as if waiting for me to gasp or plead or give him some kind of satisfying show of fear.

He'd wait forever.

Whatever he did to me, I didn't care anymore. He might as well be raping a mannequin. I looked in the direction of the hall, trying to catch a glimpse of the girl. I couldn't help but wonder how often she'd talked back to him like that. Cory chose young girls for a reason. They were pliable, easy to control. If she kept showing signs of having a will of her own, I doubted an inadequate, narcissistic shithead like Cory would keep her around much longer. And he wasn't the type to break up peacefully.

He rummaged through a kitchen drawer and pulled out a knife. A smile snaked over his lips. "Ah, this'll do." He slipped the sharp blade between the cups of my bra and sawed upward. The honed steel sliced elastic and lace. My bra flapped open and cool air rushed over my skin.

He took a nipple between thumb and forefinger and pinched hard.

Another wave of sweat bloomed over my skin from the pain, but I stared back at him as if I didn't feel a thing.

He gave the other breast the same bruising treatment. "Your nips are erect. You enjoying this, babe?"

"Sure, Cory," I said, laying the sarcasm on thick. "I'm thinking of all the things I want to do to you."

He gave me a big-ass grin, as if he actually believed those things might bring him pleasure…or involve sex of any kind. "Do you know what I'm going to do after I fuck you?"

"No, but I'm sure you're dying to tell me."

He scraped the flat of the knife blade against one breast. "I'll cut off your nipples first. Then your whole tits. Then I might just fuck you again before I slit you down the middle." His nostrils flared. His scalp pinked under the short, graying stubble. He unbuckled his belt and lowered his fly.

"Cory…"

"I'm busy, Di." Leaving his jeans gaping open, he spun around to the girl. "Watch the door."

She glanced at me, then down at Cory's pants. A flush crept up her neck and blazed in her cheeks. Her lips tightened into a hard knot.

I locked eyes with her, then forced myself to look at Cory. "Come on, big boy," I said. "Give it to me."

He chuckled. "Yeah, I know you want it, bitch."

Turning his back on Di, he started on my jeans.

With Cory hulking over me, I heard the snapping hum before I realized the girl had moved.

Cory lurched forward, his back arching, a loud growl grounding out between clenched teeth. Tendons stood out in his neck.

Di kept the stun gun's juice going.

He stumbled forward, hitting the counter. When she finally relented, he collapsed.

She stared down at the weapon, as if suddenly realizing what she was doing. Jerking her hand back, she let it clatter to the floor. She stared at him for a few seconds, as if she wasn't sure what she was seeing, then tears swamped her eyes, and she covered her face with her hands.

"It's OK, Di. It's OK." The situation was ridiculous. Here I was strapped down, half-undressed and unable to move, and I was trying to soothe this confused, jealous girl who'd just zapped her boyfriend and more than likely wanted me dead.

She lowered her hands, sniffing, her thick lashes spiked with tears. "Aw, Christ, he's going to be so mad when he wakes up."

"It's OK."

"What the hell do you know?"

"I was in your place, remember? I used to be you."

She glared at me, as if she remembered far too well and wanted to make me pay for that sin.

I pushed ahead anyway, taking a chance. "I can help you get away from him. All you have to do is cut these ties."

"Get away from him?" She shook her head. "You just want me to get away so you can have him yourself."

"Trust me, that's not it."

"Like I would believe anything you say. I should just kill you."

"Cory won't like that, and you know it."

Her lower lip trembled.

If she didn't want to escape Cory, there wasn't much I could do. Even if I could convince her to leave, she'd likely find her way back to him. And when she did, he would make her suffer for it.

"Listen, if you free my hands, you can say it was my fault. Tell him that I stunned him."

She shook her head and sniffed. "He knows you didn't have the thing."

"Stun guns cause something called critical response amnesia. He won't remember anything from the thirty seconds or so before the attack."

My statement wasn't exactly true. While some people experienced amnesia, it was far from all and generally didn't encompass that much time. But at fourteen, I doubted Di was well versed in such things; at least I hoped not. And since she needed a way out, I hoped desperation would override skepticism.

"He won't know it was you who pulled the trigger."

She wrapped her arms around herself as if she was cold. But although her body language suggested she was closed off, I could see her mind working.

I pressed on. "If you help me get out of here, when he wakes up, you can tell him I stunned him and got away. He won't blame you, and I'll be gone. You can have him to yourself. All you have to do is cut the zip ties on my wrists."

She looked at my hands, then at Cory.

"Hurry. He'll be waking soon. Then it will be too late."

She took a step closer. The fact that she didn't pick up the stun gun or the knife Cory had dropped and use them on me seemed encouraging, but the hate in her eyes hadn't faded. "He'll keep looking for you," she said.

"Let me worry about that."

She shook her head. "He always talks about you."

"That's only because he's been in prison so long, and I helped put him there. The more he gets to know you, the more opportunities he has to see how perfect you are for each other…he'll forget me."

"You think so?"

"I know so."

She nodded, as if trying to talk herself into swallowing the bullshit I was feeding her.

"It'll work out, Di. I'll make sure he doesn't find me again. I'll disappear and you two can be together."

She held out her hands, palms up. "I don't have anything to cut the ties."

"Check the drawers."

She opened drawers and raked through their contents. Finally she held up a pair of utility scissors.

"That should do it," I encouraged.

Below me, Cory groaned.

The girl froze.

"Hurry," I whispered.

The sound of my voice seemed to snap her out of her paralysis. She slipped the scissors' blade under the tie binding my left wrist and cut.

Needles of pain raced through my fingers. I pulled my arm free of the board and moved my hand, willing the blood to return. Then I took the scissors from her. My grip was weak and it took me several seconds to cut my other hand free.

"What the hell is going on?" Cory's words were sluggish, but the anger behind them rang loud and clear.

Blood tingled through my right hand. I clawed at the Velcro straps pinning my head and shoulders to the backboard.

"Di?" he bellowed again.

She stared at me with wide eyes.

I ripped the straps free and struggled to sit. My neck was still immobilized in the cervical brace. I hit my head on the overhead cabinet before I could scramble upright.

"Di? I'll fucking kill—"

I swung off the counter and landed on him, straddling his body.

He tried to bring his hands up, to grip the collar, to fight me off, but he was still recovering from the stun, and his moves were clumsy and pathetic.

I gripped his skull in my hands. I'd practiced the move many times, and I barely had to think. I gave a hard twist and felt his neck pop.

He slumped back against the cabinets. His hands spasmed slightly before falling limp by his sides.

"Cory!" Di screamed. "What did you do to him?"

I climbed off his body and took off the cervical collar encasing my neck. I tossed it to the floor and started out of the kitchen.

Di blocked my path. She held the scissors up in front of her, brandishing the blade like a knife.

"Put the scissors down, Di."

"You killed him! You killed Cory!"

"I just did you the biggest favor or your life. Someday you'll thank me."

"No!" She flew at me, the scissors leading the way.

I dodged the blades and answered with a solid right cross to the jaw.

Di hit the table and crumpled to the floor beside Kaufmann. I hesitated for only a second and then walked from the kitchen without looking back.

*"Drugs are tools," The Instructor said. "Like any tool, they can be beneficial, or deadly. To know the effects these tools will have on your body, your training will require you to sample a wide variety of them. So get ready to get high with your Uncle Sam."*

My thoughts were scrambled eggs, my fragile emotional state further degraded by pain, exhaustion, and an insurmountable list of things I had to do. Add in the norepinephrine I'd been injected with, and I was a nervous breakdown waiting to happen.

Or perhaps it already had.

Not that it mattered. I couldn't let grief and helplessness overwhelm me again. When I'd lost Kaufmann, I'd wanted to die. Cory's girl had made me realize I couldn't allow myself that luxury. Things needed to be set right, and I was the only one who could do it.

It didn't take long to find one of Hammett's bras tucked in the back of Victor's drawer. I pulled it on, along with a long-sleeved tee, and added the jacket I'd worn to meet The Instructor. The yellow bag of cash was still tucked in the back of the closet. I shouldered it and wiped down everything in the apartment that I or Hammett might have touched, then called 911 to report a multiple murder and left.

I took the stairs to the parking garage. The Instructor's car was just where I'd left it, but the man himself was gone. I'd given him a big enough dose of amobarbital to still be asleep, so either Hammett had taken him or he'd had backup that I'd missed.

The underground garage was dank and cool, chilling my damp hair and the new sheen of drug-sweat that was covering my body like an oily shroud. After checking the car over, I opened the door and slid behind the wheel. I reached under the seat. The Instructor's computer was still there, so I fished it out it and woke it from sleep.

Blips flickered to life on the touch screen. This time, an additional speck of light moved up Lake Shore Drive on her way to the John Hancock Center.

Hammett was smart. It would take her a while to discover my hiding place, but eventually she'd find the transceiver. The same thing that had hamstringed me could work both ways: we both had trackers implanted in us. If she did get my cell phone, I'd still have a chance to figure out what she was planning to do with it and stop her.

I focused on the blip north of Chicago in the ritzy suburb of Lake Forest. I'd lost Kaufmann, been set up by Victor, and had misplaced The Instructor. The only other person I had ties to in this world was Jacob.

Jacob, who was under siege.

I needed a weapon.

Though there were more Stretchers health clubs in the area with guns stashed in the lockers, I was thinking of something with a little more oomph. And I knew just where to get it. But before I could get anything, I needed to get my head straight. And the only way to do that was to neutralize the shit in my system.

I started the car and headed south. Like many large cities, the line between affluence and poverty was often just a block. I followed West Cermak to South Martin Luther King Drive, drove past Washington Park and the adjacent University of Chicago, and then left onto Sixty-Third. It took five minutes of circling the area before I found my first dealer.

A black teen, in a 4XL white tee, wearing baggy jeans that would be around his ankles if he didn't keep holding them up with his free hand. He had that thousand-mile stare of someone who had seen combat, and perhaps this kid had. I parked ahead of him, grabbed some bills from my bag, got out of the car, and approached slowly with my hands at my sides. He probably had eyes on the street, covering him, and sure enough I spotted a shorty—a child no more than eight years old and dressed the same way. He was on his cell phone, no doubt talking about the white woman approaching.

Though I'd never bought drugs in this neighborhood before, I was shaky, and no doubt looked strung out, which meant I shouldn't arouse suspicion.

"Coke," I said, stopping two feet away from him. "Blow or crack, I don't care."

"Well, what we got here?" He made a show of looking me up and down while he whistled through his teeth, showing me a gold grille. "You lost, little girl?"

I blew a stiff breath out of my nostrils. This should be a simple transaction. I had money. He had product. Let's make a deal. "You deaf, little boy? I want to buy cocaine. That's the reason you stand here all day, right?"

In a life undoubtedly plagued by bad choices, this dealer added one more. He decided to mess with me.

"You look like you need it bad, ho. Maybe I make you suck my cock for it."

"Sorry, I already blew a sociopath today. One's my limit."

"Then maybe you don' get no rock."

"I have money," I said, fighting the tremor in my voice. "Sell me something."

"Then get on yo knees, bitch."

"I have a better idea."

My palm hit him right in the upper lip, breaking both his nose and his fourteen-karat dental appliance. As he staggered back, I whipped a leg around, caught him on the side of the head, and dropped him to the street. His skull bounced on the asphalt in a way that didn't look healthy. The shorty watching took off in a run, and I squatted and searched the dealer's pockets, patting him down, rifling through nickel bags of weed, balloons of heroin, and finally a vial of crack and a glass cigarette pipe. Even bleeding like a stuck pig and with a lump on his head big enough to rappel from, homeboy made a half-assed attempt to grab my wrist. He received a broken arm for his efforts.

"Got a lighter?" I asked him.

"B...back...p...p...pocket."

I dug it out, tossed a crumpled twenty-dollar bill onto his crying face, and hurried back to my car. When I was a good ten blocks away, I pulled into a shopping center and prepared my fix.

During training, I'd sampled a wide variety of drugs. The human body was a complicated machine and could be made to run better, or worse, with the right combination of substances. I tapped the crack rocks out of the vial and into the end of the glass tube. Then I used the lighter to heat them to the melting point and quickly sucked in the vapor they emitted.

The effect was instantaneous. But rather than the euphoria normally associated with narcotics, instead I got quick relief from the norepinephrine that was causing havoc in my system. Cocaine blocked neurotransmitter receptors, preventing the reuptake of catecholamine. As a result, the shakes stopped, and I was able to concentrate for the first time in what felt like hours.

I needed one hundred percent of my focus for what I had to do next.

*"Everyone is the enemy. You can put your trust in your handler, and in God, and that's it. You may need to make allies to complete a mission, but these relationships should be abandoned as soon as the mission ends. Trust no one."*

I circled the block two times where my apartment building was located, the first in the car, and the second on foot after parking next to a fire hydrant. I didn't see any signs of cops or enemy combatants. My tablet showed no blinking dots in the vicinity.

Maybe I'd get lucky for the first time today and be able to get what I needed from my place without having to fight for my life.

As the sun dipped into the west, it grew cooler. My senses weren't functioning at peak level due to all the crap still in my system, but the familiar smells of my neighborhood were somewhat reassuring. I did a brisk reconnoiter of my building, then ducked into the alley and discreetly counted bricks in the wall until I reached twenty-five across and six up. The mortar there was actually a loose mixture of sand and clay, and hidden between bricks was a spare key. I used this to open the back door and paused before entering.

The building felt normal. No unusual sounds or scents. Not the hotbed of activity it must have been earlier. I padded in softly, making sure the door didn't slam, stopping every few steps to listen. The elevator was out of service, yellow police tape stretched across it. I slipped into the stairwell and climbed quickly, staying on the balls of my feet. When I reached my floor, I was slightly winded and had broken out in a good, healthy sweat. So far so good.

More police tape across the elevator, the doors still bent outward from the explosion. The spot where I'd killed the hit man had been cleaned. No chalk outline. That only happened in old movies. I thought back to the DOD report on him. Former KGB. Victor spoke flawless Russian with a native-born Pomor dialect, so I guessed there was probably a connection. This operation may have been too big for Hammett, and she'd brought in some hired help. Or worse, she had sided with the enemy. I didn't want to know what she'd promised those assholes in return for their cooperation. Those ex-KGB goons were bad news.

My apartment door was closed, the wall next to it still pocked with bullet holes. I crept up silently, placed an ear to the door, and when I heard nothing out of the ordinary I slipped the key in and entered.

I closed the door behind me, took two steps into my living room, and immediately all the hair stood up on my forearms. It was my proximity sense telling me I wasn't alone in the apartment.

I spun, raising my fists, falling into a fighting stance, and found myself staring at a woman with a gun.

But this one, surprisingly, didn't look like me. She was older, midforties, my size, long brown hair, a strong chin. Although her clothes were designer and her shoes expensive, I immediately made her as a cop, and a good cop at that. Calm and in control, with an assured, professional aura about her. As usual my mouth went dry, as it did whenever someone pointed a firearm at me, and I had to force myself to stand still.

"Relax," she said. "I'm one of the good guys."

I didn't relax. Instead I found myself studying her posture, looking for an opening.

"You're calling yourself Carmen Sawyer," the cop continued. "I'm Lieutenant Daniels, homicide. Are you armed?"

*Not yet*, I thought, eyeing her weapon. It was old-school, a .38 Colt Detective Special.

"I don't want to shoot you, Carmen. But you're making me uncomfortable the way you're sizing me up, and I wouldn't want to get nervous and accidentally pull the trigger, which, as you see, is fully cocked. So please answer me. Are you armed?"

"No."

"Can you do a turnaround and show me?"

I lifted my shirt up over my belly and did an easy three-sixty.

"Pants too, if you don't mind."

I hiked up my jeans on both sides, showing my socks.

"Isn't this the part where you tell me to get down on my knees, hands behind my head, and read me my rights?" I asked. I knew ten different ways to disarm a cop who tried to arrest me.

"I haven't decided yet. Right now I just want to talk."

"Tough to talk with a gun pointed at you."

"If I lowered the gun, would you relax a bit?"

I nodded. She lowered the gun. I made myself appear more relaxed, but I was still a coiled spring, waiting to pounce.

"I've had to deal with a lot of dead bodies on this shift," Daniels said. Though her weapon was at her side, she still had her finger in the trigger guard. "Not just here at your place, but all around the city. I'd really appreciate your help sorting this out."

"You're being awfully polite."

"Don't confuse that with weakness." She gave me a hard look, as if to illustrate her point. "Now please tell me what's going on."

"I've had one heck of a day, Lieutenant, and I'm sort of in a time crunch."

"Call me Jack. What can I call you? There are no public records of Carmen Sawyer. No history at all. Your ID is bogus. We had a team in this room for three hours, couldn't find a single thing about you. No pictures. No personal documents. Computer is clean. Not even a fingerprint in the place. What kind of person lives in an apartment for over a year and doesn't leave her prints?"

"Maybe I'm just exceptionally tidy."

Jack's eyes crinkled a bit, but the smile didn't reach her mouth. "You're very much in demand right now, Carmen. My superiors want you. The feds want you. Some guys in black suits who won't say who they work for want you. There are so many charges against you, you'll need a busload of lawyers just to sort them all out. You also seem to be drawing the attention of a certain criminal element." She paused, as if for dramatic effect. "Some of them look a helluva lot like you."

I gave her a one-shouldered shrug. "I have one of those faces."

"Actually, you have four of those faces. Three of them are currently in Cook County morgue."

I took a careful step forward, trying not to appear threatening.

Jack instantly raised her gun back up, aiming at my center mass. Her hand was remarkably steady. "Please stay where you are, Carmen. I don't want to shoot you, but people have a tendency to die in your presence, and I don't want to be one of them."

Contrary to the adversarial nature of our current relationship, I was starting to like this woman. "So what *do* you want, Jack?"

"To take you in."

I gave my head a small shake. "I can't allow that."

"I can promise you protection."

"No. You can't. They'll kill me."

"I won't let them."

"Then they'll kill you, too. Besides, I have things I need to do."

"Who do you work for?" Jack asked.

I let out a short, abrupt laugh. "Seriously?"

Jack shrugged her shoulders, but her aim didn't waver. "It was worth a shot."

"Let's just say I'm a public employee, like you."

"That's what I figured. And it's the only reason you aren't in handcuffs right now. Are you CIA? NSA?"

I didn't say anything.

"So far every corpse we've found appears to be a case of self-defense," Jack said. "I could be wrong, of course. According to the FBI, you're a dangerous terrorist, hell-bent on overthrowing the government. But to me it looks more like you're being pursued. So why come back here? No one thought you would."

"Why are you here?"

"I had a hunch."

"Don't you homicide cops travel in twos?" I asked.

"My partner is close by. So why did you come back here, Carmen?"

I didn't answer, watching as Jack sorted it out.

"There's still something here," she eventually said. "Something you need. What is it?"

"Floorboards, beneath you." I hoped she would look down. She didn't.

"What's there? Top secret documents? Or are the fibs right, and it's a plan to assassinate the president?"

"Just my sniper rifle."

"What do you need that for?"

My turn to shrug. "Sniping."

We stared at each other for a minute, then Jack lowered her gun again. "I want to help you, Carmen. But to do that, you're going to have to trust—"

On Jack's last word I rushed her, coming up underneath the .38, chopping at her wrist with the heel of my hand. Either fatigue and pain had slowed me down or the cop was faster than she should have been, because Jack dodged the move and brought an elbow down on my shoulder, driving me to the left. I took an extra step to correct my balance and found myself looking at the wrong end of a spin-kick. I raised up my hands, taking the hit in the forearms instead of my head, and then Jack was dancing around my other side, raising the gun again. But I anticipated the move, striking the back of her hand. The gun went flying, and for a brief, eternal moment we watched it arc through the air, then land on the sofa on the other side of the room.

Jack backpedalled, getting between me and the sofa, and then kicked off her shoes and struck a Dwi Koobi stance—a defensive posture used in tae kwon do, with one foot in front of the other and both fists raised.

"I just want my rifle," I said, blinking away some spinning motes.

"You've killed enough people for the day," Jack said. "I'm taking you in."

Since my days with The Instructor, I'd kept up with my combat training. I had black belts or equivalents in half a dozen martial arts. But more importantly, I also knew all of the restricted moves banned from competition. In a fight for your life, points didn't matter. That was something the majority of YMCA practitioners didn't understand, but something that Jack was about to learn the hard way.

I leaped at her, figuring a tae kwon do practitioner wouldn't know what the hell to do against a Muay Thai attack known as a *hanuman thayarn*—a flying knee.

She leaned sideways, my leg catching her shoulder, and her footing was strong enough that I bounced off rather than took her down. I tried to clinch her leg, do a quick judo reversal, but she punched me in the side of the head hard enough to bring the stars out. I brought up a quick elbow and hit her in the crotch—decidedly not tae kwon do—and when she grunted and doubled over, I gave her a head butt in the chin, pulling it so I didn't shatter her jaw.

Jack stumbled away, fists still up but knees wobbly. It's actually harder to knock someone out than it is to kill them, and I didn't want to kill her, so I wasn't quite sure what to do next.

My hesitation cost me. The cop apparently wasn't as hurt as she seemed, because she charged me with a flurry of punches and kicks. I deflected the first four, then had to take a step back and cover up because they were coming so fast. Expending that much energy usually wore a fighter out, leading to an opening, and when the punches started getting weaker, I struck my stance and began to push forward, waiting for them to stop so I could unleash.

When a second went by without getting hit, I opened up, ready to jab.

She tagged me under the chin with an uppercut.

It knocked me backward and doubly surprised me. First, because I hadn't expected it and thought she'd punched herself out. Second, because she'd pulled it.

"You held back," I said after finding my center and planting my feet.

Jack was breathing heavily but still seemed strong. "So did you."

I spat blood from a cut in my upper lip. "Any chance you're a crooked cop? I've got about twenty-five thousand bucks nearby. You let me have my gun, I let you have the money."

"Sorry, I don't—"

I launched again, another flying knee, but reversing it in the air to avoid her counter. I connected with ribs, basically hugging her body in a reverse piggyback. Then I brought my arms down, grabbing her around the neck, pulling her forward and flipping her over, onto her back.

While she was stunned, I scooted around on my butt and went for the grapple. The move was known as an armbar, where I got my hips and legs under her and tugged her arm back by the wrist until it was fully extended, putting pressure on both the elbow and the shoulder. If I forced it, I could both break and dislocate her arm with only a minimal application of force.

Finally I had her.

Jack groaned. "How do I tap out?"

"Do you have handcuffs?"

"My purse. The Gucci bag in the kitchen."

"How does a homicide cop afford Gucci?"

"Got a discount on the Home Shopping Network."

I applied a bit more pressure to her arm, prompting a high-pitched squeal.

"I need to incapacitate you while I get my rifle," I said. "I'd prefer using the handcuffs to do that, but snapping your arm in half would work, too."

"I vote for the handcuffs," Jack squeaked.

"I'm going to walk you into the kitchen. Any sudden moves, you wind up in a cast. And you know how long bones take to heal with older women."

"You beat me already. You gotta be mean about it, too?"

I really did like her and hoped I didn't have to blow her elbow out. Moving slowly, I released my legs and switched the armbar to a wristlock. Jack stayed compliant, letting me get behind her, not trying to fight as we both got onto our knees.

"Stand up on three," I told her. "One…two…three."

The move was smooth, and then it was just a question of leading her into the kitchen.

"Grab your purse by the bottom, dump it onto the counter."

She did, and I watched, somewhat amused at all the crap regular women kept in their purses. Besides the obligatory makeup, tissues, cell phone, mints, brush, wallet, and loose change, there was a bottle of calcium pills. I smiled.

"Those are for indigestion," Jack said.

"Really? The bottle says they help to fight against osteoporosis."

"The handcuffs are in the side pocket."

I knew it was mean, but I couldn't resist. "It has one of those easy twist-off caps, for the elderly."

"It was the only bottle the store had, all right? You want to cuff me or talk about supplements?"

I fished the pair out, Smith & Wesson, gunmetal black. I flicked a bracelet open, locked it around her wrist, and connected the other end to the handle of my refrigerator. Then I took two quick steps away.

Jack looked annoyed and humiliated. She straightened up and said, "I'll give you one last chance to surrender."

I had to smile at that. "You said your partner is nearby."

"He's across the street, getting a meatball sub with extra cheese. And meatballs. And bread. It's actually two subs he eats at the same time, one on top of the other."

"Is he going to burst in here and shoot me?"

"With the elevator out? If he bursts in here, he won't be holding a gun. He'll be clutching his heart with a myocardial infarction. Herb and stairs are old enemies."

She didn't give me any cues that she was lying, vocal or nonverbal.

"You said you came back here on a hunch," I said. I didn't need to know, but I was curious. "What caused it?"

"I saw your wardrobe. It's lacking, and that's being kind, but I found the money and wires sewn into the hems. I thought anyone who took the time to do that might have other things hidden around the place. Figured I'd poke around, see if I could find anything."

"Did you?"

Jack frowned. "Yeah. I found a pain-in-the-ass spy who doesn't respect those who came before her."

I went to the kitchen closet, took out my box of tools, careful to hold the handle by the palm so I didn't leave prints.

"I respect all of that old-school, old fogey stuff," I told Jack. "Black-and-white TVs. Those huge computers with floppy disks. Paper books."

"Paper books aren't old-school."

"Give me a break. They're so 2008. Get an eReader, Jack."

Her gaze flicked down to my hand. "No need to hold the box like that, Carmen. I already lifted one of your prints."

I paused, a spike of adrenaline shooting up my spine. It was bad enough being wanted by different agencies and authorities. As long as they didn't have my name, they wouldn't find me. But once my prints were on file...

"How?" I asked.

Jack stayed quiet.

"Don't play around here, Lieutenant. If I'm in the system, I'm fucked."

"The gun you left on the roof," Jack said. "Got a partial index on the trigger. Not enough to match it. But…"

She let her voice trail off. I felt myself go cold.

"But?"

"The medical examiner is my friend. He's doing the autopsies on those women you dispatched, the ones with your faces. He ran the prints on one. No matches in the system. But, for fun, I ran it through some POC software. Guess who it matched?"

POC was *points of comparison*, and I knew who it matched.

"Who else knows about this, Jack?"

Her eyes narrowed. "You think I'm an idiot, Carmen? That I'd offer up this information so I can get myself tortured and killed? I don't know all the powers at play here, and I'm not going to wake up one morning with assassins in my room because I stumbled across some secret government experiment and blabbed about it. You know it's statistically impossible for more than one person to have the same prints. Even twins—"

"I know," I said, interrupting. "Did the ME check the prints on the others?"

"Not yet. I had a feeling and told him to hold off. He didn't even finish the autopsy on the first one."

"You probably saved his life."

"A smart person would go to the morgue, make sure no more prints are taken. She might even find the previous autopsy records there as well."

"And what about the gun with my partial on it?"

Jack smiled. "A smart person would have that locked away in a safe place, with a note to examine it if she died suddenly. I assume we're both smart people."

"So you're asking me to trust you?"

"Yes. And to tell me what's going on."

"If you know what I know, that might put you in even more danger than having that gun."

"I like to live on the edge."

I had a choice. I could give a little, or I could snap her neck. I sighed, then gave her the Reader's Digest condensed version of the last few hours. I wasn't sure why I decided to tell her, and I was even less sure why I felt better once I had, but when I finished, Jack let out a slow whistle.

"That's a lot to swallow."

"It is what it is."

"Your code name is Chandler?"

"Yeah."

"It's a pretty cool code name."

"This from a woman named Jack Daniels?"

She rubbed her cheek, which was beginning to bruise. "So the only two left are Clancy and Hammett."

I nodded, taking my tools back to the living room. I opened the box and removed a short pry bar. "I'm going to go take care of Clancy now. I have to save my handler."

"She and Hammett look exactly like you?"

"Hammett has a small scar on her chin. If you run into her, shoot first. She's psychotic."

I measured off five paces from the far wall, then began to pry up floorboards.

"This is a bit outside my normal jurisdiction," Jack said. "How can I help?"

With the information about the morgue, she already had. "You can stay out of my way."

"Do you know why Hammett wants that transceiver thing?"

"No. Only that it would be bad if she gets it."

"Where did you hide it in the Hancock building?"

"That I can't tell you."

Three more boards up, and I saw my rifle case. I wiped the prints off the pry bar using my shirt, tossed it aside, and pulled out the case. Then I caught Jack's eye. "You know there are bad people, and even some good people, who will kill you if they find out what you know."

She gave me a brief arch of the eyebrows. "Interesting life you lead."

"Mostly it's a lot of waiting around. You caught me on a busy day."

"Chandler…" Jack's voice trailed off.

"What?"

"You should still consider turning yourself in. I could take you out of state, we could go to the media."

"Not going to happen."

"How long can you keep functioning at this level? I can see you're trying to keep it together, but right now I'm not looking at some special ops superspy. I'm looking at a breakdown waiting to happen."

"This breakdown still managed to handcuff you to a fridge."

Jack's face softened. "They're going to kill you, Chandler."

I paused. She was right, of course. Even with my training, the odds were very much against me. I doubted I had more than a five percent chance of surviving this, and that was playing fast and loose with statistics. Maybe that was why I felt OK about spilling my guts. "Have you ever faced death before, Jack?"

"Yes."

"Did that ever make you quit?"

Jack slowly shook her head. "No."

"I guess that makes two of us who like to live on the edge."

Then I tucked the rifle case under my armpit and got out of there.

*"When you're undercover, you can't pretend to be another person," The Instructor said. "You must become that person. Your success depends on whether or not people believe you. Your life is at risk if they don't."*

Hammett surveys the chaos around her, the chaos she caused, and runs the tip of her tongue across her lower lip.

*It might be more efficient to just kill them all. Or at the very least it would be more fun.*

She leans on the maître d' stand and watches the last of the Signature Room employees file into the elevator, following in the wake of diners who were evacuated from the top of the John Hancock building first. They are scared out of their minds, she can smell it, and their fear makes her pulse spike.

The world is divided into predators and prey. These men and women scurrying to escape the fake bomb threat she and Victor cooked up are weak. They are so desperate for someone to save them, they accept the fake bomb squad uniforms and generic tool boxes without a blink. They dash from their hundred-dollar meals in a scramble to catch the first elevator. They are animals begging to be culled from the herd.

And she's itching to do the culling.

Hammett is aware of the weight of the .45 on her hip, the knife in the sheath at her ankle, but she doesn't use them. As much as she would enjoy taking each of the remaining sheep out, making them beg, making them scream, she doesn't have time.

When the elevator doors close, she turns away and climbs the staircase leading to the floor above. As she ascends to the balcony, she scans the restaurant a floor below. Beyond linen-covered tables and meals abandoned in various stages of being eaten, the city shifts from day to sunset through enormous floor-to-ceiling windows. The dark void of Lake Michigan shifts and sways. Lights of ships dot the horizon, only the occasional red or blue differentiating them from glimpses of stars beginning to light the sky.

The world is a big place. And Hammett has plans a lot bigger than toying with waiters and chefs. Even the maître d' who didn't quite believe her bomb scare story, the one she most itches to kill, isn't worth it.

Maybe she'll catch up with him later.

She steps onto the balcony's marble floor and glances past the upper floor's maître d' stand. Dressed as bomb squad techs, Victor and his men started searching the bar on the ninety-sixth floor while she was arguing with the manager. She pauses to watch two of them comb the private dining rooms off the bank of elevators. Hammett doesn't fully trust them. She doesn't fully trust anyone, but since she needs the money and manpower Victor provides, she will play nice for now.

She sets off down the long hallway to the lounge to check up on Victor. He better have results.

In the lounge, the western, southern, and northern vistas open beyond the glass, along with a spectacular sunset. Victor's men dot the lounge, some searching under tables and looking under the radiator rimming the base of the room with long-handled mirrors. Some behind the center bar, moving bottles and glassware. Some probing the ceiling, checking the recessed lighting fixtures.

Victor spots Hammett and crosses the bar, the look on his face pure KGB, soulless and mean.

Hammett's not sure if she should be worried or turned on. She gestures to his men.

"Let me guess, you haven't found it."

"My people have gone over everything. It's not here. She lied."

"She wasn't lying. It's here. And we would know precisely where if you hadn't killed the old man."

He shrugs. "Accidents happen."

"Incompetence and fragile egos happen. A few jokes about your small cock and you're willing to fuck up the simplest task just to get payback. You men take size so personally." She lets a smile play across her lips. "Especially those who are not so well-endowed."

The fingers of his right hand twitch, as if they long to fondle a trigger. "I didn't hear any complaints from you last night."

Hammett cups Victor's cheeks. "A little sensitive, comrade? What you lack in size, you make up for. In speed."

Victor knocks away her hands. His dead-eyed Russian mask falls back in place. "My superiors are getting impatient. They want a return on their investment. I'm the only thing protecting you right now."

*As if I need his protection.*

"Don't threaten me, Victor."

"Then get me results."

"I did my part. Tell your men to search again. They do a good job and your superiors will have their return."

"Right. If you had let me try a few more things on Chandler, my men wouldn't have to guess the transceiver's location."

She shakes her head. Victor is pretty, but sometimes he's rather dense. "You really don't understand the training she's had, do you? The old man was our leverage. After he was gone, she would have willingly died."

"You overestimate her."

"Maybe." A buzz tickles her hip. She pulls out her cell phone and checks the display. "If your men can't manage to locate the transceiver, we'll go back to the apartment and test your theory. Now hurry. The maître d' didn't leave willingly. I wouldn't be surprised if he calls the authorities to check on our little bomb threat."

She steps away from him, walks down the hall, and ducks into the women's room. Staring out the restroom's glass wall at the city below, flaming orange in the sunset, she holds the phone to her ear. "Have you gotten inside?"

"Negative. I'm on a ridge overlooking the house. If anyone leaves, I'll know."

She knows the odds of Clancy getting inside are steep, but her sister's failure is frustrating all the same.

Hammett pulls in a steady breath. It's almost over. She almost has what she wants. She can't let impatient Russians or impenetrable bunkers get the best of her now.

"Hold your position."

Hammett tucks the phone away. Then, impulsively, she pulls out her tablet PC, just to make sure Chandler is still safe and sound at the apartment.

When she sees the blips on the screen, every muscle in her body tenses.

*You crafty little bitch. How did you get away?*

Hammett watches the blip move south and quickly figures out where Chandler is headed. She redials her cell.

"Clancy, it's Hammett. Chandler is on her way. She'll be there within half an hour."

"Shall I kill her?"

"Don't kill her. We still need information." Hammett smiles, thinking of Clancy's Hydra report. Clancy could shoot the legs off a butterfly at two thousand yards during a hurricane on a starless night. "Shoot to wound," she orders her sister. "And make it hurt."

*"In a fight between two snipers, the outcome is predetermined," The Instructor said. "The higher ground always wins. Always."*

The wind carried the scent of oak leaves, wood fire, and Lake Michigan. Driving The Instructor's car, I passed a handful of McMansions stuck into rustic settings and wound my way closer to the lake. Here gigantic homes dotted multiacre lots forested with oak and maple, most nestled so far off the narrow, twisting road that they couldn't be seen, even though tree branches were half bare. I checked the tablet PC and continued. The road flanked a forest preserve, and houses fell away to forest and wetlands. A private road turned off, and I took it.

The sun was showing off as it went down, throwing spectacular pinks and oranges across the trees, turning the horizon into a Monet painting. Soon it would be dark.

The only thing worse than a firefight during the daylight was a firefight in the dark.

I ditched the sedan in a turn off about a mile from the three blips on my tablet PC. I'd zoomed in enough to get a topical layout of the area. One was me. The other was Clancy. The third was unknown. It might be Hammett, though I guessed the blip at the Hancock Center was hers. There was also a blip at the Cook County morgue, which could indicate Forsyth, or Ludlam, or Follett. Or a combination of all three.

So why was there an extra nearby? Could one of my dead sisters be back in play somehow? Or were there more of these tracker things than The Instructor had indicated?

Hefting my rifle case, I started through the woods. Clouds scudded across the sky, dark on one side, pastel on the other as the sun dipped down. Night had its own smell, crisp and cool and dangerous.

Dry leaves skittered and skipped along the dirt. I moved slowly, watching my footing, keeping low. It wouldn't be easy to spot a sniper through the trees, especially a pro like Clancy supposedly was. I would need all my senses and a liberal dose of luck.

Make that an *extraordinary* dose of luck. Matching the blip to the terrain, I saw that my sister had taken the highest point in the area, on a ridge two kilometers to the northwest. From that vantage point, she was the master of this entire domain. My only hope was to lie low and try to sneak up on—

The shot missed my foot by only a few inches, kicking up a clod of dirt. A millisecond later, the report echoed through the trees, a thunderous boom coming from the ridge.

I dived behind a fallen tree, rolling onto my back, clutching the rifle case to my chest. I wondered how exposed I was, but didn't dare check. Since the bullet arrived before the sound, I knew Clancy was firing supersonic rounds. If I peeked my head over the rotting log, chances were I'd have it shot off before I even heard the bullet coming.

Although I'd excelled at long-distance shooting during training, the sniper mindset had never been a good fit for me. The best snipers were almost supernatural with their patience. In a full ghillie suit—a mesh covering woven with camouflage fabric and often actual leaves, weeds, and moss until the wearer looked like a swamp monster—it might take a sniper an entire day to cross a single acre of land, creeping an inch at a time, blending perfectly into the foliage. While waiting for a shot, it wasn't unusual for a sniper to bivouac for a week or more in a single area, never moving more than a few feet.

I opened the clasps on my rifle case. Working quickly, while there was still a sliver of light left, I began to assemble my M24. It was a modified takedown version of the Remington 700 rifle, upgraded for military use. This one was rebarreled for .300 Winchester Magnum ammo, had a muzzle flash hider, a Leupold day scope, and a AN/PVS-26 night vision device. I finished putting the rifle together by feel just as the sun made its exit, all the while holding my breath and waiting for Clancy's next shot. Though an excellent weapon, the M24 had a maximum effective range of eight hundred meters. I could maybe hit her at a thousand meters, but that would be pushing it.

Unfortunately, Clancy was at least eighteen hundred meters away. Not only did she have the eagle-eye vantage point, but she was no doubt using a more powerful weapon than mine. She probably had a ghillie suit as well, rendering my night vision practically useless for spotting her.

I put my chances at survival under ten percent. As for actually killing Clancy, the odds were too astronomical to even bother calculating. Add the fact that my whole body hurt and my thoughts felt sluggish after the hellish day I'd had, and I had to admit that Jack Daniels was probably right. I was going to get killed.

But I had one thing going for me.

I had nothing to lose.

And the world should fear the angry assassin with nothing to lose.

Holding the starlight scope to my eye, I took in my surroundings, deciding where to go next, wondering if it even mattered. My training dictated the best course of action would be to draw her fire, then quickly run southwest, which provided brush cover and a gradual elevation, which would put us on more even footing.

But Clancy had the same training I did. So I looked for the worst direction to go. That would be straight ahead, into forty meters of open meadow. Flat terrain, no cover at all. Suicidal, but she wouldn't expect it. If I sprinted fast enough, I could get to the copse of trees across the meadow before she could line up a shot. It was particularly tricky to hit a moving target at long distance, so I had a minute chance of making it. Maybe.

I rolled onto my stomach, my rifle on the ground in front of me, an extra magazine of ten rounds in my pocket, and I gradually spread out my legs, straddling the dirt. Staying flat, I brought my knees up until I must have resembled a bullfrog.

Then I jumped like one, springing forward over the log, feeling then hearing the shot pass under my spread-eagled leap. As soon as I hit the ground, I was tearing ass across the meadow, a full-out sprint in the dark, my rifle in one hand and my scope in the other, counting my steps until I was sure I was near the tree line, then sliding like a baseball player as another shot cracked, so close I felt it breeze by my hip.

I rolled into the tree cover, pulse pounding in my ears, amazed I was still alive. I was perhaps fifty meters closer. If I did that seven more times, and my luck held, I might get a chance to defend myself.

I stayed in the thicket, surrounded by trees, and gained another fifty meters before coming to a second clearing. This one was wider than before. It had two routes through it, neither very promising. One path had high weeds that I could perhaps crawl through, but if Clancy had a thermal camera I might as well be strolling across a football field in broad daylight. The other was a lengthy zigzag through thornbushes.

I didn't want to die tangled up in thornbushes, so I went for the weeds. The first ten strides were straight, then I cut left, then right, then right again, then left, not thinking about direction so much as trying to be random. If I didn't know my next move, neither would Clancy.

Just as I reached another tree line, I felt a tug at my leg and heard the rifle report. I put my back to a big oak, scooted onto my butt, and used the scope to check my injury.

The bullet had cut through my pants and lightly grazed my thigh, leaving a streak that looked, and felt, like a burn. It was such a minor wound I didn't even need to dress it, but it made me think.

Four shots fired, and all at my legs. Legs are much harder to hit than center mass.

Which meant my sister wasn't trying to kill me. Only disable me.

That perked up my spirits a bit. If they needed me alive, they couldn't risk a lethal hit. Which meant more careful shot selection. Which meant fewer shots. Which meant drastically increased odds of me surviving.

In an odd sort of way, it made me invulnerable.

I didn't think about my next route. I just ran like hell, straight into the thin trees, up the gradual incline, feeling completely exposed and yet bulletproof at the same time. Either my mad dash confused Clancy or she'd lost me in the darkness, because she didn't fire again for the entire length of my sprint. By the time I came to rest beside an outcropping of dirt and rocks, panting like a dog, I was unable to prevent the incredulous smile that had formed on my face. As far as I could tell, I was within a thousand meters of the ridge.

I checked the tablet PC to make sure, covering it with my shirt so the glow didn't attract attention. Sure enough, Clancy's blip was only 730 meters away. She hadn't moved. Neither had the other, unknown blip, which was 510 meters due east. I attached my night vision to the rail in front of the scope and sighted east, through crooked, green-hued trees. I saw what appeared to be the corner of a stone house, recessed into the side of a hill. If I had to take a guess, the house, and the source of the blip, was Jacob's stronghold, and Clancy was keeping watch on it.

Curiouser and curiouser.

I tugged back the bolt and loaded a round, then flopped onto my belly and set up my bipod. I was still panting from the run, and I took several deep breaths in an effort to slow my respiration and counter the rise in my heart rate. Then I assumed the standard sniping position. Body in line with the weapon. Heels flat on the ground. Elbows comfortable. The butt of the weapon resting on the fist of my nonfiring hand. My face against the cheek plate. Then I adjusted the eyepiece focus ring and the range focus ring and tried to locate my sister.

She helped me by firing once again, the round burying itself into the dirt between my calves. My pulse spiked, and I fought the urge to roll away, instead zooming in on the tiny barrel flash I'd seen.

Clancy fired once more, shooting off the tip of my right shoe. That's when I saw her in the scope, an amorphous mound of green moss draped over a gigantic rifle barrel, so far away she was barely visible. It was a calm night, with a slight northeast wind, and the elevation and bullet drop were hard to judge on the fly. I couldn't make out Clancy's features, but aimed where her head would be and exhaled while I gently squeezed the trigger.

My shot fell short by at least ten meters.

*Steady. Stay calm.*

I worked the bolt and relaxed my fist, raising the barrel a hair to account for the incline and gravity—like all projectiles, bullets moved in an arc and were pulled downward toward the earth. I hissed out a breath and squeezed another round off a bit too soon. It sailed harmlessly over Clancy's head.

*Breathe in, breathe out.*

*Relax, stay calm, don't rush it.*

*Don't think about getting shot.*

*Don't worry about missing again.*

*I'm ice, and my blood is antifreeze.*

Clancy returned fire, but my shot must have unnerved her, because her round hit a few feet to my right. That's the biggest danger in a sniper firefight. You want so badly to kill before you get killed that you don't take your time.

But she recovered quickly, firing less than a second later, grazing my left thigh with another searing burn.

That's when I decided to cheat. She might have been the better shot than me, but technology had improved since we'd been trained by Hydra.

I tugged out the tablet PC and saw Clancy was 728.5 meters away. I zeroed out my scope, adjusted for elevation, then hit the DUAL HIGH buttons on my side-mounted AN/PEQ-2. This was an infrared illumination system, only visible through night vision. The narrow beam was a laser dot for pinpointing targets. The wide beam was like a flashlight, illuminating a cone of visibility.

No doubt Clancy was equipped with this as well, but she hadn't used it because it was ridiculously easy to spot by the opposition, almost like a signal flare. But in this case, we both knew where the other person was. I just needed to be able to hit the bitch.

Letting out a slow breath through clenched teeth, I centered the tiny laser dot alongside her scope, right at her closed eye—my closed eye—and fired.

Clancy's head erupted in a brilliant green explosion of brain matter and bone.

*Adios, Sis.*

I had nothing in my stomach, but retched bile onto the dirt next to me.

That was the fourth lookalike I'd killed today. Four suicides by proxy. Four sisters I desperately wanted and never got the chance to know. I'd never met Clancy. She'd been my enemy. I shouldn't care that she was dead. But the thought that there were only two of us now—me and that psycho, Hammett—made me feel almost as alone as I had after Kaufmann's death.

Freud would have loved me.

But there was no time for distractions. I couldn't allow myself to be anything but senses, reflexes, and training. No thoughts. No feelings. It took less than a minute to pull myself together, to get my breathing and heart rate under control, to get my head back in the game and my emotions buried. When I finished compartmentalizing everything, I scrambled to my feet and headed east through the forest, toward the other blip on the screen, trying not to think about my sister's face.

The murmur of wind through branches was now joined by the plaintive hooting of an owl. Darkness cloaked the forest, the moon and stars only visible in brief flashes between the clouds. The terrain sloped upward, and I entered a clearing and caught another glimpse of the low hulk of a house, a shadow behind the trees.

The place was expansive, a block of stone and glass built into the side of the hill. Only the east side had a view, windows peering across sloped paths. The rest of the house burrowed into the earth, like the hobbit homes in *Lord of the Rings*, but without charm. I had no idea if this was Jacob's personal home or some kind of Hydra Project safe house, but clearly whoever paid the bills had cash to spare and a serious need for security.

I scooped in a deep breath of night air. If that blip was a hostile and had infiltrated Jacob's defenses, I might be too late.

Dropping to a knee, I brought my rifle to my shoulder and peered through the starlight scope. From this angle, I could see through the windows. Even though the room was dark, I could make out furniture, a few plants, a dark hall presumably leading to other rooms.

No light. No movement.

Time for me to see who was home.

I swung away from the home's interior and scanned the grounds. A path sloped upward to an entrance just to the south of the window bank. I could see scorch marks from here, along with the mangled steel that used to be the doorknob and dead-bolt mechanism. The remnants of a destroyed camera hung down from under the eave.

I thrust to my feet and moved quickly through the forest. My footsteps were quiet, although I was more worried about surveil-lance cameras than sound. As I drew nearer, I spotted two addi-tional cameras hidden in trees. Both were out of commission, like the one I'd noticed on the house—no doubt the fault of the bullet that had drilled a hole through each lens.

I approached the south entrance. Keeping low, I crept up the sloping path and stopped to the side of the scarred door. I paused outside, listening for movement, scanning for any unusual scents. The memory of stepping through Victor's apartment door and getting zapped with the stun gun was still fresh in my mind, and I waited an additional two minutes and stole another glance at the computer to be sure the blip wasn't awaiting my entrance. Finally I shoved open the disabled door and surged inside, leading with my rifle.

I moved into the living area, clearing each corner as I went. Satisfied no one was in the front room, I mentally logged my sur-roundings. A gleaming hardwood floor was broken up by two cream rugs. A cream sofa and contemporary-style chairs dotted the living area. A formal dining room complete with buffet and silk flowers on the table occupied the other side of the long room. A simple and small kitchen nestled along the back wall. Generic prints hung on beige walls, and silk greenery popped here and there. All in all, the place looked more like a furniture showroom than a home, impractical and unlived in. I noticed two more cameras, these looking as if they'd been clubbed instead of shot, then turned my attention to the dark hallway leading deeper into the house.

Four doors led off the hall, one on the left, two on the right, and one at the end. The farthest door was slightly open. A broken diamond bit drill littered the hardwood floor at its foot. A small monitor nestled in the wall, its screen shattered.

Gun at the ready, I walked to the door and swung the wooden portal wide. Behind the oak hid the type of door commonly seen at the mouth of a bank vault. Explosion burns scorched the steel, but except for cosmetic damage, the door appeared unbreached.

I could guess what had happened. Clancy had tried to penetrate Jacob's defenses. Unable to, she had taken up her position outside, waiting for Jacob to emerge or for someone like me to try to help. But that explanation didn't answer one important question.

Since the source of the blip was beyond those doors, what was it?

"Is that Xena?"

The familiar electronic male voice made me jump. Jacob! Following the sound to the side of the door, I spotted a small speaker and intercom control under the shattered monitor. I hit the speak button. "I'm sorry, she's in Oklahoma. At the baseball game."

"I prefer basketball myself."

After verifying our identities, the sports references were code that each of us was alone.

I was so relieved to hear his voice, my throat felt thick.

"Are you OK?" I asked him.

"Clancy cut the power. I got the backup generator working, but it doesn't supply power to the entire grid. Let me reroute it to the door."

A loud clack echoed through the hall, and the thick steel door swung open.

"Come inside," Jacob said.

A chill worked over my skin. Leading with the gun, I slipped through the door and found myself in a long, sloped tunnel. Steel girders reinforced the textured concrete walls and floor. The air smelled surprisingly fresh and dry and carried a hint of bacon.

Strange. I'd never pictured Jacob living in an underground bunker.

Come to think of it, I'd never pictured Jacob living anywhere at all.

The door clanged closed behind me. Heart banging in my chest, I started down the slope, holding the rifle at the ready. It wasn't likely someone else had gotten Jacob's code, but it was possible. And even though I'd heard Jacob's voice on the speaker, I had to remember the voice I'd identified as Jacob's was electronically altered. The person speaking could be him, or it could be someone else using his voice changer. Either way, I liked to have as much control as possible.

People clung to security blankets of all kinds. I preferred a weapon with stopping power.

The sloping tunnel switched back twice and ended at a door identical to the bank vault model above. As I reached it, the lock clacked and the thick steel swung wide. I paused for a second before stepping through.

A large room greeted me, much homier in feel than the furniture showcase upstairs. A living room area and a full-fledged, eat-in kitchen, the obvious source of the bacon odor. A regular apartment, not that different from mine, except for one thing.

Kitchen counters, tables, and shelves were all two-thirds the normal height.

Was Jacob a dwarf? A super-intelligent child? Who really was the man who saw me through countless ops and saved my life scores of times? I knew nothing about him. Our conversations over the years never got deeper than common pleasantries. Yet all of the sudden I felt like I was on a blind date, and I had a sudden, irrational urge to check my hair and makeup.

Then I heard a quiet whir approach from the side. Turning, I saw a person in an electronic wheelchair. A woman, with wide, expressive eyes, and a smile on her face.

A smile that matched mine.

In fact, it matched mine perfectly.

*"There will be times when you're caught off guard," The Instructor said. "Even the best-prepared operative can be surprised. It's part of being human."*

No wise words popped into my mind, no training I could fall back on to help me deal with this. I stared down the rifle sights at yet another of my sisters, this one in a wheelchair.

"You're Jacob," I said.

"Hi, Chandler." I could tell her smile was genuine. "Yes, I'm Jacob. If you'd like, I can confirm it by talking about some of the ops you've been on. Remember Lebanon, when I sent you to Beirut to replace your fake passport?"

"I remember." But my smile fell away, and I still kept the gun trained on her. I didn't trust people, not normally, and if my skepticism needed any reinforcement, today had provided it in spades. "There are only supposed to be seven," I said.

"Seven?"

"Hydra sisters. Seven. And only Hammett and I are still alive. I know. One died years ago, and I killed the other four." The words tasted sour on my tongue, but the truth behind them wasn't something I could change.

Her eyebrows flicked upward. "Who told you about Hydra?"

I didn't answer.

She left her hands on her chair's arm rests, as if she sensed how close I was to drilling a bullet through her forehead. "Was it Hammett? She's behind this, isn't she?"

"The Instructor told me."

"So he visited you. I thought he might."

"You didn't know?"

"I haven't seen him since training."

"Then you're not Jacob. Jacob is supposed know everything." Even in my own ears, my argument sounded hollow, like a child insisting on the existence of Santa Claus.

"I've been a little busy," she said in a dry tone.

An inflection I'd heard many times in Jacob's electronically disguised voice. I mulled this over and waited for her to go on.

"Normally I'm not the one playing catch-up. Everything I know about Hydra I've learned in the past few hours, digging through government databases. Why haven't you answered your phone?"

"It's gone. I thought they were tracking me with it."

"That's impossible. The transceiver can't be traced. Did you try to destroy it? The case is made out of carbon fiber, so it's resistant to—"

"I didn't try to break it."

Jacob's eyes got wide. "Does Hammett have it?"

"We'll talk about the transceiver in a moment," I said. "First, let's talk about who you are."

"I'm your handler. You know me as Jacob. At Hydra, I was given the code name Fleming."

"Fleming is dead."

Jacob stared at me for a moment. I could practically see the wheels turning in her head.

"If The Instructor told you that, he's either been compromised or fed false information. I was completing a sanction in Milan and had to hang outside of a five-story window. My support wire snapped." She gestured to her legs, covered by a blanket. "I've been your handler since then. I should debrief you, but there isn't time. We have to get the transceiver. Where is it?"

I wasn't sure what to answer. I wanted to trust Jacob or Fleming or whatever her name was. But I'd wanted to trust Victor, too. I felt like I was scrambling to keep up. After all that had happened in the past day, all I'd had to process, I couldn't seem to get my feet under me.

"Fair enough," Fleming said. "We'll talk first. Can you tell me how you found me?"

"The same way Clancy found you. The tracking chips."

"What chips?"

"Sewn into our stomachs."

"Sewn into our…?" Fleming stared down at her waist. "We have locator chips in us?"

"I've got a tablet PC. It shows where all seven sisters are. I guess you're the seventh."

Fleming shook her head. "They chipped us. Those motherfuckers."

I couldn't agree with her sentiments more. "So what is so special about my phone? Why does Hammett want it so badly?"

"Have you been in contact with her?"

"You could say that."

Her lips pursed, as if she had some guesses as to how unpleasant contact with Hammett might be, then took a deep breath. "Your phone…it's not just a phone."

"I've figured out that much."

"It's actually a highly encrypted transceiver."

Technically speaking, any phone was a transceiver. As for the encrypted part, Jacob, or Fleming, had told me that part when she had originally sent it to me. "Go on."

"I designed it. I'm a bit of a computer genius." She averted her eyes for a second, and her face tinged just a tiny bit pink. "There are only two transceivers like this in existence. You have one. The president of the United States has the other."

"An iPhone isn't good enough for him?"

Her expression remained serious. "The iPhone doesn't have an app for this. There's a hidden source code on the operating system. If accessed, it can be used to remotely launch America's nuclear arsenal."

My arms trembled, and I had to steady my weapon. "What?"

"Whoever has your phone could punch in a code and destroy the entire world one hundred eighty times over. If Hammett gets it, she'll have the power to start World War Three."

*"There is no good information or bad information," The Instructor said. "Information simply exists. It's neutral.*

*It's your reaction to information that is either good or bad. You have to bury that reaction and be neutral, too."*

I felt my stomach do some cartwheels. "So I could dial a wrong number and accidentally blow up Russia?"

"It's more complicated than that. You'd need to—"

I held up a hand. "I don't want to know."

Fleming nodded as if she'd seen my response coming. "That's why you were given the phone."

I narrowed my eyes.

"Your reaction," Fleming said. "It's less common than you think. You don't even want to know how to use the phone. Not everyone would have that response. And even while most people might not want to blow up the world themselves, they might be tempted to use the power for personal gain."

I could see Hammett blowing up the world, or at least holding it for ransom, but I couldn't be the only sister who wasn't trigger-happy or power mad. "Why give it to me? I don't want that kind of power."

"After nine-eleven, the president decided there needed to be a safeguard, in case he was compromised. Someone able to follow orders. Someone who could launch the strike in his stead. You've killed for your country. You've shown your loyalty."

"I've also turned down assignments. Maybe if given the order to blow up the world, I'd balk."

"Your psych profile says you wouldn't."

I didn't know how much I liked that. "Why not you? You developed it."

"The president concluded you were the one to be entrusted with the phone. My psych report was favorable, too, but then this happened." She glanced down at the wheelchair. "After my injury, I was determined to be too much of a risk."

"A risk? You live in an underground bunker."

"I think they half-expected me to go crazy with grief over my useless legs and retaliate by blowing up the world." She gave a laugh.

A giggle bubbled in my own throat. I'd never laid eyes on this woman until tonight, and yet I sensed the idea was ridiculous. Fleming might be new to me, but in all the time I'd known her as Jacob, she was as reliable as gravity.

I lowered my gun.

"Are we at a level where we're trusting each other?" she asked.

I hadn't realized I'd decided to take that leap until her words hit the air. I gave a slight nod, uncertain if my voice would function.

"Good," she said. Fleming took her hands off of her armrests, then lifted up the covers. Concealed beneath were two rifle barrels, built into the frame. "I was hoping I wouldn't have to shoot you. All I have to do is squeeze the armrests."

"Nice. Is that standard for that chair model?"

"I made a few minor modifications. Can I be frank? I know you don't know anything about me, but I know a lot about you and always hoped we'd meet one day."

"Maybe we can have a sleepover," I said. "Braid each other's hair and talk about boys we've kissed."

"Then we'll bake s'mores and play Truth or Dare." Fleming's face got serious. "But first...where's the phone, Chandler?"

"I hid it. But...Hammett might be able to find it." Again my throat thickened, this time with humiliation. I'd broken and done the worst thing anyone in my position could do. I'd revealed secrets to the enemy. My cheeks burned, and I felt a little dizzy.

"She got to you," Fleming said. "Was it Kaufmann?"

"You know about Kaufmann?"

"You said it yourself. I know everything. Is he...?"

"Dead." I said. "I told Hammett the transceiver is on the ninety-sixth floor of the Hancock building. But I didn't tell her where exactly."

"She was persuasive, I take it."

I nodded. "Waterboarding."

Fleming's eyes went mean. "Fucking bitch. Took that right out of our training. When we catch her, let's tie a weight to her legs and drop her in Lake Michigan."

My spirits perked up. "So…we're a team now?"

"We've always been a team, Chandler."

Fleming held out her hand. I walked slowly toward her and clasped it in mine.

It felt good.

After gathering the equipment I would need, I left Fleming at the bunker and retraced my steps through the forest. The sky was a giant, black blanket, only a glimpse of stars and moon between clouds. The wind had died down. I found Clancy's body without too much difficulty. Trying not to look too closely at the ground meat and bits of skull formerly known as her face, I grabbed her ankle and dragged her through trees and brush, fifty meters south to a dirt road.

Sweat slicked my back from the effort, cool in the night air. I had just managed to slow my breathing when headlights split the night. A green Humvee stopped near me, and the driver's window lowered. Fleming peered out from behind the wheel. "Need some help?"

I wasn't sure how my sister meant to help lift a body into the van without the use of her legs, but I had no doubt she'd find a way. I waved her offer away. "I can manage."

The Hummer's interior flatbed was lined with plastic, no doubt Fleming's plan to contain the blood and fluids. Using her arms to lift herself out of the driver's seat and into a chair, she met me in the back. For a moment, she said nothing, just stared down at the body I'd loaded inside, then I saw the shine in her eyes.

At least she didn't have to look at Clancy's face, since it was no longer there." Did you know her?"

Fleming shook her head. "Not personally."

"But you knew you had sisters."

"Only you. Until today." She glanced up at me. "I'm sorry I couldn't tell you."

I shrugged a shoulder. "I always wondered what it would be like to have a sister. I never imagined I would have six...and that five of them would want to kill me. That sort of weakens the sisterly bond."

Fleming gave me a dry smile. "Well, I'm glad to finally meet you."

My throat tightened, and all I could manage was a nod.

She returned the gesture and pulled a plastic package from a duffel of equipment she'd brought with her. "Do you want me to do it?"

"Do you want to?"

"No."

"Me neither. Rock scissors paper?"

Her eyes crinkled. "Are you serious?"

"We could flip a coin. Got a coin?"

"I don't. OK, we'll go on three. One...two...three."

I made my hand into scissors. So did Fleming. Since her hand looked exactly the same as mine, it was a pretty surreal moment.

"Once more," I said. "One...two...three."

This time we both made a rock.

"This is weirding me out," I said. "Just give me the gloves and the scalpel."

Fleming handed me a pair of latex gloves, and I snapped them on while she tore open the disposable scalpel wrapper. Grasping the ghillie suit, I stretched it away from Clancy's body and, dodging bits of stick and weeds, slit it down the middle. Underneath the camouflage, Clancy wore combat fatigues. I patted her down.

"Got a cell phone," I said, handing it over.

Fleming played with the buttons. "Password protected. I can crack it back at my place, but it'll take a few minutes."

"Later, if we need to."

She nodded. "Right. We already know where Hammett is."

A few more cuts and I exposed Clancy's belly.

"Would you look at that?" Fleming leaned forward. "Is that what I think it is?"

Her skin appeared as if it was coated with peanut butter, brownish and somewhat lumpy. Not an attractive look, but one I'd seen before.

"Liquid body armor." I scraped some off with the flat of the blade. "Forsyth was wearing it, too."

"I thought this stuff only existed in theory." Fleming pinched some between her fingers. "It's a sheer thickening paste. Semisolid now, but watch." She flicked her fingernail at it, and it made a clicking sound as the paste became rock hard. "Add energy, it becomes a solid. I also feel some iron filings in the mixture, so it could be magnetorheological as well. Amazing."

"Yeah. Well, she should have smeared some on her face."

Fleming glanced at me, and we shared a small laugh, one that was surprisingly comfortable. Then I turned my attention back to the task at hand. Once I'd finished scraping off the body armor, I positioned the blade above Clancy's belly button. I tried not to think about how her belly looked like mine, and how I also had a tracker in me, and then I made my first cut.

Dead hearts no longer pumped blood, and so dead bodies didn't exactly bleed. Instead they oozed. Blood reddened my fingers and seeped out onto the plastic as I widened the incision, past the layers of skin and fat and muscle, until her insides were exposed.

"Check the duodenum," Fleming said. "I see a scar there. And try not to nick the intestines. This smell is bad enough."

"You can jump in at any time," I said, breathing through my mouth.

The odor of blood and death and digestive tract was nearly overwhelming. I palpated the tissue, finally feeling a very small but hard nub beneath the slick scar tissue. I sliced carefully and finally freed the tracking device.

The thing was a small, round chip of clear plastic, the size of a penny, but several times as thick. I brushed off some blood and saw the circuit panel inside. Fleming pried it from my fingers, even though she wasn't wearing gloves.

"The weight is lopsided. I think it has a rotor in it, like a self-winding watch. That keeps the battery charged."

"Fascinating," I said, pulling the ghillie suit closed. Then I wiped my hands with some paper towels and fished in the duffel for what I needed next.

I chose a hand clipper, the kind used to prune rose bushes. A branch nipper would have been easier, with its extra leverage, but for all the tools Fleming had in her bunker, she was woefully short on garden implements.

Ironic, since she lived in the middle of a forest.

It didn't take long for me to snip off the ends of Clancy's fingers and plop them into a jar filled with hydrochloric acid. Then I cleaned up the mess and encased my dead sister in a body bag.

I was grateful that part was done, but the first step in our plan was far from over.

"Were you able to get the paperwork?"

"I have everything we'll need." Fleming handed me a pile of clothing and then climbed back behind the wheel. Instead of using a foot pedal for brake and gas, she maneuvered the vehicle with hand controls, and soon we were cruising down the lonely road.

Time for me to get dressed.

By the time we reached the city, rush hour was long since over and traffic was heavy but flowing well. We made it into the city in good time. Fleming drove like she was pissed off at the entire world, and maybe she was. But being in a Humvee, with a horn stolen straight off a freight train, motorists gave her a wide berth. A good thing, too, because I could easily have pictured her driving over some of the slower, smaller cars in her way.

Fleming pulled into the hospital's rear parking lot and up to the double doors. After offering to help my sister into her wheelchair—which apparently was akin to spitting in her face—we headed toward the morgue entrance. This chair was manual, not electric, and had angled wheels and a lower profile.

"Does this model also have the guns in the armrests?" I asked.

"Among other modifications. I don't like being unarmed."

We both signed in with the attendant, a sleepy-eyed dough-boy with greasy hair. The morgue was off-limits to the public, but cops, doctors, and morticians were granted entrance. Our fake credentials said we were doctors, and we were dressed appropriately in white lab coats.

I kept my head down so the attendant didn't notice we were twins, but it didn't matter because his eyes were glued to a television showing, of all things, an Animal Planet special on otters.

I let Fleming deal with the paperwork—a bogus autopsy order—while I used one of the morgue's stainless steel gurneys to fetch Clancy and wheel her inside. When I returned, Fleming was waiting for me at the entrance to the cooler. She went in first, and I followed.

There are not many smells worse than the stench of the morgue. Underneath the bleach and antiseptic was a sickly-sweet odor akin to rotting carnations. It coated the insides of my nostrils and clung to my skin, and I knew from experience it would stick with me long after I had left the building.

In the massive walk-in cooler, the dead were stacked four high on wire racks, many of them leaking fluids onto the sticky floor. They were naked, bluish-colored regardless of race, and many were still stuck in the odd positions they'd died in: on their sides, arms and legs akimbo, curled up as if in sleep. Cook County morgue was one of the biggest in the nation, and it was operating at full capacity, which meant over three hundred bodies. We were the only two live ones in the place.

Fleming picked up a stray bottle of bleach and began spritzing down Clancy's body bag, destroying our prints. I ducked into the autopsy room—which was devoid of any medical examiners as Jack Daniels had promised—and found two of my sisters on the cutting tables. Follett, whom I'd putted the grenade at, was missing a good portion of her legs. The other, whose head wound indicated she was Ludlam from Stretchers, already had the standard Y incision on her chest. Luckily, she hadn't been opened up yet. I swallowed the bad taste in my mouth and took the hand clippers out of my lab coat.

"Forsyth is missing," I called over my shoulder to Fleming, "so check the racks. She'll have on liquid body armor."

"I'm on it. You know, this may sound stupid, but it feels good to be in the field again. Nice to get out of the bunker and stretch my legs. Figuratively speaking."

I might have enjoyed the small talk with my sister more if I hadn't been snipping off my other sister's fingertips. We needed to get rid of all fingerprint evidence, or both Fleming and I were in deep shit.

Well, *deeper* shit. Things were pretty dire already.

I finished up with Ludlam, then got to work on Follett. She only had seven fingers, the explosion apparently having taken care of the other three.

"Found her," Fleming called out. Less than a minute later it was followed by, "Someone's coming."

I snipped off the last digit and placed it in a plastic baggie. Then I scanned the nearby table, looking for paperwork. Jack had said one of my sisters had been printed. I needed to find the card and—

"Well...look at what we have here."

I spun, looking at the cop who had just walked into the autopsy suite. He was midforties, unshaven, his uniform a bit too tight around his belly and badly in need of ironing. He wore a leer normally reserved for striptease venues.

"Can I help you, Officer?" I asked, using my polite voice.

"You've got to be one of the cutest doctors I've ever seen. I may have to call heaven, see if Jesus filled an MAR." He winked. "A Missing Angel Report."

Normally I didn't tolerate the loud, obnoxious type. But seeing as how I was impersonating a doctor, it wasn't in my best interest to piss off a cop.

"Looks like we're both working late," I said. "You here for take-out or delivery?"

He smiled wide. "Neither. Just needed to check up on a case."

"Don't let me keep you." I gave him a quick, saccharine grin, then stuck a scalpel into Ludlam's Y incision with more verve than I felt.

Horny Cop didn't take the hint. "Say, that's some hottie you got there on the table. You know who she looks like?"

I tensed, waiting for the obvious, thinking of my next move.

"That chick who played in *Tomb Raider*," he continued. "Smaller tits, though. And paler. And not nearly as active. You don't mind if I observe, do you?"

"Be my guest." I offered a crocodile smile and yanked out Ludlam's stomach by the esophagus.

"Hey, lookie here, another cutie. Nice wheels, Doc."

I glanced up and noticed Fleming had her hands on her armrests, right on top of the rifle barrels. I gave her a discreet head shake, imploring her not to shoot him.

"You guys related? You look kinda alike. Except for the wheelchair thing."

"We're sisters," I said, palpating Ludlum's duodenum.

"Sisters. That's hot. So would it be out of line if I asked you guys out?"

*Is he serious?*

"Are you serious?" Fleming asked.

"Yeah. It would be like a double date, but just me and you two. I've always wanted to date sisters. It's on my checklist of things to do before I die."

"I'm afraid you're not going to be able to check that one off," Fleming said, eyes mean and hands squeezing her rails.

I needed to defuse this fast, before we had to dispose of another body.

"You're ten kinds of sexy," the cop said to Fleming. "I like a woman who can't run away."

Then again, a morgue was a pretty good place for body disposal.

"You are the biggest, rudest—"

"Let's cut the crap here, ladies," the cop said, interrupting her. "I know you two aren't doctors. You, Wheels, were snipping off someone's fingers when I came in. And you, Dr. Incompetent, you're apparently practicing for the movie *World's Worst Autopsies*. You hold that scalpel like it's some guy's johnson. Which, I admit, is arousing, but not very effective."

Shit. Now we probably had to kill him.

"But all that is none of my business," he went on, "and I certainly wouldn't use my authority to force you both to go out with me. On Thursday night, say eightish. I have tickets to the game. Box seats. That means I give you the seat, you show me the box."

"Look, Officer…" I squinted at the name on his shirt, "McGlade. We really have a lot of work to do here and—"

"Your badge is plastic," Fleming said.

McGlade nodded. "Yeah. They took my real one when they kicked me off the force. The uniform still fits, though. Mostly. I'm in the private sector now." He gave me what he probably thought was his serious face. In reality, he looked constipated. "I'm here to check on a teenager. Suicide. Parents suspect foul play. I snuck in to take a look. So what's your story? Some sort of creepy, sister-on-sister necrophilia stuff? Because that's hot."

I glanced at Fleming, who mouthed, *Let me shoot him.*

"Here's the thing, McGlade…"

"Call me Harry."

"…I know I speak for both me and my sister when I say we don't find you attractive."

"I'm also rich. They made a TV series about me."

"And we're so very happy for you. But we've got some shit that needs to get done, you've got that suicide thing to work on, and the chances of us ever hooking up are less than zero."

"That's cool," he said. "So how about I pay you each two hundred bucks to French kiss?"

"You can leave now, McGlade."

He threw a salute. "Message received. And if you change your mind, just Google me. Reference this morgue thing, though, so I remember. I ask a lot of women out."

He shot me with his index finger, did the same to Fleming, and then strutted out of there like a delusional peacock.

"I almost killed him about four different times," Fleming said. "You know, I actually saw his TV show. *Fatal Autonomy.* I don't even know what that title means."

"Did you get the chip from Forsyth?" I asked, getting us back on track.

"Not yet."

"I'll do Follett and meet you there."

When I was finished, I tucked both trackers in the plastic bag, then helped Fleming remove the third from Forsyth. We dodged a winking Harry McGlade and got the hell out of the morgue.

Our next stop was the Hancock building, to retrieve my phone. But…

I checked my PC and saw two blips. Me, Fleming, and my dead sisters constituted one of them. The other, Hammett, was a mile distant and heading this way. If she was still after me, it was a good indicator she hadn't found the transceiver yet. I guessed she was with Victor and who knew how many of his men.

Fortunately, I had a plan to throw them off our trail.

"Have you ever been to Buckingham Fountain?" I asked Fleming.

*"When defeating the enemy isn't possible," The Instructor said, "confusing the enemy is the next best thing."*

Hammett stares at the screen of her tablet PC, unsure of what is happening. Normally, depending on how closely she zooms into the map, there are anywhere from five to seven blips, each representing one of the sisters.

But now there are only two. Hers, and another.

Hammett has no idea what this means. But she's about to find out. Driving in a cargo van with Victor and his thugs, she's closing in on the mysterious second blip. "Turn here," she orders.

When she gets within ten blocks, the blip begins to move east. They fall into pursuit.

So far, this op has been a catastrophe. One fuck-up after another. It was all so eloquently planned, too. Thought out down to the smallest detail. The only wild card was Chandler.

And what a wild card that turned out to be.

Hammett hasn't heard from Clancy and can only assume she's the latest casualty.

It's a shame. The Hydra Project was a wonderful idea, and might have still had a few good years left. Hammett easily imagined controlling a crime syndicate with her sisters. Or staging a coup and running a small country. But their deaths put an end to any future plans.

Fortunately those plans paled in comparison to acquiring the transceiver.

Victor believes his people will have access to the phone. He even has a team of scientists lined up to reverse engineer it. They care less about its nuclear capabilities and more about its encryption, which is supposedly unbreakable. At least that's his story.

Hammett assumes Victor will kill her as soon as the transceiver's delivery is assured.

She assumes this because she plans to do the same to him. Him and his tiny prick.

Hammett allows herself a smile. For now she and Victor are the best of allies, joining forces to reach a mutually beneficial end.

Victor takes the PC from her. He is so keyed up he's nearly vibrating.

"It appears they've stopped," he says. "At the Buckingham Fountain."

"Let me see."

He tilts the screen toward her, offering a glimpse. She grabs the PC from his hands, eyes on the now stationary blip.

Victor orders his man to turn onto Columbus Avenue, the street flanking Grant Park. The night is cool and only a couple dozen people mill around the fountain to watch its nightly light show. Classical music jangles through the air, accompanying the dance of water lit from all sides, turning the fountain into a rainbow of color. Vapor rises into the cold night, giving the Chicago landmark a dreamlike quality.

"What's happening?" Victor asks, leaning close to Hammett and eyeing the tablet PC.

In front of their eyes, the single blip becomes four distinct blips, separating in different directions.

Victor gestures to the driver. "Pull over."

They pull the van up onto the sidewalk and quickly pour out onto the park grounds, guns concealed in jackets, eyes alert for anyone who looks like Hammett. The gravel on the path around the fountain crunches under combat boots, pigeons scattering at their approach, and Hammett holds the PC in front of her like a talisman, tracking the nearest blip. It's close, moving slowly, erratically. The other three have dispersed, fleeing to other parts of the city.

Hammett zooms in to the maximum resolution of the tracking map, wondering why the powers that be, in their infinite wisdom, gave each of the Hydra sisters an identical chip, rather than a unique one that could be linked to a specific identity. Of course, that was years ago, and technology wasn't as advanced as—

"There!"

Victor, the fool, whips out his gun in public. Several spectators turn and stare at them with wide eyes. Hammett combs the small crowd, trying to focus into the darkness and pick out the familiar shape of a sister. But there's nothing there. Nothing but—

"Pigeons," Hammett says. She checks the tablet, then confirms it with a forward glance. There's a loft of pigeons ahead, dozens of them, feasting on what appears to be small, bloody pieces of steak.

Correction. She spies a bird with something in its beak. Something that is quite obviously a piece of a human finger.

Hammett laughs, so loudly and profusely that she disturbs the loft, which takes flight and spreads out over Chicago.

"What's going on?" Victor asks.

"This bird has flown," Hammett says.

"What?"

"Your piece of ass. She played us. Played us good."

"What are you talking about?"

Hammett realizes her laughter has attracted even more attention, people backing away as if afraid she has lost her mind. She turns to Victor, her mood suddenly souring. "Put your gun away, you idiot."

He tucks it back inside his jacket. Hammett folds her arms, tries to concentrate, but anger clouds her thoughts. Staring at the PC again, she resists the urge to throw it into the dancing waters of Buckingham Fountain. Instead she looks at the blip moving north on the screen and then gazes in at the Magnificent Mile, all lit up along Michigan Avenue. Chandler told the truth about the Hancock building. They hadn't found the transceiver, but that didn't mean it wasn't there.

"Call your men. We're going back to the ninety-sixth floor."

Victor's brow furrows. "My superiors—"

"Fuck your superiors," Hammett says. "You either come with me, or you go back to them empty-handed. Now move your ass, *comrade.*"

Hammett strides back to the van, indulging in a private smile. It has been so long since she's faced any sort of challenge. Tragic as the current events have been, she has to admit, she's having fun.

Almost as much fun as it will be to launch one of those nukes on some unsuspecting country, once she gets the transceiver.

After all, what's the point of having ultimate power, unless you exercise it?

*"Always prepare for the worst," The Instructor said, "because the worst is usually what happens."*

When I was growing up, my wicked stepfather used to call pigeons *rats with wings*. While I didn't share that sentiment, pigeons were undeniably scavengers, and they had made quick work of the fingertips and the tracking devices, gobbling them up with ratlike efficiency.

"You know what you just did?" Fleming said, pulling the Hummer onto Columbus and heading north.

"What?"

"You killed two birds with one stone."

I allowed myself a small smile, then turned my attention to the substantial armory Fleming had in the back of the truck. I packed a rucksack with two Sig Arms P220 Combat Pistols, loaded, and four eight-round magazines. I also added an M18 green smoke grenade and a Taser M26.

"Is this Tec-9 converted?" I asked, holding up a submachine gun slightly bigger than one of the Sigs.

"Full auto," Fleming said. "Squeeze the trigger and it fires a thousand rounds a minute."

I didn't see any thousand-round magazines, but I found some thirty-round sticks. I put the Tec-9 and the mags in the sack. I also strapped a wicked-looking Mercworx VORAX double-edged combat knife to my right calf under my pants leg, using a Velcro holster. On my left leg went a retractable police asp. It weighed about half a kilogram, and when fully extended, was over two feet long.

"You've got a full case of M67s back here," I said, eyeing a crate of hand grenades.

"Leave them. If one explodes on the ninety-sixth floor, it would blow out windows, and the cross breeze could sweep us outside. Or worse, it might cause some structural damage."

I left them. A moment later, Fleming hit a pothole, making the crate bounce. I winced.

"You sure it's safe to drive like that when you've got all of this ordnance back here?"

"If you're worried, you could sit up here where it's safe."

If the Humvee blew up, I doubted anywhere within a hundred meters would be safe. But I climbed into the passenger seat just the same.

"Maybe I can drive on the way back?"

"Sure. And there's an extra key in the trailer hitch in back, under the tow ball, just in case."

I knew what *just in case* meant. Just in case Fleming didn't make it.

I didn't like that scenario at all.

We arrived at the Hancock Center a few minutes later. As we drove up the spiral ramp to the parking levels, my thoughts drifted to Kaufmann. Earlier that day, we'd escaped the men in the black SUV on this ramp. It seemed so long ago.

So much had changed since then.

And yet, everything remained the same.

The Instructor once told me that the game never changes, only the players.

Poor Kaufmann. Poor goddamn Kaufmann.

The sixth-floor parking lot was closed, so Fleming parked on the fifth, the wide Hummer taking up two spaces. She crawled into the backseat with me, opened the rear door, and set her wheelchair onto the concrete. As she lowered herself into it, her right foot snagged on the door handle.

"Ow…"

"You can feel that?" I asked.

She shot me a look. "I'm maimed, not paralyzed."

I wondered what the true extent of her injuries was. "So, can you walk?"

"Walking is for suckers," Fleming said. "But I can swim like a son of a bitch."

"Can you—"

"Enough about me. Get your mind on op. We take separate elevators. I cover them. You get the transceiver. If things go sour, we'll rendezvous in the lobby of the Congress Hotel at eleven hundred. Oh, and I almost forgot." She pulled something from her pocket and dropped it in my hand.

It was a cell phone and an accompanying Bluetooth earpiece no bigger than my pinky.

"How far we've come," I said. "Remember those big radio headsets?"

She nodded and pulled a matching set out of another pocket. "These are trac phones, never used before, bought them at a drugstore. I already synced the earpieces."

Pushing my hair back, I screwed mine into my ear and watched Fleming call me. A moment later I heard the ringing.

"Tap the button to answer."

I did. "Hello? Can you hear me?"

Fleming made a face. "Of course I can hear you. I'm standing right in front of you."

She attached her earpiece and rolled a few meters away.

"What's Hammett's position?" her voice said in my ear.

I checked the PC blips. One was moving in a straight line toward us. "She's seven blocks away, approaching fast. We have a few minutes at most."

"Then let's move."

I stuck the tablet in the rucksack, and we took the parking elevator down to the lobby. The place still smelled like dusty marble, but now the scent was overlaid by the odor of human stress. Several cops dotted the lobby, talking to a handful of people, and the Best Buy was closed off.

The building had been a hotbed of activity today, and after the mess I'd caused earlier, I expected extra security. Of course, Hammett and Victor had just left. I could only guess what they'd been up to.

I circled to the tiny express elevators to the top floors, Fleming rolling behind me. We ran into more cops before we reached them. A man with short blond hair and the black suit of the Signature Room held up a hand, his gaze hovering somewhere to the side of Fleming, as if too uncomfortable to look directly at the woman in the wheelchair. "Sorry ladies. The upper floors are closed."

"But we have a reservation," Fleming said.

"The restaurant and lounge are closed for the evening. We are very sorry. If you'd like, I can rebook a table for you, say for tomorrow night?"

"What happened?" I asked, shifting the rucksack behind me and hoping he'd just think it was the latest style of oversized handbag. I had no doubt that whatever had closed the top floors was Hammett's doing.

"There was a bomb threat earlier."

"Don't worry." He shifted his gaze up to me, whether trying to be polite and address us both or avoiding the handicapped woman, I couldn't tell. "It seems the threat was bogus, but…" He narrowed his eyes.

*Oh, hell.*

"You look familiar."

"I have one of those faces."

I turned to push Fleming's chair, but she was already heading in the other direction. I hurried to keep up.

I remembered the women I'd followed this morning when I'd been looking for a place to stash the phone. I was fairly certain the elevators they'd first approached had led to residential floors, the floors immediately under the restaurant and observation deck. I motioned to Fleming. "This way."

We ducked behind a planter just in time to avoid two officers, then made a dash in the direction of the residential elevators.

A short, squat woman wearing a black vest and pants stood in front of the elevator banks. From first glance, she seemed to be armed with a radio, a name tag, and nothing more. Noticing our approach, she glanced up. "May I help you?"

"I got this," Fleming said out of the side of her mouth. She tapped her right ear, referencing the earpiece we each wore. "Meet you at the Congress."

Then she rolled up to the security guard, hit the brakes on her chair, and flopped onto the floor. She began to writhe around and moan, a definite Oscar-worthy performance.

As the guard rushed to her aid, I slipped past. I hit the up button and stepped into an open lift. The buttons went up to ninety, so that's the one I pressed.

I caught one last glimpse of Fleming, lying on the ground, her eyes rolled back in her head, and then the door closed. The elevator lurched, then took off on its ascent.

I forced myself to breathe, to concentrate. I took out the tablet PC and saw that Hammett had arrived. Once she entered the building, I wouldn't be able to tell which floor she was on. The computer would be all but worthless to me. I stowed it back in my rucksack and strapped the Tec-9 across my shoulders. I stuck extra magazines for that, and the .45s, into every available pocket of my jeans, and then jacked a round into the Sig and held it alongside my body.

Watching the numbers climb, I focused on slow breaths and equalizing the pressure in my ears. This elevator was much slower than the express, and I hoped it wouldn't stop before reaching my floor. My appearance would probably unnerve a civilian.

Luckily, the car took me all the way to the ninetieth floor. The bell chimed, the door parted, and I stepped into the hall, gun at the ready.

---

"When we get there, Chandler is mine. I don't want you messing things up."

Victor ignores Hammett and feeds the full magazine into the Brügger & Thomet MP9. Aware of the glitzy shops of the Magnificent Mile whizzing outside the van, he longs to open up on unsuspecting shoppers at nine hundred rounds per minute. He's been living in America for too long, and he's had enough. Americans are lazy, ignorant pigs who think they are entitled to all that is good in the world. More than anything, he has thirsted for this moment, his chance to set them straight.

Too bad he can't start with Hammett.

"I've provided money and men," he says, a temple of infinite patience. "I've done my part. You promised to deliver the transceiver."

"Your part? What was your part? Fucking my sister?"

"She's a better fuck than you are. Apparently she's better at everything else as well."

He says it to get her to shut up, but realizes it is true. Hammett, sexy as she is, doesn't even seem to realize he is in the same room as her when they make love. She uses him like a piece of gym equipment. At least Chandler seemed to want to please him.

Of course, he doubts that would be the case now, especially after the whole torture thing. But if she comes out of this alive, he'll take her along with the transceiver. He could have fun with her, at least for a little while.

Hammett, he'll dump in the lake as soon as the prize is in hand.

In the back, his men pretend they didn't hear, but Victor can feel them grin.

He is going to enjoy killing her.

"Let us out here," Hammett orders. She turns to Victor. "I'll go after Chandler. You watch for the police. Try not to fuck it up."

Victor clenches his jaw and doesn't answer. He is the one giving orders. He is the one who found the investors. He is the one who gets the transceiver when it's all over. Somehow the bitch always forgets she depends on him.

The van stops. He, Hammett, and his men jump out. Best case, they find Chandler, find the transceiver, and escape without a shot being fired.

Worst case, they'll draw attention to themselves, and people will have to die.

Victor smiles privately, his hand gripping the MP9.

Worst case doesn't seem bad at all.

———————

Leading with the Sig, I stepped out of the elevator and into a wide hall. Various prints depicting Chicago hung on the walls, and my feet sank into plush carpeting. The air smelled of lavender and money. No telling how much it cost to live in a landmark like the John Hancock building, but my nose told me the people who made this their home rarely stooped to do something as middle class as cook dinner.

The sound of strings filtered into the hall from the closest condo. "The Jupiter Symphony," if I remembered my Mozart. No one was in the hall. Hopefully the late hour would keep it that way, at least until I could find the stairs.

Picturing the layout of the Signature Room above, I headed left. Sure enough, the third door I passed was marked FIRE EXIT. I ducked inside, the alarm ringing briefly. Springing on the balls of my feet, I started up the remaining five flights.

I reached the top, my heart rate slightly elevated, and pushed into the restaurant.

A man around my age stood near the maître d' stand. "Ma'am, I'm sorry but we're…" His voice trailed off and mouth froze open as his stare alternated between my face and my weaponry.

"I'm sorry, I'm going to have to ask you to leave. It's for your own safety."

"Again?"

It took me a second to realize he was probably reacting to an earlier run-in with Hammett and assumed I was her. Wouldn't he be surprised when she turned up, which I was sure would happen soon.

"Get the fuck out," I said, pointing my weapon at him.

He got the fuck out.

"I'm in on the ninety-fifth floor," I said to Fleming.

Then I went to find my cell phone.

———————

After flailing around and looking appropriately pitiful for the time it took Chandler to get into the elevator, Fleming allowed the security guard to help her back into her chair. A small collection of gawkers had gathered, and even though Fleming had been faking her helplessness, she still felt a small sting of humiliation.

*One more indignity to add to the list.*

She listened to Chandler announce her arrival, and for a brief, self-indulgent moment, Fleming pretended she was up there instead. After the fall, and the countless surgeries and hellish failure that was rehabilitation, Fleming had sworn off feeling sorry for herself. She refused to allow tragedy to limit what she could do. As a result, she'd worked harder and accomplished more than she probably ever would have if her legs had still functioned.

But that was all behind-the-scenes stuff. Even the encryption code for the transceiver—a brilliant combination of mathematics and programming—was for someone else to use. Fleming longed to do something active. To be viable again. But instead of taking the lead, she wheeled back into the lobby and played the backup role, watching for Hammett.

She didn't have to watch long.

Hammett strolled in, wearing an ankle-length brown duster, a beige top, and black leather pants. Fleming had always flirted with the notion of buying leather pants, and seeing them on Hammett, decided they were a bad idea. Hammett was flanked by six men, walking in groups of two, looking very much like a military unit even though they were in civvies. Slung over each of their shoulders was a duffel bag, and judging by their weights Fleming guessed they held automatic weapons.

Keeping her head down, she backed around the corner and watched as they approached the bank of express elevators. One of the men began to speak to the maître d' they'd run from a moment earlier.

Hammett reached inside her duster, no doubt putting her hands on a gun.

Fleming gripped the arms of her chair, but she didn't fire. This was not ideal. Hammett and Victor stood between her and the cops. If she stayed in position and tried to take Hammett out, she might hit the innocents behind her. If she did nothing, Hammett would likely get through, and if everything went to hell, she could kill those same innocents on her way to interfere with Chandler.

Footsteps sounded to the side of Fleming. Two more officers.

She took her fingers from the triggers and gripped the wheels. Where shooting at Hammett's men didn't bother Fleming in the least, the thought of getting in a firefight with police officers who were just doing their jobs was another story. She'd have to find a different position and figure out another way to keep Hammett and the men from reaching the restaurant, at least until Chandler had a chance to get the phone and get out.

"She's here," Fleming whispered. "Six men with her, all armed and—"

That's when Hammett pulled out a semiautomatic pistol and shot the maître d' in the head.

---

After Hammett caps the rude maître d'—and let's face it, the son of a bitch had it coming—she sidesteps the police line and goes to the express elevators, ignoring Victor and his shouts of rage.

A firefight breaks out, Victor's men and the police in the lobby. Hammett slips into the first lift that opens and hits the button for the restaurant. Then she does a quick check of her weapons. A 9mm Beretta, loaded with hollow-points. A carbon fiber Spyderco Navaja. One of Victor's MP9s, hanging from a shoulder sling inside her coat. And something with a bit more stopping power in her right pocket.

"Ready or not, dear sister, here I come."

---

Fleming spoke in my ear as I was racing up the stairs to the balcony overlooking the restaurant. "Six men with her, all armed and—" Gunfire exploded in the background, making her words hard to hear. But reading the alarm in her voice was easy.

"Fleming?"

More gunshots. My stomach clenched like a fist.

As I approached the top of the stairs, I forced all thoughts of what my sister was going through from my mind. I needed to focus. I needed to get the phone.

After contemplating and rejecting various hiding places, I had decided to take a more direct approach and had given the phone to the bartender, feeding him a story about finding it in the ladies' room. Then I'd hung around just long enough to see where he kept the lost and found.

Now I dashed straight for the maître d's stand on one end of the balcony.

The top drawer was locked. Hands shaking, I started feeling along the hem of my T-shirt before I remembered I wasn't wearing my own clothing.

Yet my fingers hit something stiff. Wires.

Of course. This was Hammett's shirt. Hammett, who had gone through the same training I had.

I ripped the stitching and removed the picks, letting the fifty-dollar bill fall to the floor. The lock was a simple one and only took seconds. I pulled the drawer open and stared at over a dozen cell phones jamming the small space.

How did so many people manage to lose their phones?

I clawed through the collection. Seven iPhones, a Droid, at least six of the old flip models—who knew how long those had been there—and a variety of odds and ends, including a Kindle. Finally I located mine. I dropped it in my rucksack and zipped it up.

Just as the elevator door chimed.

---

Victor curses that *shalava* Hammett and then fires ten rounds into a wide-eyed cop who has barely cleared leather with his weapon. He also dispatches the cop's partner, who manages to get off two ineffective shots before doing the machine-gun boogie. Then Victor's men form a half circle around him and lay down a burst of suppressive fire. The two dozen people in the lobby who haven't fled or hit the floor yet get the hint. All except some cripple in a wheelchair, who seems to be rolling their way with an expression of—

*Chto za huy! I know that face!*

Victor rolls out of the way as a barrage of bullets fires from the armrests of the wheelchair, mowing down three of his men. He slides across the tile floor on his shoulder, bringing up his MP9, but Hammett's sister is already in motion, barreling toward his men, who duck for cover. She steers toward one who took a dive and then—*what the fuck is that?*—a long, thin blade comes out of the chair's axle and neatly slices Sergei's throat and then severs Nikolai's hamstring.

Peter comes up behind, spraying bullets. They clang off the back of her wheelchair, apparently bulletproof.

She taps her armrest again, and a long jet of fire hits the poor bastard square in the face.

*Holy shit.*

The woman spins around, lifting up her footrest, which concealed another blade, and as Yuri rushes at her, she guts him.

That leaves Victor and Karl, and Karl is backpedalling as fast as he can move his feet, his shots flying harmlessly over the crippled woman's head as she accelerates toward him, now brandishing a .45. She shoots Karl in the forehead, then whirls around, seeking Victor.

But he's already in motion, raising his weapon, stitching rounds up her legs and across her chest.

The woman slumps in the chair, her gun clattering to the floor.

Victor looks at his fallen comrades, spits in disgust, and then storms over to her, ready to put the coup de grâce into her head.

---

The gunfire began when the elevator doors opened just a sliver. I immediately dropped behind the maître d' stand, crawling away as bullets chewed into the wood and flung sawdust into the air, the tattoo of automatic weapon fire drowning out all thought.

I reached the stairs, flipping onto my back, freeing the Tec-9 and aiming with my left hand while the right held my Sig.

The shooting paused, and for a moment, all I heard was the ringing in my ears.

"Where was it?" Hammett called out.

I kept my arms extended, fingers on the triggers. "Lost and found."

"Clever girl. Clever, clever girl."

I caught the movement peripherally, Hammett rushing in low to my right, the muzzle flash of her machine gun preceding the barrage of lead pocking the floor in front of me, coming my way to cut me in half.

*Ah, hell...*

I swung the rucksack in front of me, using it as protection. The punch of a dozen rounds peppering it, I pushed myself backward, scooting down the stairs. Still being chased by bullets, I tucked my legs up to my chest and began to roll, feet over head. I bumped into the railing and kept somersaulting, each step bruising my spine, my skull. By the time the steps spit me out onto the lower floor, my sense of balance and direction were completely gone.

My skull ached, adding to the disorientation, and after a quick self pat-down, I found I had somehow lost my Tec-9, and—

*Oh, no.*

My rucksack.

My rucksack, with the transceiver in it.

I cast a frantic look around and saw it, sitting midway on the stairs.

I got my legs under me, ready to make an attempt, but Hammett suddenly appeared over the railing above, her face shiny with excitement.

Still dizzy, I fired my Sig and then dived to the side as more lead rained down on me. I made it to the edge of the carpeted dining area, crawled under the closest dinner table, and upended it, sending silverware flying. Hunkering down behind it, I replaced the magazine in my weapon and willed the world to stop spinning.

"Please tell me the transceiver is in that backpack." Hammett's voice carried a teasing edge.

She'd seen my face when I realized it was gone. She knew something important to me was inside. I wasn't about to give her any more hints. "Why don't you go and check?" I taunted, the Sig now loaded and ready.

In my earpiece, more gunfire and screaming.

I peered around the table, eyes on my rucksack, then looked left to the expansive wine cellar, stocked to the ceiling with bottles behind glass doors. I crawled over to it, broke the glass with the butt of my .45, and snatched a bottle of Merlot by the neck. Hammett was no longer at the railing, but I knew if I were up there, about to make a run at the rucksack, I'd be close to the stairs, yet behind cover. The only thing on the balcony that qualified was the splintered remains of the maître d' stand.

So that's where I threw the bottle.

As it sailed through the air, I quickly grabbed a replacement from behind me, then aimed and shot the Merlot. It shattered near where I guessed my sister to be, spraying glass and wine. I tossed the second bottle, grabbed a third, shot the second, tossed the third, grabbed a fourth, shot the third, and then I stormed the stairs, taking them two at a time, emptying my magazine as Hammett brought her gun up and began to blind fire. Discarding my Sig, I snatched the rucksack strap. Bullets cut the air around me. I flew up the last three steps, leaped past the maître d' stand, and, just as my sister stuck out her head, I cracked her in the face with a 2007 MacPhail Pratt Pinot Noir.

I landed on my side and tugged the rucksack onto my shoulders. Then I pulled up my leg and freed the asp.

Hammett was on all fours, shaking wine, glass, and blood out of her hair like a wet dog.

I got my feet under me and sprinted at her, extending my telescoping baton with a *chhhht-chhhht* sound like a shotgun being racked.

Hammett brought up her MP9, and I swung the asp with all I had. It hit hard, bending both it and the barrel of her gun. Then I drew back a foot, aiming to kick her in the throat.

She twisted her body and caught my leg in her armpit. She thrust to her feet, and I fell backward, over the broken stand. Grabbing her jacket, I pulled her with me, and we both tumbled down the stairs.

---

Victor raises his weapon to the woman's head. He pauses for a moment, savoring. The bitch destroyed his men. Only Nikolai is still alive, writhing on the floor, whining and clutching his useless leg. But in the end, Victor took her down, and now he will blow her goddamn face off. The fact that she looks like Hammett is a bonus.

He smiles.

Before he can pull the trigger, he hears the click, feels the twin prongs jab into him, and when the electric charge rips through his body a split second later, there's nothing he can do.

His teeth clench. Every muscle seizes. A guttural groan bounces off the marble, coming from his own throat.

The woman opens her eyes and stares at him, very much alive, as the Taser pumps juice through his body.

He manages to stumble backward, ripping the darts from his flesh, but he can't regain his balance and goes down, hitting the floor hard.

The force knocks the air out of him. He gasps for breath, but he's not done. He still holds his weapon. Bringing it up, he sprays rounds in her direction. Bullets fly everywhere, uncontrolled; his muscles still in spasm.

Her .45 lies useless on the floor, out of reach, and she spins around, shielding herself with the armored chair. She takes off in the other direction.

*She's out of ammunition.*

She has to be. It is the only reason for her to turn tail while he is down and wheezing and out of control.

Victor scrambles to his feet and starts after her. He feels stronger with each step, and he closes the gap between them despite her surprising speed. He has her now. This time he will not hesitate, he will not assume anything. This time he will shoot her in the head first and savor the kill later.

He pushes his legs to move faster, running all-out, gaining.

Small pieces of something fall from her chair and skitter over the marble. He doesn't fully grasp what is happening until his foot comes down on one.

The spike drills through the sole of his shoe and knifes into his foot. Cold slices his flesh, chased by pain. He bellows and pulls up short.

The chair keeps moving, rolling around the corner.

Hammett releases her sister as they tumble down the stairs, spreading out her limbs to stop the rolling. She snatches the railing, the world a blur, and watches Chandler reach the bottom floor and begin to crawl away.

*Oh no, you don't.*

Hammett unholsters her Beretta. She fires, pinging Chandler three times in the left side.

They're hollow-points, meant to open up on impact and cause massive internal bleeding. A hit to a limb at this range should prove fatal, let alone three body shots.

Chandler cries out but keeps crawling.

Body armor? Perhaps the liquid prototype Hammett stole?

No matter. She's got something stronger than hollow-points.

Slapping at her pocket, Hammett removes the grenade. According to The Instructor, the transceiver has a diamond-hardened case and is practically indestructible.

Chandler, however, is not.

She pulls the pin and throws it, fastball style, at her sister's head.

---

Fleming took a turn into the main lobby, leaving the Russian behind.

She couldn't help wondering how Chandler was dealing with their dear sister. Right now, she'd give nearly anything to be able to get upstairs to help. When Hammett's men had started shooting, she hadn't been able to hear much over the earpiece. Now her pulse was beating so hard in her own ears, all she could make out was a loud explosion.

She hoped to hell it was only gunfire.

"Chandler? What's going on?" Her voice sounded shaky, even in her own ears.

There was no answer.

Fleming's arms felt weak, as if all the adrenaline was suddenly draining from her system. Her chest and legs hurt like hell. While the liquid armor she'd borrowed from Forsyth's body had stopped the Russian's rounds, they'd still left countless deep bruises in their wake and what felt like at least one cracked rib.

Approaching one of the building's exits, she slowed the chair and took several shallow and painful breaths. She should head for the Congress Hotel as planned, but the thought of wheeling out the door and leaving her sister to face Hammett alone left her cold.

But could she really help? She was injured, and while she normally wouldn't let that stop her, she had the extra problem of being out of ammunition.

When they'd arrived, she'd had to stay on the ground floor because cops had closed off the restaurant and the express elevators leading to the top floors. Now those cops were dead. The elevators were accessible. And the bodies of Hammett's men were scattered around them.

Hammett's *armed* men.

A few of their weapons and a short elevator ride, and Fleming would be back in business.

She turned away from the exit and headed back into the building.

---

Getting shot while slathered in the liquid body armor felt a lot like getting hit with a bat.

Then, a moment later, the ball hit me as well.

But it wasn't a ball. It was heavier and green and unmistakably a grenade.

It cracked into my hip, then rolled a meter to my left on the black marble floor. My heart froze in my chest. I had no time to think, no time to get a safe distance away, so instead I crawled toward it. No time to even pick it up, I swatted it and covered my head as it rolled into the corner of the restaurant.

The explosion was epic, impossibly loud and bright, the light blinding me even though I had my hands over my eyes.

Then came the wind.

I blinked away motes and saw that the grenade had blown out two of the floor-to-ceiling picture windows. The wind was gale force.

I crawled away from it, not anxious to get sucked outside.

Hammett, still on the stairs, had to grab the railing so the gust didn't knock her over. I dug into my bag, pulling out the spare Sig, and unloaded on her. It took a few shots before I was able to adjust to the crosswind, but then I began pegging her like a tin bunny in a shooting gallery.

She dropped her gun, but the rounds didn't drop her, and I guessed she must have slathered herself with the body armor as well. So I went for the head shot.

That's when she charged me.

I tried to adjust, but I was dizzy and hurting; add the wind and my shot went wide, and then Hammett was throwing a tackle, lifting me up off of the ground, driving me toward the broken window.

---

Victor pries two spikes from his foot. The hot ooze of blood soaks through his sock, and he curses the bitch and her tricked-out chair.

She's long gone now, he's sure.

He's not happy.

He turns and hobbles back to the express elevators. Bodies litter the floor, blood pooling on light marble. Nikolai is still wailing, his leg dragging behind him as he tries to crawl.

Victor doesn't feel like carrying him, but although he wants to put a bullet in the worthless man's brain, he resists, instead kicking him in the ribs. "Shut up and pick up your weapon," he says to the man in Russian. "Be ready."

Dialing his wails down to whimpers, the man does as he's told.

"When Hammett steps off those elevators, shoot her." Victor has had enough. He's going to collect his transceiver.

He picks up an AR-15 off Sergei and hits the UP button. The chime sounds, and the elevator door slides open. He steps in just as shots squeeze out from Nikolai's position.

*What the hell?*

He peers out in time to see the cripple roll in from the opposite direction. Nikolai is shooting, but she is not dying. She rolls past the open elevator, leans down, and scoops the weapon from Peter's dead hands. She empties it into Nikolai.

She has her back to him, either not yet aware he's there or confident her chair will protect her.

He steps up behind her. Keeping his body out of range of whatever blade she might produce, he flings the assault rifle's shoulder strap over her head and yanks.

Her head slams against the back of the chair.

He keeps the pressure on. Once she stops struggling, he tips the chair forward and dumps her onto the floor.

She lies limp on the marble.

He levels his weapon on her, waiting for the slightest twitch.

A cough shakes her body. She's still alive.

His first inclination is to end her before she tries something else, but then he notices her earpiece.

This one might be more useful alive.

Victor hears a police radio crackle. Any second, the cops will be swarming the place.

He drags the cripple over to the express elevators and hits the call button, reopening the doors.

It's time for this debacle to end.

Hammett aches all over from being shot, and this little game has gone on long enough. The wind is howling and whistling, whipping through her hair. She body slams Chandler to the floor, pinning her down, and Chandler's gun bounces across the floor and out the window. Then Hammett reaches for her Spyderco knife, wanting nothing more in the world than to slit this bitch's throat, get the phone, and get the hell out of Dodge.

Chandler grabs her wrist, trying to leverage Hammett away, and Hammett drops a knee onto her stomach, provoking a lovely grunt of pain.

"Didn't you hear, Chandler?" she shouts above the wind, raising the blade up. "You're second-best. I'm number one."

"This…this is what you are," Chandler says, punching Hammett's knife hand.

Hammett almost laughs at the attempt, and then feels the spike of pain, accompanied by a roiling nausea. She looks at her hand and sees Chandler has stabbed her with a piece of silverware.

Chandler grins, her face manic. "You're forked."

Then Hammett's nose explodes when it meets Chandler's fist.

Fleming woke up to pain. Excruciating, unrelenting pain.

It took her back years, to waking up on the operating table, her shattered bones poking through her skin in so many places her legs looked like cacti. She screamed so hard her throat bled, screamed while the nurses scrambled to put her under, screamed even as she slipped into unconsciousness.

This pain was similar. Except she wasn't in a hospital. She was in an elevator. And her legs weren't the cause of her agony. It was her finger.

Her broken finger, that the Russian was twisting back and forth, pulling it and snapping it again and again.

Fleming tried to claw his face, his goddamn smiling eyes, but he easily slapped her hand away, twisting even harder, prompting the biggest scream of her life.

———————

Hammett pushed herself away from me, and I rolled to all fours, taking a quick look over my shoulder at the howling Chicago skyline, the building's edge less than two meters away.

My stomach twisted into a vertigo knot, and then I scrambled after Hammett. She was staring at the fork in her hand as if it had magically appeared. Her nose was a mashed tomato, leaking down her chin.

I bent down, reaching for my VORAX blade, when my head was pierced with the most horrible sound I'd ever heard. A scream in my earpiece. So sharp and shrill that it drowned out the whooshing wind.

*Fleming.*

———————

Victor twists the cripple's finger once more, grinning at the screams he provokes. Then he snatches the earpiece from her and shoves it into his own ear.

"You hear that, Chandler? That's your sister. You couldn't save your dear Kaufmann, but I'll give you a chance to stop her pain."

He twists so hard he hears the knuckle pop out of place. The high-pitched keening is probably waking up every dog in the building.

"I want the transceiver, Chandler."

---

For a moment, I was unsure what to do. Fleming's cries cut me to the core, and suddenly I was back in that helpless place, watching Kaufmann break down, lose his humanity, knowing it was me who'd betrayed him. In that instant of inaction, Hammett pounced on me, throwing a reverse kick. I managed to catch it on my shoulder, bunching up my muscles. She followed with a knife thrust, and I managed to block that, too.

Another scream threw off my concentration, and this time Hammett used a Muay Thai kick known as a *Kradot thip*—a jumping foot-thrust. It connected with my thigh, forcing me backward, backward toward the edge of the world.

"Don't give him shit!" Fleming cried out, followed by more shrieks of agony.

I took a quick glance behind me, the night wind slapping my face, the ninety-five-story drop so steep I couldn't see the ground.

Hammett took two steps toward me. She'd yanked out the fork and was slashing her knife in front of her, cutting the air. Not any martial arts move I was aware of, but terrifying nonetheless.

I dug the cell phone out of my pocket and held it up. "Come closer and I throw it off the building."

Hammett stopped, but her face morphed into a bloody sneer. "It will survive the fall."

"Maybe. But how long do you think it will take to find? If ever?"

I was liking the idea more and more. I had never asked for this responsibility in the first place. I didn't want to be the president's backup plan. I didn't want to have the fate of the world resting on me. Better to chuck the transceiver as hard as I could and hope it would be lost forever.

The elevator chimed, first on the floor, then in my ear. Victor stepped out, dragging a still-crying Fleming across the floor by her hand.

"Hold it," Hammett warned. "She's got the transceiver."

Victor scowled at her. "I know, you ass. And look what I've got." He raised up Fleming, holding her like a prize fish.

"Give me the phone, Chandler."

"Don't do it," Fleming gasped.

Victor kicked her, then dropped her to the floor and stepped on her neck. He unslung the AR15 around his chest and pointed it at Fleming's head. "The phone! Or she dies."

Fleming's eyes found mine. I saw fear there. But also resolve. She was willing to die so the transceiver was safe.

*I should be the same way.*

*I need to think of the greater good.*

*These maniacs can't have access to nuclear weapons.*

*I have to throw the phone away.*

*I have no other choice.*

*They're going to kill Fleming anyway. Fleming, and me.*

*The world is more important than we are.*

But I couldn't drop the phone.

I'd only known Fleming as Fleming for a short time, but I'd known her as Jacob for years.

I couldn't watch her die. I couldn't watch anyone else I cared about die. Never, ever again.

"Let her go," I said, with more bravery than I felt. "Or I'll drop it."

Hammett began to creep closer to me. I took a step back, my heels on the windowpane. For a millisecond I wondered if I should just keep going, plummet to my death with the phone. Then I wouldn't have to watch Fleming die, and this worst day of my life would be over.

But my tank still had a bit of hope in it. And where there's hope, there's always a way.

"Here's how it will work," I said, staring at Hammett. "You let Fleming go and throw me your gun, and I'll throw you the phone. Or I chuck it out the window. Am I bluffing, Hammett? Do you see anything on my face that indicates I'm lying?"

Hammett narrowed her eyes. "She's telling the truth."

"I will drop it, Victor. And you can spend a few months combing the entire block looking for it. That is, if someone doesn't pick it up and take it home."

"Do it," Hammett said.

Scowling, Victor released Fleming, then tossed his gun my way. It didn't reach me, coming to rest on the carpet two meters from my feet.

True to my word, I tossed him the phone.

Hard.

Real fucking hard.

Victor did what anyone would have done. He ducked.

Hammett and I both went for the gun at the same time. She reached it first, but I was ready with a punt to the head. She bunched up, and I connected with her shoulder, then drove an elbow down on the back of her neck.

"Broken!" Victor yelled. "The phone is broken!"

It was broken because that was the trac phone Fleming had given me. The transceiver was still in my backpack. As Hammett ate the ground, I got a hand around the sling of the MP9, tugging as hard as I could even as she grasped the butt of the weapon. I saw Fleming crawling toward us on her elbows, her face a stone mask of determination, and then Victor was on me, hands around my throat, his eyes bulging with rage.

He tugged me off of Hammett and pushed me back, back, toward the broken window.

Gunfire, behind Victor. Five or six shots.

*Oh…no…*

Although I was getting strangled and about to be thrown off the building, I strained to see what happened, blinking away the encroaching darkness.

*No...no...*

Hammett was standing over Fleming, the barrel of the MP9 smoking, Fleming still trying to slink away, leaving a thick streak of blood across the floor.

"Don't drop her, you idiot!" Hammett called. "The transceiver is in her backpack!"

Victor reached one hand down for the bag, and I raked my fingernails across his eyes, then tried to kick him in the crotch. He pushed me back farther. My feet were hanging in open air. I was going over the side of the building.

He released my throat and I fell off the ninety-fifth floor and into open space.

I had a moment of pure, animal terror, rivaling drowning, then I jerked to a stop and slammed into the side of the building. Pain yanked through my bad shoulder. My elbow was hooked around one of my rucksack's straps, and Victor held the other.

Legs kicking, feet scrambling to find purchase, I reached for Victor with my free hand, stretching to grab his arm or shirt. He swatted my attempt away and tugged down the zipper.

The stun gun began to slip out of the opening, then tumbled toward me.

I reached for it...

...missed.

Victor dug around. He pulled his hand out, the transceiver clutched in his fist. He gazed down at me, his eyes glinting.

"See you at the bottom."

Then he let go of the strap.

---

It was over.

Fleming was unarmed and outnumbered, and even if she'd had healthy legs before, they certainly weren't healthy now. She hadn't smeared liquid body armor on the backs of her legs, since they were already protected by her chair, and Hammett had shot them full of holes. Then Fleming had watched Chandler—poor, dear, heroic Chandler—fall out the window and felt something inside of her die.

"Hello, Fleming," Hammett said, gazing down at her. "Apparently you survived that fall in Milan. My my my, how pathetic your life must be."

Hammett nudged Fleming's legs, and she set her jaw to avoid crying out.

"Don't worry," Hammett said. "We're not going to kill you yet. We have one more use for you first." She turned to look at Victor, who had walked over.

"It wasn't working out between me and Chandler," he said. "So I had to drop her."

Victor eyed the MP9 dubiously, but Hammett was wiping it down with her shirttails, then she tossed it off to the side. "We carry her down in the elevator. If the police stop us, we're taking a wounded woman to an ambulance."

"What if she talks?" Victor asked.

"She won't talk," Hammett said.

Fleming saw Hammett's boot come down, and then everything went blessedly black.

*"You shouldn't fear the inevitable,"* The Instructor said. *"And it is inevitable that one day you'll die."*

For the second time that day, I was falling off a building into open air. But the Hancock Center was a lot taller than my apartment, and I had been in much better shape earlier.

Panic making it impossible to breathe, I hugged the rucksack to my chest like a teddy bear. Cold wind beat my face, my body. My fall felt slow, painfully slow, each fraction of a second stretching out into hellish, terrifying infinity. Tears streamed from my eyes and I saw nothing but a swirling mosaic of darkness and light.

Then something skimmed past my leg.

I didn't think, just grabbed it.

Fire seared my palm.

A cable! A goddamn lifeline!

*The window washers.*

An image flashed through my mind, earlier in the day, searching for a place to hide the phone, noticing the cables outside the restaurant windows, the ones that lowered the window washers' suspended scaffold.

I couldn't hold on—I was falling too fast—but I felt the cable or rope or whatever it was still whizzing by, still near. Thoughts blasted through my brain like machine-gun fire:

*Can't grab the scaffold—can't hold on—hit it square and I'm dead—thrust an arm through the rucksack strap—push it tight over my shoulder—one shot, just one shot at this—might rip my arm out of the socket—gotta try—scaffold rushing up at me—the whole city beneath my feet—dizzying height—stretching—reaching out with the other strap—timing it just right—even with the scaffold—streaking past—looping the strap around the corner winch bracket—*

A force ripped through my arm, my shoulder, my back, my neck. For a moment, all I felt was excruciating pain.

When my brain kicked back in, I realized I had stopped. Motes swam in front of me in the darkness, and I struggled to assess what had happened.

I hung on the side, one handle of the rucksack caught on a bracket at the base of the platform. The force of my fall had unseated the scaffold, and it listed sharply to one side, hanging from the safety cable. The wind and reverberation thrashed it against the side of the building.

I gripped the rucksack strap with every bit of strength I had left. It took a few seconds for my heart to catch up and feel as if it was part of my body again. It took longer for the scaffold's bucking motion to slow to a dangerous sway.

Then the rest caught up to me as well.

*Disbelief. Amazement. Exhilaration.*

*Terror. Panic.*

*Anger.*

*Loss. Sadness.*

*Pain.*

*Too many kinds of pain.*

Wind whipped around me, over me, through me, twisting me left and right. The backs of my eyes hurt like they'd been wrung out, and tears froze to ice on my cheeks. I no longer had the strength to sob, but my breath hitched painfully anyway, in my throat, in my chest, in my gut, as if it would never stop.

Fleming was gone, almost as soon as I'd found her. I could picture her body, crumpled on the floor of the restaurant, life draining from the holes Hammett had punched into her. She'd be dead soon, if she wasn't already. Just an anguished, lifeless face, staring into nothingness.

Like Kaufmann.

Kaufmann…Fleming…

*Oh, God.*

Maybe it didn't matter. Hammett had the phone. It was only a matter of time before she used it.

Maybe soon the world would cease to exist.

Maybe Kaufmann and Fleming had just escaped first.

Maybe I should let go of the strap and let everything fall away. Simple. Final.

Against all common sense, I chanced a look down.

Tiny pinpricks of light unfolded below me, as cold and far away as the stars. I should have felt panic, dizziness, the moment of weightlessness before the roller coaster plunges.

Instead, I felt nothing. I felt dead.

Over the wind's shriek, I heard the sound of canvas tearing, and I dropped several inches lower.

*The rucksack.*

I craned my neck, aching from the abrupt stop. My backpack had a tear in it. As I watched, the rip extended, making my heart leap up out of my throat. I thought I'd run out of adrenaline hours ago, but fear grabbed me, full body, and shook the living hell out of me.

If I feared death that much, I obviously wasn't ready to call it quits. At least not yet.

Keeping perfectly still, not moving my neck, I peered over at the building, hoping to see a window with a bunch of people staring and pointing.

Instead, the window was black, reflecting a mirror image of a terrified woman whose life was hanging by a thread.

Far away, I heard a car honk. I glanced down again, seeing the traffic beneath my feet. Too small to even look like toys. The wind kicked up, making me sway.

Another tearing sound.

Another small drop.

Another notch of sheer fucking terror.

Moving slowly, deliberately, I eased my free arm up over my head. I could barely touch the platform, but not enough to get a grip on it.

Instead, I cinched my fingers around the strap, and carefully removed it from around my armpit.

Which was when the tablet PC fell out of the tear in the bag.

Not stopping to think, my other hand lashed out, pinching the corner of the PC before it dropped out of range. If I were to live through this, I needed the tablet to find Hammett.

I took a deep, cold breath, let it out slowly, then did a one-armed pull-up on the strap, grateful I could rely on my good arm. Slipping the tablet PC snugly into the back waistband of my pants, I grabbed the bracket the strap was hooked over. It was freezing metal with a sharp edge, but it would hold me. I released the strap with my other hand, gripped the platform, and did a slow, painful chin-up.

On the platform was a locked metal box for cleaning supplies, an automatic winch system, and a dual rope, which I guessed was for the Bosun's chair—a pulley system that carried workers to and from the platform.

I let my body down again, moving carefully, and lifted my right leg up to get a heel onto the platform.

Then the wind hit.

A freezing updraft, actually lifting me away from the platform. I lost my right-hand grip and clung to the bracket with four fingers of my left hand.

Three fingers…

The wind wouldn't let up.

*Oh, sweet Jesus…*

Two fingers…

Then, finally, when I couldn't hold on any longer, the wind died down—

—causing me to swing toward the building—

—pulling my fingers off the platform.

For a crazy millisecond, I hung in the air like a trapeze artist between partners.

A whimper escaped my mouth, and I frantically scrambled for a handhold on something, anything, catching the torn hole in the rucksack.

My fist closed around the canvas, increasing the rip, making the hole larger, the rucksack tearing down the middle. I was sure it would pull right in half, but at a double-sewn seam, the tearing stopped.

I dangled, one-handed, above ninety-four floors of open space, unable to catch my breath. Then I clasped my other hand around the rucksack and waited for another fierce wind to assault me.

The wind didn't come. But something dark and heavy slipped out of the hole—*oh hell no, the smoke grenade*—and smacked me right between the eyes.

It hit hard enough to bring out more stars than there already were. My grip slipped, my hands burning down a length of strap to the very end. For a long moment, I twisted in one direction, and my dizzy head spun in the other. My fingers cramped, begging for relief, and it almost seemed like a good idea just to let go and be done with it.

Then the impact confusion passed, chased away by a jolt of adrenaline, a lot like waking up suddenly when you realized you were late and had overslept.

Hand over hand, I inched my way up the backpack, eyeing the hole, anticipating the moment the rucksack would totally give out and send me sailing down to the pavement.

But the moment never happened, and once again I gripped the platform and eased up my right heel.

A minute later, I was lying on my back, chest heaving, the cold air freezing the sweat on my body. Something midway between a laugh and a sob breached my lips, and I stared up the side of the building, up into the night sky, feeling a deep-core sense of relief that I'd never experienced before.

Then I set my eyes on the ropes.

Thin rope was impossible to ascend without proper equipment, such as a Bosun's chair. But the dual ropes might be thick enough for me to make the climb.

I let my heart rate return to a manageable level, then I sat up and squinted into the darkness above me. Eight meters, maybe less, to the ninety-fifth floor and the broken window.

After the day I'd had, piece of cake.

I stood up on the platform, legs shaky, feeling very much like I was riding a surfboard. The ropes were each ten millimeters thick with braided nylon sheaths. I stretched my sore hands up over my head and sandwiched the ropes together, letting them hold my body weight. Then I clamped my legs around the dual rope and began to inchworm up.

When I reached the halfway point, I almost began to laugh at how easy this was.

Then the wind kicked up again.

I crossed my knees, locking them together, holding on for dear life as the gust blew me sideways until I was on a forty-five-degree angle to the ground, staring down at the tiny traffic on the street below. I was terrified, for sure, but the truly frightening moment happened when the wind died down.

That's when I began to swing.

I saw it coming before it happened and could only watch helplessly as momentum kicked in and I picked up speed, heading right for the Hancock building.

I hit one of the reinforced windows so hard it felt like it knocked out my fillings. The impact was brutal, making my entire left side go momentarily numb. Then I began to twirl uncontrollably, faster and faster, until I couldn't hold my position any longer. I began to slide down the rope, my hands and thighs burning until I had to let go.

Then I was unattached to anything, plummeting toward the ground.

I landed on the scaffolding platform, right on my butt, an instant pain shooting from my coccyx up to the base of my neck.

For a moment I just lay there and soaked in the fact that I was still alive. Waiting for my orientation to return, I stared up at the swaying ropes.

*Piece of cake, my ass.*

I carefully stood up, and before I let my brain talk me out of it, I again began to ascend the ropes. I moved faster than before, trying to get to the broken window before another gust blew me off the building.

Halfway up, the wind began to challenge me once again. I kept climbing, upping my pace, gritting my teeth as the building gale slapped me around.

*A little farther...*

I could see into the ninety-fifth floor, the interior restaurant caked with broken glass and bits of exploded tables, carpet, and floorboards.

*Almost there...almost there...*

The wind died down again, and I began to swing toward the building. But this time, I was heading straight for the opening.

At least, that's what it looked like until I got close enough to realize I was about half a meter short.

Sticking out my feet like I was rappelling, I braced myself for impact.

Before I hit, my body turned. First sideways, then one hundred eighty degrees.

I was going to smack into the side of the building backward.

*If I live through this, I swear I'll never set foot into a building higher than three stories.*

Once the rope was perpendicular to the ground, I released it. Then I twisted my body in the air, momentum carrying me toward the opening, stretching out as far as I could—

—and catching the edge of the window frame.

Buoyed by the amazement of surviving, I quickly chinned up, threw a heel over, and pulled myself onto the ninety-fifth floor.

Hammett and Victor were gone.

And so was Fleming.

I set my chin and headed for the fire exit, knowing what I had to do.

It was time to visit my parents.

*"There's a time to mourn,"* The Instructor said, *"and a time to fight."*

I stopped at gas station near the Indiana border and bought a bottle of Advil, some caffeine pills, and a black T-shirt to replace the torn top I had on. I also had a rip in my jeans—Hammett's jeans—but bottoms were harder to come by.

When I arrived at my destination, I parked the Humvee in the empty visitors' lot. As expected, the cemetery was closed. But the wrought iron fence was easy to climb, especially compared to everything else I'd been through tonight. My individual pains had all conspired to combine, and my entire body throbbed. But I knew it was going to get worse.

I let my feet carry me along the path I'd taken many times. The tombstones were hard to read in the darkness, but I didn't need to see the names. I remembered the location. The names were probably fake anyway, if what The Instructor had told me about my early upbringing was factual. Hard to tell. It seemed nothing I had learned to count on in my life was true.

Well, almost nothing.

I wound through large family monuments and small, humble benches, the feeble glow from the back of the neighboring strip mall my only light. A cornfield stretched on the other side of the rural cemetery, dried stalks rattling in the wind, the blades of a wind turbine turning eerily slowly against the dark, lonely sky.

I found the gray marble stone I was searching for. For a moment, I could only stand and stare, my chest aching, experiencing a pain deeper than the agony caused by anything else that had happened today. I'd relied on a handful of people in my life, and I had none left. Not my dear Kaufmann, not that psycho prick, Cory, not my sister, Fleming. I imagined what Hammett and Victor were doing to her, if she was even still alive. I also imagined what Hammett would do with a damn cell phone that could blow up the world.

How could everything have gone to hell so quickly?

When I was a girl, I was happy. Whatever doubts I harbored about my assigned parents' real names, I couldn't doubt that they'd loved me. I'd felt it every day. Now standing at their grave, I longed to be close to them once again. I longed to lie down on the leaf-strewn grass beneath their headstone and cry myself to sleep.

"Hi, Mom. Hey, Dad. I know I don't visit you guys too often. But I think of you, a lot. I learned…I just learned…that you aren't my real parents. That's OK, though. You'll always be my parents to me."

A coyote howled in the distance. Mournful. Lonely. Thunder rumbled, a storm moving in. I reached over and brushed a stray leaf from the tombstone.

"I screwed up. Big-time. People have died. And more people are going to, before this is over." I stared up into the dark, black night, eyes glassy, trying to find the words.

"Part of me just wants to give up. I hurt…I hurt so bad right now. But I need to make this right. It's stupid, but do you remember when you were teaching me how to ride a bike? I was seven years old, and I kept falling off, and I skinned my knee and was crying and wanted to quit and Mom, you kept telling me, 'As long as you keep trying, honey, you won't fail.' And Dad, you smiled and put a bandage on me and said, 'Stiff upper lip, soldier. Failure is not an option.' "

The tears were coming freely now, and I didn't brush them away.

"So I'm gonna keep trying, Mom. Dad. I'm gonna try my damnedest."

I turned and started for the cemetery garage only a few gravesites away. It held a garden tractor for mowing the grass, a backhoe, and garden tools for trimming and digging. The door was locked, but the simple side-hung windows easily lifted from their tracks. I grabbed the top frame and swung myself in feet first, gritting my teeth at the pain seizing my…well, every part of my whole damn body.

The tiny structure smelled of dried grass, dead flowers, and gasoline. I located the tool rack, selected a shovel, and let myself out the door. Once back beside my parents' grave, I finally swiped at tears winding down my cheeks. Then I shoved the blade into the earth. Sweat slicked my skin as I cut through sod and scooped out shovelful after shovelful of black dirt. The sharp stab of pain in my chest grew into an all-encompassing ache, a pain I couldn't escape, and I no longer even tried.

Three feet down, my shovel hit something hard. I kept working, uncovering the large fiberglass box, digging out the edges to expose the whole thing, then stepping down into the hole. I lifted off the lid.

The red fabric was still inside, untouched from when I'd buried it originally. I pulled it all out, and then lifted the small Evinrude boat motor free.

My upper lip was stiff. Failure was not an option.

*"I've done my best to train you," The Instructor said. "The rest is on your shoulders. You can either sink or swim."*

Fleming didn't have to open her eyes to know she was on some kind of boat. Either that, or death felt like the rolling toss of waves, accompanied by a lilting sickness in her belly.

The anchor she was handcuffed to was another clue, as was the distinctive smell of a large body of fresh water, she'd guess Lake Michigan.

*A boat, then. Death will have to wait.*

She managed to force her lids open, only to be rewarded with claustrophobic darkness. Fleming felt around with her free hand, the one the Russian had mangled. Each bump made her gasp. The pain was bad, but she'd had worse. She kept probing.

It turned out she was in a small enclosure, probably a pantry or closet. The anchor was a modern one, maybe half a meter high. Fleming gave it a shove with her shoulder, figured it weighed about forty pounds.

In her condition, it may as well have been four hundred.

Using her unbroken thumb, she gingerly prodded at her legs. They were bandaged, but only to control the bleeding. The wounds were open, some slugs still lodged in her flesh. They obviously didn't intend for her to live long enough to heal.

The last she remembered, she'd been in the restaurant at the top of the Hancock building. Hammett was shooting her, kicking her. And the Russian, Victor...

Victor had thrown Chandler from the window.

Fleming closed her eyes once more. That image was burned onto her retinas and ten times worse than any physical pain. Chandler had been everything to Fleming these last years. Unable to be in the field after her accident, she'd lived through Chandler. She'd gotten to know her sister better than she'd known anyone.

Fleming loved her.

And now she was gone.

Fleming let the tears come, not even trying to check their flow. But even in her anguish, she held on to a certainty. If she was the one who'd died, Chandler would never let those responsible walk away.

*And neither will I.*

Fleming had wanted another chance in the field, and she'd gotten it. Now it was up to her to make Hammett and her Russian stooge pay.

*You're an operative. Use your training.*

She continued her exploration of the space. One of the sides of the enclosure moved—the door...and it wasn't locked.

*Oh, so I'm so harmless you don't even have to lock me in?*

*Big mistake.*

*Big fucking mistake.*

---

Victor reclines in a white leather swivel chair at the helm, one hand on the wheel, and navigates the Sea Ray 610 Sundancer across the expansive darkness of Lake Michigan. The water is choppy, the pickup in wind and rumble in the distance signaling a storm. Suddenly he's glad to have the nineteen-meter yacht, even if it is too big for his current needs.

Of course, when he arranged for it, he assumed he'd be traveling with six more men. Such a waste, dying so badly.

*That's what they get for being incompetent.*

He pulls in a deep breath, double-checks his GPS coordinates, and turns up the state-of-the-art sound system. Rachmaninoff swells through the room. Passionate. Powerful. Russian. And loud enough to rattle the instrument panel.

*This is the life.*

He still wants to kill Hammett and knows she aims to kill him. As he stares through the windshield and out over the black, undulating water, he imagines how he'll do it. A knife would be fun, carving her up, bit by bit, until she begs him to end it. He'd like to hear Hammett beg. That would be the ultimate turn-on. And he always had a thing for knives.

Of course, since it's Hammett he's plotting to kill, he'll probably just shoot her. He reflexively checks the Glock on his hip.

*Yes, shooting is best. Anything else is too risky. I've seen what she can do.*

However Victor does it, he's content to leave her alive for now. Now that they have the transceiver, things are a little more relaxed between them. She did as he told her, bringing her sister along, and for the past hour, she's been on the phone with his tech team, figuring out how the transceiver works, leaving him to relax and think about what he'll do next.

He's a rich man now. He can do whatever he wants.

Hell, maybe he'll start off by getting laid.

He smiles, liking that idea. The only question is which sister does he have a taste for? Hammett? Or her crippled look-alike belowdecks?

As if on cue, Hammett saunters into the cockpit, clad in silk and leather. She is sexy despite her battered face, or maybe because of it. Her cheeks are flushed and her eyes gleaming, and for a moment, he half expects her to start stripping right there. Instead she holds up the transceiver.

He turns down the music.

"I've figured out the launch application." Her tongue flicks out, running across her lower lip. "Let's nuke a city."

---

*How much did it cost to put teak flooring in a boat?*

Fleming shook her head, hoping to rid herself of inane thoughts. The pain was messing with her mind. She focused on her senses, trying to concentrate.

She was in a cabin, a platform bed to her left, stairs to the right. Classical music came from above deck, Rachmaninoff, no doubt the Russian's choice, and she could hear the slap of waves against the bow. Fleming also detected a growl of thunder, but no rain. At least not yet. She could smell a hint of it on the air.

Before she went any farther, Fleming had something to do. Something awful. She sucked up her courage, then took a look at her hand.

*Oh...boy.*

Two of her fingers were bent at crazy, unnatural angles and swollen like overcooked hot dogs. Her thumb, pinky, and ring finger remained unscathed, and if Fleming bit her lower lip to stop from crying out, she could pinch them together like a lobster claw.

But that wouldn't be enough. For her to have a chance, she needed to have a greater range of motion in her hand.

She started with her index finger. That one appeared to be in slightly better shape. At the second knuckle, it bent backward at almost a ninety-degree angle. Fleming moved her hand to the anchor, gripping the digit tightly, squeezing her eyes shut—

*—this is going to be bad—*

—and then bent it the right way.

There was a sound like a walnut being cracked, and then the wave of pain hit. She had to turn her head and bite her left biceps to keep from howling. When the worst of it faded, she peeked a teary eye at her middle finger.

Two bends in this one, each in the opposite direction. It looked like a bruised, misshapen Z. Fleming knew the thing to do was pull on it to align the bones, then snap them back into place. But neither of her hands moved.

*All pain is temporary. Bad as it gets, I can get through it.*

Her body still refused to obey.

*Do it. Just do it, goddamnit.*

Such a small part of the body, a finger. Yet when she tugged it straight, the entire essence of Fleming's being was reduced to white-hot agony. Her vision swirled, and then the darkness came in from all sides, making her already-aching head vibrate like a church bell being rung. The little bones inside her middle finger were so shattered it reminded Fleming of a beanbag.

She chanced a look, both hands quivering. Her middle finger was more or less back into position, but it still needed a lot of work.

*There's no way I'm touching that again. I'll make do.*

Fleming dragged herself through the closet door, going from teak flooring to thick carpet. She sank into the pile like it was deep sand, fighting the weight of the anchor for every inch. It was slow going, and she needed to be quick. If Hammett or the Russian discovered she'd escaped the closet, there wasn't much she could do to protect herself, let alone bring the hurt to them.

And she wanted to deliver some hurt.

What Fleming needed was a weapon.

She struggled between the galley and a seating area and stopped at the base of the stairs, straining to catch her breath. The seven small steps loomed above her like Mount Everest. As she sized up the challenge ahead, her gaze rested on the large cabinet seated into the wall. It was marked EMERGENCY.

Gritting her teeth, she plopped the anchor on the first step, then dragged her body up after it. The steps were wood, hard, making her miss the thick pile carpet on the floor. A chrome handrail framed one side, the perfect height if she'd been standing. But as things were, it was as good as worthless.

She mounted the second the same way, then the third and fourth. When she reached the fifth, she could reach the emergency cabinet. Leaning on one hip, she gripped the latch.

The boat rolled hard to the starboard side, almost sending her careening down the steps. She clung to the anchor with her good hand and tried to quiet her stomach before reaching for the box again.

This time she managed to get it open before another heave from the waves. And as she clung, her eyes locked onto a silver blanket, a waterproof radio, and a bright orange, plastic gun.

That would do.

She pulled out the signal gun and loaded a magnesium flare. Fleming had never fired one before, but the mechanism was simple. Point and shoot.

She tucked the gun in her waistband and turned her attention to the remaining two steps. The boat continued to pitch and sway, and the climb seemed to take forever. With each sound, she braced herself, expecting Hammett or Victor to suddenly appear and put a bullet in her, ending it all.

Fleming made it to the deck, lifting the anchor, placing it in front of her, then dragging her body after.

Lift, place, drag.

Lift, place, drag.

Voices carried on the wind, over music and waves.

She tucked herself behind a small beverage fridge and strained to hear.

"No, Victor! I love Paris!" Hammett. Her tone was a mock whine.

"You women and Paris." A man. The Russian, Victor.

"How about London?" Hammett said. "Rains all the damn time."

"I can live without London. Do it."

A chill ran the length of Fleming's body. The transceiver. Hammett had figured out the launching sequence.

*And she was launching a nuclear strike on London.*

She struggled to breathe. *Please, let me be wrong. Let it not be true.*

Once again, the boat rolled hard to the side, and she held on to the side of the refrigerator.

If they were indeed launching a strike, Fleming had to find a way to stop them. No doubt they were armed. The cheap plastic flare gun in her crooked hand suddenly seemed like a cruel joke.

"Why don't you try to steady this damn boat? I'll look up the latitude and longitude." The heels of Hammett's boots clicked across teak. A second later, she let out a startled noise. "Oh, hell. That bitch."

Fleming gripped the flare gun. She was almost certain the refrigerator blocked her from their view. Hammett couldn't have seen her. But if not her, who could she be talking about?

"What is it?" A second set of shoes scuffed over the floor, Victor joining Hammett at the cockpit's control panel.

"Look for yourself."

"Chandler!" Victor shouted.

Fleming's heart stuttered.

"It can't be her. It has to be one of those pigeons."

"You really think a pigeon is going to fly out over the lake, Victor? It's Chandler, and she's coming right at us."

———————————

Hammett grabs a set of binoculars from the cockpit and races out of the deckhouse.

"Hold her steady!" she yells at Victor through the side windshield. Then she grips the guardrail and walks along the narrow port gunwale, stepping onto the yacht's expansive, twelve-meter bow. It's a perfect place to sunbathe, but not a perfect place to stand during choppy water. Especially when it's wet, and the rain had begun to fall. She plants her feet and scans the horizon.

The water churns white behind them, the Chicago skyline barely visible through the storm clouds rolling east over the lake. She searches the waves in the direction of the blip, but sees nothing.

Impossible.

She looks again, sweeping slower this time. Lightning flashes, and the rain kicks up.

"Where in the hell is she?"

As soon as the question leaves her lips, Hammett knows the answer. The tracking devices don't show height...and they don't show depth, either.

Chandler is coming at them from under the water. She's using scuba gear. Or, considering her speed, a submersible.

*No problem. I can deal with that.*

She makes her way back into the cockpit and grabs a duffel.

Victor glances at her and raises his brows.

"She's underwater," Hammett tells him. "Kill the engine, and let her come." She pulls two grenades from the bag. "Are there more in the staterooms?"

"Yes," he answers, but the lazy bastard doesn't move his ass off the swivel chair.

"Then get them, damn it."

She grabs the tablet PC out of the duffel before she spins around and returns to the boat's bow. Chandler's blip is nearly below them now. Time for Hammett to give her sister the welcome she deserves.

She pulls the pin on one of the grenades and throws it into the waves.

The explosion is powerful enough for her to feel the concussion shake the hull and vibrate in her chest. Water erupts into the air, meeting the rain falling from above.

She throws another off the starboard side, right where the blip should be.

The *whump* hits the ship like a slap from an angry god, causing it to pitch, then roll. Hammett points the deck spotlight on the water and smiles when she sees something float to the surface.

*Hell. It's a salmon. Son of a—*

"Freeze!"

Hammett glances portside, sees her disabled sister holding an anchor in one hand and a flare gun in the other. The image is so ludicrous, she begins to laugh.

"I want the transceiver," Fleming says. Her hand is shaking badly.

"Or what?" Hammett asks. "You'll signal for help?"

"How about I shoot you with a flare instead? Magnesium burns at three thousand degrees, and I'm aiming at your fat head."

Hammett considers her next move. Getting hit with a flare doesn't sound like a good time. She has a .45 in her shoulder holster, under her jacket.

"Fair enough," Hammett says. "I'll give you the phone."

She casually slips a hand into her coat.

"Hold it! I saw you put the phone in your side pocket. Take your hand out slowly, and give me the goddamn phone."

Hammett blows a snort of air out of her nostrils, annoyed. They really don't have time for this. But, impaired as she obviously is, Fleming is one of the Hydra sisters. Hammett respects the training she's had and follows her orders, slowly holding up the phone.

"Now toss it to me," Fleming says.

"How about instead you toss me the flare gun," Hammett smiles wide, "or I'll press the touch screen and destroy London?"

---

Fleming wasn't sure what to do. She should probably take the shot, but her aim wasn't steady, and she had no idea how accurate flares were.

Last she checked, there were more than seven and a half million people in London. Their best chance at survival depended on the next decision Fleming made.

"What the hell?"

Now Victor was coming across the gunwale, reaching for his sidearm.

Fleming had no choice.

She had to take the shot.

She aimed.

Let out a breath.

Squeezed the trigger.

The flare exploded out of the gun. Hammett ducked below its arc, and it sailed out across the water, a bright orange streak, before falling into the lake a hundred meters away.

Then Victor was on her, kicking the useless gun away, putting his foot on her chest, pointing the Glock in her face.

"You lose," Hammett said.

Fleming glanced at her, and watched as—

*Oh no.*

—she pressed the screen. "In seven minutes, London bridge is falling down."

Tears erupted from Fleming's eyes. She could imagine all of the people, the innocents, the children, swallowed up by an atomic fireball. Black-and-white images of Hiroshima and Nagasaki flashed through her mind. The horror. The tragedy. The misery. The senseless waste.

*All because I couldn't aim a goddamn flare gun.*

She stared up at Victor, into the barrel of his pistol, trembling and broken and beaten but still defiant.

And then she saw something.

Something above Victor.

Something black and red and plummeting down to earth like Satan getting booted out of heaven.

*Chandler!*

---

Flying an ultralight trike at night was hard enough. Especially this junker, which had been buried on top of my parents for six years and had seen much better days. I throttled the modified Evinrude motor, slowing down the rear prop, and took another glance at my PC to see if I was on course. According to the blip, I was right on target. But I couldn't see a damn thing below me, and missing would be deadly. I was too far out to swim back to shore.

I had to be at a high enough altitude to prevent Hammett from seeing me coming and so I could get the drop on them. The altimeter had some water damage, being exacerbated by the rain coming down. It said I was at eleven thousand feet. I was betting my life that it was right.

Then I saw the flare, bright orange, my own personal landing strip.

I killed the engine, ditched the PC because I had no way to carry it, and unbuckled my seat belt. Beretta in hand, I rolled out of my seat, falling into open sky.

As soon as I dropped away from the ultralight, I pulled the ripcord on my parachute. It took about nine hundred feet for it to fully open, so I was cutting it close.

I quickly fell through the haze, then saw the lights below me, following them to a white yacht. My chute deployed, making me jerk and rock in my harness. Still clutching the gun, I snatched the brake handles. Once I had control I steered toward the boat, sighting Victor on the bow. Victor, Hammett, and...

*Fleming!*

My aim was for shit, but I emptied my magazine at Victor, forcing him away from my sister. He fired back, his bullets whizzing past me, and then I had my feet out in front of me, and I planted both on his chest just as I hit my buckle release.

Victor went flying, and I rolled onto the bow, out of control, crashing into the raised pulpit, the guardrails stopping me from falling out.

I turned around, scanning for Fleming, and instead saw Hammett, drawing a gun from her leather jacket, pointing it at my head.

I fired at her. No rounds left. Then I reached for the extra magazine in my pocket and found my pocket had torn off.

---

Hammett doesn't believe this is happening. Chandler swoops onto the deck like a bird of prey, firing wildly, then knocks down Victor.

She unholsters her .45 and aims carefully, anxious to put this unkillable bitch out of her misery.

"Hey!"

Hammett looks to the right, sees Fleming, who has crawled up next to her.

"Anchors away, Sis!"

Then she sees the anchor, Fleming swinging it like an Olympic hammer at Hammett's legs. She jumps back, but not in time, and one of the pointed flukes catches her calf, digging a bloody rent across it.

Hammett slams into the bow, her gun falling overboard, the transceiver skipping across the deck. She quickly pulls the Spyderco blade from her sheath, ready to gut Fleming, then sees Chandler coming closer.

*Fine. First Chandler. Then the cripple.*
Hammett stands to meet her sister.

---

Fleming locked eyes on the transceiver as it skittered aft, down the bow.

"The phone!" she yelled at Chandler. "That psycho launched a nuclear attack on London!"

Then she crawled after it, her legs begging for mercy, her swollen hand slapping torturously against the teak as she dragged her broken body, and the anchor, closer and closer.

A wave hit, splashing over the port side, cold water spraying her in the face. The boat tilted, and the phone slid back toward Fleming. She reached out her broken hand, and it bounced off her screaming fingertips, sliding off the bow—

—across the narrow gunwale—

—and skidding onto the stern, where it came to a stop at the edge of the transom. Two more inches and the lake would have it.

Fleming pushed herself harder, fighting the pain, using the handrail to pull herself and the anchor along the gunwale, past the deckhouse, across the starboard-side windshield, and finally flopping onto the stern next to a cheap, folding metal deck chair.

The boat heaved up, then down, taking Fleming's stomach with it. She bit back the rising gorge and got within two meters of the phone, so close she could see the bright glow of the touch screen counting down in large, red numbers.

3:55...3:54...

She continued her trek toward it.

*Almost there. Almost...*

That's when her anchor got snagged on a cleat, preventing her from getting any closer.

———————

I lifted my knee and pulled the VORAX knife from its sheath, focusing on Hammett. The boat rocked gently, back and forth, and my stance was wider than normal so I didn't fall over. Fleming, the boat, the transceiver, the guns on the deck, Victor—none of it mattered. The whole world was nothing but me and Hammett.

And I was going to kill her.

She lunged at me with her Spyderco blade, almost a fencing move. I parried appropriately, steel clanging against steel, the impact so hard and fast it made a spark. The bow was slippery, but there was enough space for us to circle each other.

"You're like a cockroach," Hammett said, her eyes venomous. "You just won't die."

I cut in close, slashing at her face, then back-slashing at her knife hand. Hammett pulled back, my attack narrowly missing her, and then dropped to one knee and cut me across the chest. But liquid body armor worked as well with blades as it did with bullets, especially as hard as Hammett was striking. I popped her under the chin with my left hand, making her stagger back, and then did a quick spin kick and solidly connected with her cheek.

Hammett fell backward onto her ass. She stared up at me with a look of shock.

"But... I'm better than you. The Hydra reports..."

"...are years old," I interrupted. "That was then. This is now. And now, right now, I'm going to kick your ass, cut you into pieces, and feed you to the fish."

I took a step forward and then noticed Victor, coming at me from the side.

———————

Fleming pulled, hard as she could. No good. Her handcuff chain was wedged under the stern cleat.

She turned her attention to the transceiver, resting on the very edge of the transom.

2:12...2:11...

Fleming reached for it, stretching out her arms as far as they could go.

Not enough.

The cell phone was still a foot out of her grasp.

Fleming looked around the stern for something to extend her reach, and her eyes locked on the deck chair. She grabbed it with her thumb and pinky, but it was a folding model, and it snapped closed around her broken fingers.

Her scream was drowned out in the clapping of thunder.

———————

Once Victor gets up, the rage overpowers him. His only goal in life to choke the living shit out of Chandler, make her pay for all she has put him through.

She's preoccupied with Hammett, so Victor sprints at her, grinning, already picturing her neck breaking between his hands.

Chandler spins around and lashes out at him—*oops, she has a knife*—and Victor quickly dodges back.

"Ha! You missed!" he yells.

But the words don't sound right.

Because they aren't coming out of his mouth.

They're coming out the gaping slit in his throat.

He brings his hands up to his neck, feels something hard and wet. *That's...*

*That's my thoracic vertebra.*

That's also his last thought, and then he flops over and bleeds out onto the bow.

———————

Hammett watches Victor drop, and she stares at Chandler and feels something she hasn't felt in a very long time.

*Fear. I'm afraid of her.*

The Spyderco knife isn't enough. Hammett needs a gun. No, she needs a goddamn bazooka.

*Or some grenades.*

*There are grenades in the staterooms.*

She sprints aft, over the windshield and the roof of the deckhouse, dropping onto the stern. Hammett sees Fleming, straining to reach for something.

*The transceiver!*

Then Chandler is on the roof, jumping down—

—and a swell hits the boat, making it roll starboard, so fierce it knocks Hammett and Chandler to the deck.

Hammett wants the transceiver.

*But Chandler is in the way.*

*Indestructible, angry, scary-as-hell Chandler.*

Hammett scurries away, heading belowdecks.

———

1:19...1:18...

The wave unhooked the handcuff chain from where it had been hung up on the starboard stern cleat, and Fleming was free. She tugged her battered hand out of the folding chair and strained to grab the phone—

—missing as it plopped into the dark water.

Fleming quickly glanced at Chandler, and the two locked eyes.

Chandler's eyes told her, "*No, please don't.*"

Fleming's answered back. "*You know I have to.*"

And then she pushed the anchor over the transom and sank beneath the waves.

———————————

Watching Fleming go after the phone, I realized what it all meant.

All of our training. All of our sacrifices. All of the pain we'd endured.

We were the good guys.

Not because our government used us like pawns in some grand, worldwide espionage game.

Not because we could kill on command.

Not because we were unfeeling, uncaring machines, programmed to follow orders.

We were the good guys because we did the right thing.

No matter the cost.

Which was why I dived into the water after her.

———————————

Fleming sank fast, the anchor dragging her down into the cold, murky depths. She managed a deep breath before she went over and knew from experience it would last about ninety seconds.

Ninety seconds left to live.

Ninety seconds to save more than seven million.

The water was freezing, black, and when she hit the bottom, the pressure in her ears was excruciating. She pinched her nostrils with her thumb and pinky, equalizing the pressure, and figured she was perhaps thirty, thirty-five feet deep.

Lucky. Some parts of Lake Michigan were over nine hundred feet deep.

Fleming squinted, looking for the light of the phone, turning in a complete circle.

*Nothing. There's nothing. It's darker than a grave down here. The phone could be right next to me and I still wouldn't—*

*There!*

Two meters away, three, tops. She could make out the glow-ing red touch screen.

0:57...0:56...0:55...

Fleming began to crawl toward it, ignoring the pain, dragging the anchor through the muck behind her.

---

I decided, right then, that I truly hated water.

The icy blackness fought me, not letting me in. I swam down two meters, but I couldn't get any deeper. I was too buoyant.

It was my lungs. Filled with air, it was like trying to sink with two basketballs.

I peered down, not knowing how deep it was, unable to see Fleming or the phone.

And I made a choice.

*If the air in my lungs is stopping me, I need to get rid of it.*

I blew out a big breath, about half of my reserve, and then continued my descent.

---

Hammett hurries past the bridge, hearing the marine radio crackle. The coast guard is hailing the ship that shot the flare.

*Damn Fleming.*

*Damn Fleming, and damn Chandler, and damn this entire op.*

*It's time to cut my losses and get the hell out of here.*

*But first...*

Hammett barges into the stateroom, finds the duffel bag filled with grenades.

Four of them.

More than enough.

_____

0:11…0:10…

Dizzy from exertion and oxygen deprivation, Fleming reached the phone. She picked it up in her bad hand.

0:09…0:08…

Bringing it over to the anchor, she used her good hand to exit the countdown screen, bringing up the manual override.

Because the nuke had been launched from this transceiver, this transceiver was the only one that could disarm it. It was a simple, four-digit code.

Fleming accessed the keypad, finger raised.

0:07…0:06…

*Oh, hell. Brain fart.*

*What the hell is that code?*

0:05…0:04…

*Think! You designed the damn thing!*

*Duh!*

Fleming punched it in: 5-9-3-1.

*Missile disarmed.*

She smiled in the darkness. Then she turned the phone upside down, looking what the numbers spelled.

IE65

Legs.

And then Fleming started to laugh.

*I did it.*

*I really did it.*

*Hell yeah!*

*Ladies and gentlemen, boys and girls, the worthless cripple who got shoved behind a desk has saved London!*

As the air bubbled out of her lungs, Fleming felt no fear. No panic.

Her legs and ribs and hand no longer hurt.

All she felt was joy.

Pure joy.

And that was a damn good way to die.

Then something grabbed her in the darkness.

---

Dizzy, my lungs screaming for relief, I continued to swim downward, into the deep, not knowing where the hell I was going until my face was bathed by something warm.

Bubbles.

I followed them, then made out the tiny spot of light only a few meters away.

Fleming. Still handcuffed to the anchor. The transceiver in her hand.

I fought to reach her, struggling against the water, mustering up my last bit of strength. Much as I feared what was coming—the terrible panic and unbearable pain of my lungs filling with liquid—I had to save her, or die trying.

I grabbed her arm and tugged. Maybe the two of us, both swimming hard as we could, would be able to get her to the surface.

Fleming shook her head, then pointed a crooked finger up, her eyebrows furrowing in the soft glow of the phone.

*She wants me to leave her.*

I pulled her again, but this time she shoved me back, shaking her head.

We stared at each other for a moment. I watched her face relax. She showed me the phone.

MISSILE DISARMED.

Then she mouthed, quite clearly, "I love you."

I threw my arms around her, hugging her, hugging her so hard and never, ever wanting to let go.

And then I remembered my jeans.

*Hammett's jeans.*

Body shaking from lack of air, my thoughts beginning to scramble, I felt along the pants seam of the denim and found it.

A wire.

Even nearly dead, I could pick a handcuff lock. I popped her wrist free, thinking that maybe we actually could make it out of this—

Then the lake exploded.

The shock wave hit me hard, knocking the precious bit of air out of my lungs. Making my ears pop and ring, and rattling my body so hard I bit my tongue.

*Grenades.*

I covered up Fleming with my body, and another shockwave hit.

And another.

And another.

By now, I had no choice. I had to breathe, and my body sucked in the lake.

And then I was back on Victor's kitchen table.

Back at Hydra training.

Back in Cory's car as the water came in.

My whole body shook in panic, and I choked and tried to cough, and once again I was going to die a mindless, panicked animal.

That's when I felt it.

My hand.

My sister, holding my hand.

And for the briefest moment, I had the childhood I had always wanted. A safe, caring home and a sister who loved me.

I clasped my fingers in hers and let the water take me.

*"Sometimes you win, and sometimes you lose," The Instructor said. "Winning is better."*

The first thing I was aware of was an antiseptic smell. Then I opened my bleary eyes to a bright light and immediately gasped for air, my heart beating like hummingbird wings.

When I was able to focus, I realized I was in a hospital room. And I wasn't alone.

The cop, Jack Daniels, was sitting next to my bed in a plastic folding chair. Jack held a syringe, and I realized she'd just injected something into my IV line. I tried to sit up and found I'd been handcuffed to the bed.

"Your sister is some swimmer," Jack said.

"Yeah," I said. "She can swim like a son of a bitch. Where is she?"

"The coast guard saw a flare and picked both of you up. You had to be resuscitated. That's twice you drowned, isn't it?"

*Actually, more like a dozen times.* "Where's my sister?"

"She's being debriefed by some serious-looking men in suits. They won't let me, or anyone else, inside, not even a lawyer. Thing is, I can't tell if they're good guys or bad guys."

I eyed the syringe. "What'd you give me?"

"Adrenaline. They put you under and have been keeping you drugged. I assume they'll interrogate you next, but I wanted to talk to you first. We've got a minute, tops, before they find out I'm in here."

I blinked, my vision slowly sharpening. I still tasted the mucky water of Lake Michigan. "How long have I been out?"

"About nine hours. Long enough that you missed the breaking news."

Jack held up a newspaper, the *Tribune*. The headline read: "US Accidentally Launches Nuclear Strike on London."

"The president deeply apologizes for the mistake. The nuke was disarmed in midair and no one was hurt." Jack looked up from the article to meet my eyes. "Am I wrong, or does the world owe you and your sister a big debt?"

"Was anyone else picked up? Someone who looks like me?"

"Just you two."

"Did you recover a phone?"

"I heard something about a phone. I think the suits with your sister have it."

I took a shot. "We're so far off the radar, we don't even exist. They'll send my sister and me abroad, to a CIA prison. No trial. No due process. We'll be left there until they forget about us or we're executed."

"Oh, you exist. I called in a favor, got a peek at your juvie record."

And then she called me by something I hadn't heard in a long, long time. My real name. Then she folded over the paper and showed me another article.

Two Killed in Streeterville Apartment.

It was about Kaufmann and Cory.

"Looks like the world owes you another debt, taking out that piece of trash. I'm sorry about your parole officer. He seemed to be a good man."

"He was. What happened to the girl?"

"Her name is Dione Simowicz. Runaway. Her parents have been notified."

"She'll need counseling."

"She'll get it. Court ordered. A local 7-Eleven has her on video sticking the place up with that Cory creep. She kept going on and on about you, how you killed her boyfriend in cold blood."

I let that sink in. "So they know all about me."

"No. *I* know all about you. No one else does. You're listed here as Jane Doe."

I raised an eyebrow.

"Your juvie record is still sealed," Jack went on. "For as long as you've been here, the only one who took your prints was me."

Good thing I'd had the wherewithal to wipe down Victor's apartment before I left. "What about Mozart?"

Jack shot me a questioning look.

"Was there a fat calico cat hiding in the apartment?"

"One of the cops at the scene took it home."

Good. She was a sweet cat. She deserved a good home. "How about the gun? From the roof of my apartment building?"

Jack shrugged. "Apparently that gun with your fingerprints on it got lost in the evidence room."

I tried to figure out where she was going with this and could only come to one conclusion. "You're letting me go?"

"I can't. I'll probably get fired just being in here. But I did bring you some of your clothes." She looked at me, pointedly. "From your apartment. They're in the bag, on the chair. Being executed is bad, but the real tragedy here is that hospital gown. Now at least you'll die looking sharp."

Jack stood up.

"The suits have closed off the west wing on the sixth floor. That's where your sister is."

"I need a gun."

"I'd prefer you stop killing people in my city, if you don't mind. Besides," her lips curled into a smile, "didn't you say you liked to live on the edge?"

"Thank you, Jack," I said. And I meant it.

The cop walked to the door, then stopped.

"If you need a friend someday, I work out of the Twenty-Sixth District. Look me up."

"I will."

"And nice work saving the world, Chandler."

Jack left.

I hurt in a billion places and was dog tired. No doubt the hospital was crawling with operatives, and I probably had less than a five percent chance of getting out of there alive. The odds were even worse if I tried to rescue Fleming.

But my parents would have been proud, because even after all that had happened, after the hellish day I'd had, after all I'd done and all I'd lost, my upper lip was as stiff as could be.

Quitting was not an option.

I opened the bag Jack had left, found one of my shirts, and felt along the seam until I reached the fifty dollars and the lock pick.

"Hold on, Sis," I whispered. "I'll be right there."

*THE END*

**Chandler, Fleming, and Hammett will return in Spree.**

# Authors' Note

We truly hoped you enjoyed *Flee*. While it can be read as a stand-alone thriller, this is the first part of a trilogy featuring Chandler, Hammett, and Fleming. If you like to read things in order, it is: *Flee, Spree, Three*. Chandler also appears in the short novel *Exposed* and in the short novel *Hit*. Hammett appears in the short novel *Naughty*, all of which take place prior to *Flee*.

The characters of Jack Daniels and Harry McGlade appear in *Whiskey Sour, Bloody Mary, Rusty Nail, Dirty Martini, Fuzzy Navel, Cherry Bomb*, and *Shaken,* written by J. A. Konrath. They also appear in *Stirred* and *Serial Killers Uncut*, written by J. A. Konrath and Blake Crouch.

Harry McGlade also appears in *Babe On Board*, written by J. A. Konrath and Ann Voss Peterson.

**CAST OF CHARACTERS**

**CHANDLER** is an elite spy, working for an agency so secret only three people know it exists. Trained by the best of the best, she has honed her body, her instincts, and her intellect to become the perfect weapon.

**VICTOR CORMACK** meets Chandler online and wants to date her.

**JACOB** is Chandler's handler and speaks to her in an electronically altered voice over the phone. They have never met face-to-face.

**CORY** is a psychopath from Chandler's past. He has a penchant for girls who have just reached puberty and cutting off the body parts of others, though not necessarily in that order.

**MURRAY KAUFMANN** works as a parole officer and is the only man Chandler trusts. After her arrest at age fourteen,

Kaufmann helped her pull herself together and make something of her life.

**HAMMETT** is a dangerous psychopath with all the training of Chandler and none of the moral fabric. She's a superassassin, and she loves it. Unsympathetic to her fellow human beings, she has a soft spot only for animals.

**JACQUELINE "JACK" DANIELS** is a Chicago cop who appears in *Shot of Tequila*, *Whiskey Sour*, *Bloody Mary*, *Rusty Nail*, *Dirty Martini*, *Fuzzy Navel*, *Cherry Bomb*, *Shaken*, and *Stirred*. *Flee*, *Spree*, and *Three* take place between *Dirty Martini* and *Fuzzy Navel*.

**HARRY MCGLADE** runs a private investigating firm with Jack Daniels. McGlade is possibly the most offensive human being of all time.

**THE INSTRUCTOR** trained Chandler to be a superassassin. He admits that in his thirty-eight years in the military, she was the second best spy he's ever trained.

### The Code Name: Chandler Series
By J. A. Konrath and Ann Voss Peterson
*In chronological order*
*Exposed*
*Naughty*
*Hit*
Flee
Spree

# ALSO BY THE AUTHORS

**J. A. Konrath and Ann Voss Peterson**

**J. A. Konrath/Jack Kilborn Works Available on Kindle**

Jack Daniels thrillers:
Whiskey Sour
Bloody Mary
Rusty Nail
Dirty Martini
Fuzzy Navel
Cherry Bomb
Shaken
Stirred
Killers Uncut (with Blake Crouch)
Serial Killers Uncut (with Blake Crouch)
Birds of Prey (with Blake Crouch)
Shot of Tequila
Banana Hammock
Jack Daniels Stories (collected stories)
Serial Uncut (with Blake Crouch)
Killers (with Blake Crouch)
Suckers (with Jeff Strand)
Planter's Punch (with Tom Schreck)
Floaters (with Henry Perez)
Truck Stop
Symbios (writing as Joe Kimball)

Flee (with Ann Voss Peterson)
Babe on Board (with Ann Voss Peterson)
Other works:
Afraid (writing as Jack Kilborn)
Endurance (writing as Jack Kilborn)
Trapped (writing as Jack Kilborn)
Draculas (with J. A. Konrath, Jeff Strand, and F. Paul Wilson)
Origin
The List
Disturb
65 Proof (short story omnibus)
Crime Stories (collected stories)
Horror Stories (collected stories)
Dumb Jokes & Vulgar Poems
A Newbie's Guide to Publishing
Wild Night Is Calling (with Ann Voss Peterson)
Shapeshifters Anonymous
The Screaming
Visit the author at www.jakonrath.com

## Ann Voss Peterson's Works Available on Kindle

Thrillers:
Pushed Too Far
Flee (with J. A. Konrath)
Exposed (novella) (with J. A. Konrath)
Short stories:
Babe on Board (with J. A. Konrath)
Wild Night Is Calling (with J. A. Konrath)
Romantic suspense novels:
Gypsy Magic (with Rebecca York and Patricia Rosemoor)
Claiming His Family
Incriminating Passion
Boys in Blue (with Rebecca York and Patricia Rosemoor)

# About The Authors

John Peterson, 2011

Award-winning author Ann Voss Peterson wrote her first story at seven years old and hasn't stopped since. To pursue her love of creative writing, she's worked as a bartender, horse groomer, and window washer. Now known for her adrenaline-fueled thrillers and Harlequin Intrigue romances, Ann draws on her wide variety of life experiences to fill her fictional worlds with compelling energy and undeniable emotion. She lives near Madison, Wisconsin, with her family and their border collie.

Maria Konrath, 2010

J. A. Konrath broke into the writing scene with his cocktail-themed mystery series, including *Whiskey Sour*, *Bloody Mary*, and *Rusty Nail*—stories that combine uproarious humor with spine-tingling suspense. Since then, Konrath has gone on to become an award-winning and best-selling author known for thriller and horror novels. He is also a pioneer of self-publishing models and posts industry insights on his world-famous blog, *A Newbie's Guide to Publishing*. He lives in Chicago with his family and three dogs.